THE LAST SONG OF DUSK

Also by Siddharth Dhanvant Shanghvi

The Lost Flamingoes of Bombay

The Rabbit and the Squirrel

Loss

PRAISE FOR *THE LAST SONG OF DUSK*

'Full of sharp wit and the kind of tantalizing writing that fills you with certain envy and delight at the simple pleasure of a well-told story'—*The Economic Times*

'The quality of prose is of the highest order—it is, in fact, poetry'—*The Hindu*

'Shanghvi knows how to wield a magical pen ... a promising debut'—*The Telegraph*

'A magical piece of storytelling'—*The Sunday Times*

'Shanghvi has extended the boundaries of the Indian novel in English ... as style goes, it is Mendelssohn plus a sprinkling of Marquez, and for the sensuality part, Kundera has a tropical heir'—*India Today*

'A masterpiece'—*Pioneer*

'A magnificent debut'—*Wall Street Journal*

'[A] colourful first novel ... what begins as an erotic fairy tale grows into an exploration of love and loss, sexuality and innocence, friendship and solitude ... Shanghvi's loose, poetic style ... [is] cut with a dash of magical realism ... [and his] story has eloquent insights into the nature of love'—*The Times Literary Supplement*

'A magical debut. Madcap characters shimmy across the pages, throwing out slangy witticisms with insouciant charm, but underneath the glitz the mood is mythically melancholy. Delicious'—*Elle,* UK

'Shanghvi carves a magic-realism-tinged niche for himself between Salman Rushdie and Arundhati Roy ... a sensual, delectable debut'—*Publishers Weekly,* USA

'A cross between Zadie Smith and Vikram Seth'—*Hindustan Times*

'A spell is cast: you enter Shanghvi's idiom, and you are snared' —*Tehelka*

'A mini marvel ... Shanghvi's debut still fulfils the most essential covenant of storytelling ... it spins a story well and keeps the reader hooked ... *LSD* is a recommended trip'—*The Times of India*

'It is one of those stories you want to read in one breath—and then you want to read again'—*Corriere Della Sera,* Italy

'The whole book sparkles with energy, and is by turns cheeky, funny and achingly sad ... a story to treasure' —*Literary Review,* UK

THE LAST SONG OF DUSK

SIDDHARTH
DHANVANT
SHANGHVI

HarperCollins *Publishers* India

First published in 2004

This edition published in India by HarperCollins *Publishers* 2024
4th Floor, Tower A, Building No. 10, Phase II, DLF Cyber City,
Gurugram, Haryana – 122002
www.harpercollins.co.in

2 4 6 8 10 9 7 5 3 1

P-ISBN: 978-93-5699-856-8
E-ISBN: 978-93-5699-896-4

Typeset in 11.5/16.2 Garamond Premier Pro at
Manipal Technologies Limited, Manipal

Printed and bound at
Thomson Press (India) Ltd

To Padmini, who, in her waltz with Fate,
found her toes stepped on
And for Pappa, who brought along the music

I don't know why it should be this way,
But I am so sad; an old time tale,
Will not leave my heart.

Heinrich Heine 'Lorelei'

PART ONE

Violins and Frangipani

1

On the day Anuradha Patwardhan was leaving Udaipur for Bombay to marry a man she had not even met in the twenty-one years of her existence, her mother clutched her lovely hand through the window of the black Victoria and whispered: 'In this life, my darling, there is no mercy.' Anuradha nodded respectfully and ached to ask her what exactly she meant by that. But even before she could articulate her question, Mrs Patwardhan's large, oval eyes, the hue of liquid soot, misted over and she shut them with gracious restraint. At that moment, young Anuradha decided that her mother had never looked lovelier: robed in a cobalt-blue sari with a gold-leaf border, she was a woman of altitude although not imposing, slim but with pertinent parts of her biology eye-catchingly endowed, and a certain gift of Song that was, to say the least, legend in Udaipur.

It was this same simple but inexplicably alluring beauty which her daughter had inherited. Indeed, Anuradha Patwardhan's looks were so fabled that more than a few young Romeos of the Udaipur Sonnets Society categorically claimed her as their Muse. Was it her hair, that dense, fierce swathe of it—a poem in itself? Was it Anuradha's red bow lips, as thin and stencilled as Urvashi's—the Seductress to the Gods? Or was it her presence itself: assured, controlled and elegant, as though a hymn wrapped in a sari—which, this January morning, in the deep spleen of Rajasthan, was an easy pearl white. It duly complemented the pale yellow duranta flowers billeted in her thick chignon, flowers with such an aptitude for fragrance that several bees grew dizzy and promptly fainted in mid-air.

'Maa ... I will always cherish all that you have given ...' she blurted as the horseman belted the black stallions with a whip made of carefully twined camel's eyelashes.

'*Never* forget the songs,' Mrs Patwardhan counselled as the stylish Victoria kick-started with a jolt.

In the carriage, Anuradha sat opposite her father, a man she loved but did not like. A tiny rotund creature with thinning grey hair and a nose curved like a macaw's beak (Anuradha frequently thanked the Lord Shreenathji that she had been spared her father's awkward lineaments), Mr Patwardhan grinned at her with a politesse bereft of all warmth. In any case, she cared not two bits for the clumsy, hollow manoeuvres of masculine sympathy and hurriedly turned to notch up the fading sight of her mother. Mrs Patwardhan was standing on the last step of the marble portico, erect as an obelisk but with the grace of a swan, the silken pallo of her sari drawn over her head: a sigh of sartorial grace. As the carriage trotted down the snaking drive, the wind picked up pace and crumpled into dust the image Anuradha was taking in with the fervency of a cyclone on the rampage: snatching every detail into the centre of her. She recorded the regality of the house, its scrollwork windows, the shaded long veranda as consoling as a paragraph from one's favourite novel. She recorded the glistening belly of Lake Pichola which hemmed their estate, the pergola she used to sit under to watch the dazzling saffron strokes of the sunsets of winter. She recorded the texture of air, its depth of character, the songs that the women of her family had sung inside it.

A weep gathered in her chest like the white crest of a wave.

The grand old Marwar Express, painted black with gold accoutrements, would bring them to Bombay inside two days. The platform itself was narrow, long and littered with an assortment of corpse-like beggars and lifeless Britishers. Several travellers stopped in their tracks to nail glances at Anuradha, at the animal fluidity of her movements, her noble stride, the carriage of her lovely head, all various aspects of one mesmerizing concerto. Her neat leather luggage stood by her side; her father had fallen into conversation with an acquaintance. She crossed her arms and thought about how her mother had promised to come to Bombay as soon as she had conducted the delivery of her youngest daughter-in-law—her due date and Anuradha's leaving had crossed like the tributaries of two rivers: unknowingly, ferociously. Mrs Patwardhan had assured her that no matter what ('I shall grow wings and fly, if need be'), she would be in Bombay if Anuradha's marriage was decided, which, of course, seemed most likely: only a monumental fool would ever turn down someone like her. The irony, of course, was that Anuradha had scant idea of her own charms: she was under the impression that all women inspired sonnets; all women had received marriage proposals since they were four years and thirty-nine days old. As a result, modesty trailed her as the most dignified of chaperones in her candlelight tryst with Destiny, and it was *this* unassuming humility, an ingenuous unpretentiousness, which elevated her from merely being attractive to being—yes, let us bow our heads and admit it—downright irresistible.

A little ahead of her, she noticed someone feed coal into the throat of the train and a minute later a swaggering cockade of smoke billowed over its haughty metal head. Behind the iron paling of the station was a cluster of resilient acacia trees, hammered by the sun, bitten by wandering camels. Now, just after she and her father had boarded the train, and as they were arranging their luggage under the seat, everyone on the platform started whispering and pointing towards the clutch of trees: naturally, even Anuradha rose to see what the hullabaloo was all about. Her eyes fell again on the acacias behind the station, where peacocks had gathered—and not one or two, mind you, but dozens of them. An ostentation of peacocks that, just as the Marwar Express snorted its way out of Udaipur, unleashed their rain-beckoning cries of *Megh-awuu, Megh-awuu, Megh-awuu* ... bit by bit, sounds of the train, its metal rancour and romantic whistle, the awed gasps of passengers, the sweet traces of the roving flute-caller—in fact, all sounds—were doused by peacocks unfurling a melody one would not normally associate with such pavonine braggarts.

Anuradha's father looked at her with slanted eyes; his daughter had fed these birds from the high balcony of her bedroom for the last sixteen years.

'I suppose they have come to say their farewell?' he said before opening the *Times of India*.

'Actually,' she clarified, her hand on her breastbone, 'I called them.'

It was much later, after a horrendous twist in Anuradha Patwardhan's kismet, when she would return to Udaipur with a splintered heart and sullen despair, that the peacocks would seek her audience again. But then, as if to honour the anguish she had tripped into like an animal walking into the metal fangs of a poacher's trap, they were unsettlingly silent in her presence.

2

It was rumoured that Vardhmaan Gandharva was so highly thought of as a doctor that more than a few nubile lassies of Dwarika—the quaint, plush arm of north Bombay he had been born in twenty-seven years ago—feigned fevers and simulated stomach aches only so he might measure their excited pulse or even—praise the Lord Shiva!—glide his stethoscope over places no man had ever touched before. Dr Vardhmaan Gandharva, the only son of the Gandharva clan, was, in all honesty, irritated by such juvenile attention: he was of the firm conviction that his time could be better spent than in reassuring the child of some loaded cotton trader that her bellyache was only gas caused by chewing on far too many boiled peanuts. Eventually, after one annoying 'patient' requested his attentions for the eleventh time in two weeks, his fortitude snapped and he leaned forward and whispered into the maiden's ear, 'I'm afraid, my dear, you are pregnant.' Almost instantly, her fever vanished and her stomach pains never returned for as long as she lived. Thrilled with the success of his new technique, he began using it on all his female patients—with very good results. Never again did one of the Dwarika virgin lassies pester him with that pathetic request uttered in a throaty, breathless tone, *Put the metal thing all over me, will you, Doctor?*

Dr Vardhmaan Gandharva had heard about Anuradha Patwardhan from the frighteningly corpulent Ghor-bapa—Bombay's most eminent matchmaker. Dubbed 'Mr Thunder Thighs' in good humour, he was said to have broken a chair or two in every household he had graced, which *he* claimed was a good omen—the devastating harbinger of a wedding—although one glance at him and you knew it was only because of his epochal ass.

'I have heard,' Ghor-bapa had whispered into the ear of the young Vardhmaan, 'that when Anuradha sings, even the moon listens.'

One line.

That was all it took for Dr Gandharva to tender a formal proposal to the Patwardhan family in Udaipur. Anuradha's father was ecstatic, for he had heard tomes about Vardhmaan Gandharva and his family: how they had originally made their fortune in rare stone trading, the propriety of Vardhmaan's character, the valued prudence of his medical opinion. Other bits of scuttlebutt recovered informed them that Vardhmaan's mother had passed away when he was a boy of six, and a few years on his father had married a younger woman, his stepmother, Divi-bai, of whom disconcertingly unsavoury things were said (but the Patwardhans ignored this crucial splinter of data since they presumed that all stepmothers, from time immemorial, were a tainted lot). Vardhmaan's father had died a few years ago, and the Gandharva household, consisting of a motley of relatives, was a pyramid—and the ice queen located at the very top was the legendary Divi-bai.

After Patwardhan's enthusiastic response to the proposal was conveyed back to Bombay, after their horoscopes were matched and approved, an auspicious date was set for the intensely eligible duo to meet at the house of Mrs Patwardhan's sister, Radha-mashi. Anuradha and her father, Vardhmaan had been told, were arriving in the port city on Thursday of that week: they were to meet the same evening. In the days leading up to their meeting, tense with this information, Dr Vardhmaan felt his own pulse rise and his heart smote inside him like the heart of a wolf under a full moon.

On the day that he was to meet Anuradha, Vardhmaan was plucked out of his sleep at dawn, overwhelmed as he was, by the unforgettable scent of cinnamon. A lush fog of a scent, it reminded Vardhmaan of the day his mother had died, oh, around twenty-one years ago. That fateful morning, his mother was sweating streams on the four-poster teak bed and her body was shivering, having perceived the menacing footsteps of her incipient Death. In her intolerable anguish, she extended her hand towards little Vardhmaan, and grasped his wrist: a cold, poignant touch; a love letter from someone drowning.

All of Vardhmaan's Destiny woke to that one desperate caress.

'Can you save me, Vardhmaan, please?' she pleaded to her boy. The answer, only a minute later, came from Reality: *no.* At that instant, Vardhmaan's father returned to the room—for he had gone down to get her a tumbler of water—but the tableau of his dead wife's hand clutching the six-year-old child's wrist caused him to drop the tumbler: this steel reverberation, two decades on, still woke the hound of History sleeping inside Vardhmaan.

They all thought he had trained as a doctor because of an intrinsic love of medicine or some desire for the respectability that came with a doctor's life: no one once guessed his *real* intention, his *real* hope.

At exactly seven-thirty that morning, Vardhmaan bathed and dried his body in front of the five-foot almari mirror with bevelled edges. As he ran the white cloth around the bend of his muscled calves, the limp leg hair rose again. Then he daubed the delicious dimples of his buttocks, the incline of his back, the coltish nape of his neck, and with every movement over his lovely form, bath water found itself slowly exiled to the lobes of his ears. The mirror revealed a fine specimen: a tall, muscular man with broad shoulders and a gallant puff of chest, a jaggery-brown skin, and a member between his legs that was lonely and strong willed and *utterly* gorgeous inside its own confusion. After putting on his dapper suit and linen shirt, he walked along the corridor outside his room, went down the steep stairwell and entered a kitchen with four dormer windows and tessellated flooring. He sat at the head of the rosewood table and downed his seera and bananas, and it was not until just before he left for work that he casually asked Sumitra-bhabhi, a widowed aunt who lived in the gardener's quarters at the back of the house, 'By the way, do you smell cinnamon?'

She handed him a glass of chassh and said, 'So what time are you meeting Anuradha?'

'At eight,' he answered. 'At her aunt's house. In South Bombay.'

'All love is a storm,' she said, and left the room.

3

Anuradha and her father were staying at Radha-mashi's—Mrs Patwardhan's sister—whose grand mansion sprawled out with such decadence that it took up half of Gulmohar Road, from where it commanded a view of the Arabian Sea through every one of its sash windows on its three elaborate storeys. The Patwardhans arrived on Thursday at six thirty, and Anuradha noticed that her eyes smarted from the salt in the air, and she worried that it might, perhaps, interfere with her capacity to sing.

'Anuradha!' Radha-mashi gushed, her hands around her niece's flawlessly boned face. 'My d*arrr*ling, I heard about the seventy-seven men who fainted at the train station from the sight of your maddening loveliness.'

'Lies!' she countered, hugging her flamboyant aunt, whose vermilion-red sari and backless blouse caused even the houseboys to flush.

'I *never* lie!' her aunt said. 'I merely make the truth what it hopes to be.'

Anuradha laughed. Radha-mashi turned, and when she did, her panatella puffs uncurled on to the face of her brother-in-law—a man she had long disregarded: 'And how are you, my dear?' The indifference in her voice was not disguised.

'I am perfectly fine,' Mr Patwardhan replied coldly.

'I wouldn't go *that* far,' she sassed, and returned her attentions to her niece. 'My little girl ... how you have grown ... and your eyes are *so* ... Never mind all that because Vardhmaan arrives here in an hour. Why don't you go up and have a bath and change.'

'An hour!' Anuradha cried, her hand on her chest. 'I thought it was not until tomorrow. Friday. At seven.'

'You know how I am with dates ...' Her aunt waved her hands as if to dismiss Anuradha's apprehensions. 'Now go up and get neat, *quick*!'

Almost instantly, all the fatigue of the trip whooshed out of Anuradha; in its place a frenzy stormed up to her head. She rushed to her room to change into the turquoise tussore sari and meenakari jewellery that her mother had suggested she wear for the meeting. As she sat in front of the dresser, pegging on her earrings, applying a little kohl, entirely unsure of how to conduct herself in front of a man she had never even seen before, she remembered what Radha-mashi had once told her: 'A man is like a carpet: lay them once, and you can walk on them for the rest of your life.' Such brassy snatches of counsel were hardly any balm for her troubled mind. How would Vardhmaan look? she mulled. Was he a decent man? Left-handed or right? How big were his ears? Did he shave?

And tell me, *who* in these times could you entrust with the safety of your heart?

Downstairs, Radha-mashi arranged yellow canna lilies in fluted copper vases in the lounge. She asked one of the houseboys to sway open the French doors so as to engage the manicured majesty of the lawns. Walking into the library, Radha-mashi noticed that her brother-in-law, seated in a cane recliner, was absorbed in a copy of the *Bombay Gazetteer.* She was briefly flustered: she hoped he would not be reading the piece that documented her life as one of this city's more worldly hostesses. But that was *precisely* the article—'The Canapé Maharani: Why *Everyone* Wants to Attend Radha Divan's Thursday Salon!'—that Mr Patwardhan was reading, shaking his head at the outré details of her life. Nearly twenty years ago, the article in the *Bombay Gazetteer* revealed, Radha-mashi had lost her husband when they were out on tiger shikar in the Shivalik Mountains; since then, she had had the fortune of being a widow, a young widow, and a *rich* young widow: the combination could not be more favourable. After her husband's death, the reportage continued, Radha-mashi didn't just give parties: she *threw* them. With resounding aplomb. Every chutney mary and every chi-chi memsahib worth her rickshaw change clawed for an invite to a single do at Radha-mashi's place during Bombay's famous 'December Soirée Season'. She had strengthened her reputation as a society hostess in inventive ways ... take, for instance, how, in the year 1901, Radha-mashi introduced the local palate to the chop-smacking charms of a newly discovered Italian delicacy: the *pizza*. It was a smack-your-lips, drool deliriously, double-barrel hit. Not that it stopped the bitchy South Bombay hostesses from gossiping under the laburnum trees that the pizza was nothing but a 'burnt chapatti topped with burnt tomatoes topped with burnt milk'.

Mr Patwardhan's eyes nearly tumbled out of their sockets when he saw a stylish monochrome of Radha-mashi arm in arm with, why!, none other than the reclusive Afghani painter Khalil Muratta and the notorious Patron of the Arts, Libya Dass. He read that Khalil Muratta—a despondently good-looking man with Devdas eyes and a faraway deportment common to artists—was considered to be among the greatest living painters, a reputation he fortified by not once lifting the paintbrush following the death of his wife: his Only Love. Subsequently, the rich heiress Libya Dass had looked after him, providing him with the solitude that his compelling melancholy required to mature into some epic art. What shocked Mr Patwardhan most was the fact that Libya Dass had a string of English lovers, all of whom were women. Libya Dass had famously argued that English women were homosexual by choice simply because the prospect of fornicating with a male member of their own ilk was a suitable deterrent to the comforts of *La Vie Breeder.*

'Is *she* really ... Mr Patwardhan struggled for words, 'I mean ... is Libya Dass ... queer?'

'Not at all,' assured Radha-mashi, smiling. 'I know for a fact all her bedfellows are women ... oh look, I believe our young suitor is here.'

Sure enough, a regal three-stallion buggy was clip-clopping its way up the drive. Inside it, Dr Vardhmaan Gandharva realized that the troubling scent of cinnamon that had plagued him since dawn had abruptly vanished: the clarity of air and its minted dignity frightened him before its coiled calm swathed him with the felicity of a shawl. The horseman stopped. Vardhmaan opened the door and stepped out. Tacked up in a faded grey suit with a single white tumescent rosebud in the slit of his vest, he looked clean and handsome. His hair was combed neatly back, his brow gleamed, and as a finishing touch a smother of jasmine attar had been rubbed under his elbows. He stood at the steps of the portal before he took a deep breath and looked up: there, at the last window in the room above, the other end of his Romantic Destiny had found the daring to pull back the quince-red damask curtains and steal a glance at the man who had come to ask her hand in marriage. Vardhmaan's eyes bolted a gaze into the eyes of the woman whose face he could only half see, and blood rushed to his temples like an avalanche.

He smiled; she let the curtain close.

During their first, brief meeting neither Vardhmaan nor Anuradha exchanged anything of worth. In fact, their closest interaction was when he said to Mr Patwardhan, 'I have heard that when your daughter sings, even the moon listens.'

'That is nothing but a gross exaggeration!' Anuradha was mortified that someone had spread such tattle about her.

'Absolutely!' Radha-mashi stepped in. 'The last time she sang, only a few stars stepped out to listen.'

It was Radha-mashi who insisted that the couple ought to spend some more time together since they had not been given any space to really communicate. So later that week, they met again, this time just the two of them, at the Billingdon Clubhouse, a plummy Victorian creature that had only recently lifted its ban against 'Indians and Dogs'—as part of the Visiting Whitepeople's new progressive policy.

On the flat-stone patio of the clubhouse, they sat around an antique trestle table.

'You look very ... beautiful,' Vardhmaan said, finally.

'They think so too,' she responded playfully.

'*They*?' His eyebrows arched up with the awareness that she was far more fascinating than he had presumed her to be.

'What is the music that finds your notice?'

'Mendelssohn. Beethoven. Bach ... a few young Parisians who are only now making their mark.' Each evening after work, he listened to his Shor Bazaar gramophone, which unleashed a tide of violins and pianos and cellos that spellbound him, and took him outside the banality of existence, to a place where things lay in tune and melody, and outside all that which language aspires to but never achieves.

'So does Bombay find your favour?' He grinned; he knew what a dull question this was: but then what could he say under such tricky circumstances?

'I know very little of this city,' she replied. 'I've stayed here, with my aunt, a few times when I was younger. And I hold the Sea in considerable esteem.'

Both grew conscious of how stilted and starchy their interaction seemed—to the point that it was exasperating. The conversation paused. As silence stretched out before them, Vardhmaan decided to take a risk. 'Did I tell you about the time I flew a kite so high it stayed up in the sky for a week?' Her interest was piqued. This, to her knowledge, was not how first meetings between prospective life partners were supposed to go: from what little she'd heard from her friends, most suitors had asked whether they knew how to make 'very thin chapattis' or whether they would press their father-in-law's feet after dinner each evening!

Vardhmaan continued: 'I was nine at the time, and full of piss and vinegar. I suppose because I was the local chilli-eating champ *and* the kite-flying champion. But it was the kite-flying that gave me an edge. You see, one January I hoisted up a large black kite and, because the wind was on my side, it soared easy and high. The more string I allowed it, the higher it went, past the clouds, punching the blazing blue sky with its cheeky black whimsical dance. At one point only its long tail was visible, and that was when everyone in Dwarika gathered around. "We've never seen a kite go up this high," they said. "But what will you do when night comes?" Someone suggested I bring it down,' he said, shaking his head. Anuradha marked the sparkle in his eyes as he recounted the joy of his growing years. He said that he tied the kite's string to a hook on the wall and decided to let it be: if the kite was to come down, it would do so by itself;

as far as he was concerned he was happy letting it go. For a week the kite flew by itself and even now, he said, he could clearly recall the *phhd-phhd-phhd* of the string vibrating to trade winds. Anuradha closed her eyes to imagine a pitch-black kite vanishing into the blue sky, only its fluttering tail vaguely visible: the skin on her nape thrilled in marvelment. She hadn't expected a doctor from the suburbs of Bombay to possess such a different side. 'And then?'

Certain that his little story had hooked her, he leaned closer: 'And then the strangest thing happened.' His voice dipped here, taking on a mysterious cadence. 'You see, because the kite was so high, it could take on many weights. So one night I started to tie small lanterns to the string and let them go up. One lantern after the next went far up—and before you knew it, the glimmer of lanterns floating in mid-air competed with the shimmer of the stars above them. Everyone watched with open mouths.'

'I'm sure!' Anuradha said eagerly.

'Before long I was tying bits and bobs to the string. Someone suggested an old chair and that too went up. A chair in the sky! Can you beat that? The next day, someone tied a bright pink sari and that went up too. These were just one of the scores of things tied to the string of this kite, and it seemed to take everything into the endless blue of the sky. But then one day, it all changed.'

'What do you mean?'

'Oh, I'm sorry,' he apologized. 'What a fool I've been—going on and on like this, monopolizing the conversation when I ought to be listening to you.'

'Not at all,' commanded Anuradha. 'Please do finish with your story. In fact, I insist!'

'Oh, it's nothing really. Our neighbour, Neeta-ben, came in one evening and seeing that the kite was taking up almost everything tied her haggard mother-in-law to the string and she was just about to hoist this hapless old widow into the air when I stepped on the scene. Seeing that any moment now her mother-in-law was going to take off, I slit the string with my hands, and there, once and for all, the legendary kite with its miles and miles of string petered out into the sky never to be seen again.'

'Is this all true?' a dazed Anuradha asked after a minute. But she hastened to add: 'Never mind that.' It occurred to her: what did it matter? 'How utterly spectacular!'

Now, she knew, it was her turn to speak (lest the conversation acquire a lopsidedness) and she spoke warmly of her growing years in Udaipur, the clan of songs handed down from mother to daughter, a dowry of descants passed on by tongue to ear. She told him about the three friends she had in Udaipur and that she had no need for more since solitude always had a place at her dinner table; about how lucky she was to have attended college at a time when women were barely entering educational institutions and duly credited her mother's foresight in such matters. Vardhmaan listened without saying a word, mesmerized by the sincerity of her gesticulations, how carefully chosen her words were, the seduction of her humility. Anuradha, on the other hand, was quite taken in by her suitor's sophisticated demeanour, his genuine interest in the account of her life, his dignified pauses (more important even than the words he spoke). In this way, snippets of their pasts were traded in clean, detached flashes, and they each forgot that they were talking to the person they might, in all certainty, have to spend the rest of their lives with, individuals whose morning breath they would learn to tolerate, whose moods they would bear and understand with rapid acuity. In fact, if the prospect of such breathtaking intimacy had ever been made obvious to them at the time, they'd surely have clammed up. He told her how he had trained as a doctor (but kept secret the reason *why he* had trained), how his practice at the Nanavati Hospital in Dwarika, very near to his house, was as busy as a koli fish market, how he hoped to travel all over the country one day ('But I will save it for when the times are calmer,' he said; it wouldn't be until years later that the uncoloured tyrants were cleaned from the Land, but by then his travel dreams—Hey Bhagwan, *all* dreams—were folded and put away in a valise in the attic of a ghostly house).

Each, it was now obvious, was quite enamoured of the other—but there was one thing that Anuradha just *had* to authenticate. Early on in life, she'd decided that she could be with any species of man but *not* a coward: the lowest class of any living thing that ever breathed. So taking a deep breath she braced herself and put him to the test. When the turbaned waiter came to take their orders, she told him with an air of uncanny confidence, 'Oh, and I shall have a plate of chicken club sandwiches—but please leave out the lettuce.'

The waiter nodded politely and left.

The air was bursting with tension, like the navel of a pregnant male sea horse.

'I do not know a single Hindu woman who relishes the flesh of another living being.'

'And we're talking food here, right?' came her somewhat scandalous repartee.

No word was exchanged until the sandwiches arrived, and Anuradha ate them without the slightest discomfiture; Vardhmaan had withdrawn into a cape of amber-hued silence. *It was over before it even started,* she thought as he led her out. On Peddar Road, passing the row of bare gulmohars, she wondered whether her recklessness had been too much. Perfectly aware that his family were strict vegetarian Brahmins—they balked at the sight of an egg, let alone the innards of a feathered fowl—putting Vardhmaan through a test of such endurance was a tough call. But ascertaining his reaction now rather than later was a wiser alternative: she would not marry a man who was merely an updated version of her father. She disembarked at the steps of Radha-mashi's house; he bade her farewell, and they went their separate ways.

Of course, she never told her father about what she had done with Vardhmaan; she did, however, confide in Radha-mashi, who put her elegant fingers over Anuradha's brave shoulders and comforted, 'Well done! A man who can't stomach a woman who eats chicken club sandwiches has no guts to his name.'

'But I *liked* him!'

'I have to admit,' her aunt said, looking down, 'he was certainly one of the more pleasant of his sex.'

'I've ruined it, nè?' Her eyes were crestfallen.

'No, my dear,' Radha-mashi assured. 'Life only gets exciting when it gets tough.'

Mr Patwardhan was deadly curious as to why Vardhmaan never even rang back. But after his curiosity waned, humiliation took root: why had the good doctor not furthered the invitation of marriage with a more official offer? What had he seen in Anuradha that he had not liked? After a week had gone by since that evening at the Billingdon Clubhouse, it became apparent that there would be no wedding: Dr Vardhmaan Gandharva had, it was all too obvious, backed out. Meanwhile, upstairs, in her room, Anuradha was packing away her saris and her blouses and her cotton salwar kameezes that she thought would have been perfect for the vindictive summers of Bombay. What a waste it all seemed now! And what a pity to have lost out on a man like Vardhmaan—or was it? His fear of the chicken club sandwiches made her uncertain. All she knew was that she liked him, a place far more important than that nebulous geography of love.

What she was *really* moonstruck about was his knack for telling stories, those dazzling, dramatic anecdotes still vibrantly alive inside her, like fireflies ensparkling the forests of her heart. *I want you here,* she brooded, *I want to hear some more, Mr Chilli Champ ...* She remembered the account of the black kite, and the tales that Vardhmaan had told her about the folks he met in the course of his practice: including one Ramu-aunty, a notorious three-breasted shaman of Juhu who competed for his patients and who was working on the one cure that seemed to elude her: the Cure for the Broken Heart. *Oh, how wonderful it is,* Anuradha remarked to herself, *to be absorbed into the folds of someone's life.* Somehow a man who could tell stories and tell them *well* suggested to her that the innate, terrorizing silence of life might be conquered—even if only for a few wondrous moments. As she recalled all this, Anuradha was overcome, and hot, lovely tears fled down her soft cheeks—but she did not pause to wipe them dry for that would only have taken her into a darker cave of dejection. Instead, she started cleaning the table, making the bed, arranging her green glass bangles—anything to get her mind away from the sorrow billowing through her chest like a bush fire of late summer.

That same afternoon at four, just as Anuradha was boarding Radha-mashi's stylish black Rolls that was to drop them at Victoria Terminus, a horse-drawn carriage came careening up the drive with a dashing wildness she would have associated with a far more romantic period in history. From that carriage, out jumped a red-faced, sweaty Vardhmaan, who looked at Mr Patwardhan and panted, 'I want to ask your daughter's hand in marriage.' In the stunned pause that followed, smiles spread over several faces. However, before Mr Patwardhan could shake his hand and accept on his daughter's behalf, Radha-mashi strode on to the scene and commanded, 'Well, then ask *her*, for Shiva's sake.' Overwhelmed by the simplicity of a woman's logic, Vardhmaan turned to Anuradha, who, in a pale yellow sari with a border of miniature purple peacocks, stood in calm splendour by the buggy door, her wide, delicate eyes resolute in expression, a smile aching to erupt under the nonchalance of her bow lips.

'Will you please marry me?' He had the most pleading eyes she had ever seen.

'But *only* if I get the right side of the bed,' she declared.

4

After a honeymoon that comprised of lodging in the converted wing of a bankrupt maharaja's palace in Mysore, of riding a tusker who, in an earlier life, had ravaged several plantations and crushed to death four sleeping tribal women, and of evenings spent listening to the music of his stories, Anuradha and Vardhmaan Gandharva returned to his ancestral house in Dwarika. At first sight, Anuradha found the off-white U-shaped house with a sky-winning atrium slightly daunting: her worry only ripened when she looked at one particular window and touched her husband's arm.

'Why!' he said, delighted. 'That's my room.' He was surprised that she had picked it out of a fleet of bedrooms. '*Our* room,' he corrected, and put his arm around her.

'I know but ...' She could not complete her sentence.

That window, the shingh tree arching up to it, the scary height it stood at, all formed a viscous, bubbling terror at the base of her long neck; it was years later before she would realize how the house, at their first encounter, had told her about the mischief it could unravel with impassioned deviousness.

'Welcome home!' he said as they stepped into the portal, instantly deluged by adults and children eager to see her—and in their presence she felt festive and light and important, and she embraced those younger than her and took the blessings of those older. A few minutes into her entrance, she noted that her new house, painted limestone white, was casually furnished with two Ahmedabadi settees, a carved divan and three teak rockers with silk cushions; intimidating portraits of Gandharva ancestry hung on the walls (on seeing the curved noses of the men she secretly prayed that when she had children, her brood would escape this rhinal heritage). Inside an hour, Vardhmaan noted that most of the family members had taken to her: she had even swapped recipes and notes on good books with one of the cousin's wives, Taru, and the children of the neighbours crowded around her as she entertained them with ghost stories. His chest swelled up with pride, and he remembered how she had touched his arm a short while ago, the casual intimacy of it, that recherché idiom of lovers. And with her arrival, the grumpy Gandharva house had opened its dusty eyelids, intrigued by the tinkling of her new bride's silver anklets, the consolation of her smiles.

In the two months that swept by, Anuradha found the company of two women in particular much to her liking: Sumitra-bhabhi, a young widow ripened into wisdom by the bulk of her grief; and Taru, a talented dancer married to a cousin who had failed second grade so many times that the school officials defied policy and suspended him (thus rendering him the only chap in Bombay who never made it past second grade). Anuradha found that Sumitra-bhabhi had the quietness of someone who had seen the ghastly face of Life, from which there really was no mercy: a few days after her marriage, Sumitra-bhabhi's husband had died from cholera and she was returned because her mother-in-law claimed that her feet left black marks that brought bad luck. Sumitra-bhabhi retold Anuradha the account of her dismissal with bleak detachment, as if she were speaking of someone else's life. In the end, she concluded: 'The women in our land all have black feet. But it is not bad luck that they bring but bad luck that they must endure. *That* is the Fate of women.'

Hearing that, Anuradha fell into an instant abiding respect for Sumitra-bhabhi.

Taru, on the other hand, was a chirpy little thing, a Bharatnatyam dancer trained under the legendary Pandit Jagdamabba, who had famously swirled in a temple courtyard for seventy-two hours continuously until he eventually vanished into the blur of his own swirling, having attained a rare artistic nirvana. When Anuradha asked her why she did not dance any longer, Taru did not at first react but after a little coaxing she admitted that Divi-bai, the matriarch of the

Gandharva household, had forbidden her from practising. It appeared to Anuradha that Divi-bai—who was, even now, settling some long-running property dispute in her native Jafrabad—did not find the happiness of someone else to her tolerance.

'When is it that Divi-bai will return?'

'When she will find there is too much joy in this house.'

'And when will that be?' Anuradha asked innocently.

'I believe *that,*' Taru said, lowering her voice, 'has already happened.'

Vardhmaan loved most how his wife brought the civilization of her femininity to his life. He delighted in the Nottingham lace that she darned into the cushion ends, the melodic humming of a raga as she cooked, the concentration of her face when she was reading a Sharat Chandra novel. In her, he found an eager audience for the events of his day, its regrets and successes. How adroitly he would noose her attention: 'Do you know, Mrs Patel's daughter nearly died after a crazed bull gored her in Dwarika market?' He would make her giggle like a convent nun by narrating how Mr Shah's villainous incontinence revealed itself at the most importune of times: his son's wedding! Anuradha laughed sincerely, listened astutely and spoke with the class of words that rose from a mysterious wisdom (which he thought was perfectly befitting to a Hindu woman who had the nerve to eat, of all things, chicken club sandwiches).

No wonder, then, that he wanted to embrace her, besiege her with kisses—although he wisely kept such displays of vulgar affection in a little sealed envelope in his chest. For her part, each evening Anuradha awaited her husband's return with an anticipation she had not expected to encounter so early in her married life: she understood that she had not merely married a suitable man but found in him the building blocks of a dear friend. Her mind thrilled from the awareness that her initial instincts about him proved truer as the days went by: she liked him.

He, on the other hand, was floating in an entirely different boat.

'I love you,' he mumbled one night, half asleep.

'You don't know what you're saying.'

He woke up with a jolt; he sat with his back to the bedstead, his arms folded in a huff. 'I believe that's the most insulting thing you have said to me so far.'

Tickled by his sharp response, she put her fingers on his torso and then pulled on the chest hair with a daring that silenced him because both were aware that this was the closest display of physical intimacy the couple had shared until now.

Many nights they sat on a large wooden swing on the bedroom balcony, where Vardhmaan sought her approval for a composition from one of the new stars of bohemian Europe. A particular favourite was 'Träumerei', a tune of various enchantments. Music unfurled in calm waves, a cool wind blew, and Vardhmaan asked, 'Do you know how to waltz?'

'No,' she replied.

'I could teach you.'

And so started their nightly lessons of dancing in secret, and although he tried his best, she never seemed to learn, not because she had scarce interest in waltzing or because she was a bad student but because the longer she feigned her incapability, the longer their delightful lessons lasted (in the end, she never told him that after their third lesson she could waltz like a dream—and if need be, give lessons for three rupees an hour). *But why bother,* she thought with a sly grin. The combination of her ample breasts nudging into his chest while the restless, hungry baton in his trousers pressed into her sari brought loaded intent to their post-midnight dancing lessons. On many occasions, Anuradha would surrender to the strong hold of his arms and melt inside the moment simply because she was overcome with the conviction that he would never let go *ever.*

'Would you sing for me, then?' he asked one time.

'Why?' She figured maybe it was a form of repayment for the dancing lessons.

'Because I hope to meet your essence through it.'

She nodded with a smile, and sat him down on the swing. Then, with her fingers clutching the copper chain of the swing, she closed her eyes: it was as if she were gathering the bones of her song in the pit of her navel, and her brow creased as she focused on her search. He cracked his fingers impatiently. Wind picked up breath, and the moon stepped out from behind cloud cover. A moment later, she unleashed a song of such resplendent, tender measure that not only did it bewitch Vardhmaan entirely, it also impelled him to lean forward and kiss her upon the song's completion. Then he stood up and walked to the edge of the balcony, overwhelmed as he was by the burden of her talent, the opaque exquisiteness of the melody. Of course, he wanted to ask her more about the songs, why she had inherited them, what they really meant, how could they be *this* mesmerizing ... but he decided to wait for another, more opportune occasion.

Two weeks later, one late afternoon, Anuradha was quite abruptly heckled out of her siesta by the neighing of horses under her balcony. Swamped with curiosity, she got up to investigate the medley of noises: the restless hoofs, the screechings of a bird, the groaning wheels of a buggy. Grasping the fleur-de-lis metal railing of her balcony, she peered down and saw necklaces of agitated foam dribbling down the noses of the sweaty roan mounts; the horseman was attempting to whip them back into control but was failing miserably. Suddenly, the buggy door swung open and a woman in a starched white sari stepped out, her back curved, her grey oiled hair plastered over her gleaming skull like rail routes over a map. She whacked one of the houseboys with her walking stick, to motion him to unload her luggage. Anuradha noticed an ashen parrot in a large copper domed cage yelling invectives at the servants like a haggard pimp who has done business with every kind of whore in the trade. But it was the old woman, her arresting authority, her icy deportment, who troubled Anuradha the most. Pulling back the swathe of her hair, Anuradha watched more intently, and at that moment, as her gaze rammed into the old woman's skull, she looked right up. Anuradha shuddered from the ferocity of such a stare, the spite that travelled through it as clearly as a doe in a python's belly, and understood that from today her life would *never* be the same again.

5

Perhaps it was only a vicious rumour that Divi-bai, as a girl of five years in her native Jafrabad, had fed her twin sister to the crocodiles of the river near their house. Her simple defence, allegedly, had been: 'That's what you get for nicking my colouring chalks!' which, to Divi-bai's mind, was a perfectly sensible reason for flinging her sibling into the River Kali. And not only that, the story went, just as the poor girl came up struggling for air, her hands clutching the stern of the boat for dear life, Divi-bai dashed forward and slit her sister's wrist with a knife so that the blood might attract a pack of crocodiles upstream.

Sure enough, her ambition was promptly realized.

Inside the next two minutes, as the girl pleaded that she had *not* stolen the colouring chalks ('I swear on the Lord

Shreenathji—*please* believe me!'), scaly-black crocodiles with calmly malevolent slit-eyes came swarming towards her, and in one wide-mouthed gesture smashed her skull like an egg under a speeding train. The river's currents thrashed as the reptiles wrestled for parts of her anatomy: an arm; the neck; some thigh too—a sight that so amused Divi-bai that, even now, decades later, on some evenings when she was bored, her mind raced back to the image of how easily, how deftly, how impeccably her sister was ripped apart. The reed-thin boatman watching Divi-bai was too stunned to do anything, simply because the ingenuity of such wickedness was as hypnotic as it was heinous.

She looked at him. 'Shall we call it an accident and forget all about it?'

'I will never be able to live with myself if I do.'

'Oh,' Divi-bai said, smiling. 'One look at you, and I wonder how you do so even now.'

He dropped her off on the shore.

'You'll be sorry,' she said before she vanished into the gloomy thickets. There she tore off the gauzy hem of her rice-white boat-neck dress, loosened the red ribbons in her thick black plaits, and let brambles graze her arms till she was a grisly smudge of blood and bruises. Then she sprinted home and wept as she told her oily, flabby father how the boatman had tried to molest her honour—and yes, how the rogue had stolen the dignity of her twin sister.

'And it was a good thing that *she* jumped into the river—and drowned,' Divi-bai justified in between her sobs. 'What'd we have done with a tainted girl anyway?'

Her father nodded grimly and, before dusk, he sent out a gang of thugs to beat all life out of that harmless, haggard boatman. His cataleptic, bloody body was dumped into the nearby jungle, where the same night a snigger of hyenas ate him even as he struggled back into consciousness, wondering why on earth he had stumbled into this nightmare called Life in the first place.

When she was in her early twenties, Divi-bai's beloved father was turned to ash, leaving her distraught. But after her year of mourning reached full circle, along came the proposal to marry a well-to-do widower from Bombay; she accepted without batting her thin, smoky eyes that had no lashes (her most halting feature, everyone said). Vardhmaan's father had recovered from the passing of his wife and now needed someone to help him shoulder the responsibility of the household. She stepped right in, and with her eye for detail, her unflinching capacity to achieve what she set her mind to, she made a fitting if disturbingly malicious addition to the Gandharva household.

A few years later, her husband died; her stepson trained to be a doctor and in the time that went by Divi-bai achieved total control of the house. She caned the servants, insulted relatives from her husband's side, and gained a propensity for deep sleep only the truly nasty enjoy owing to the catharsis they experience so regularly.

Everything was flying just fine.

Until, that is, Vardhmaan decided to marry.

The prospect of having to share her territory, perhaps even negotiate her role in the house, caused her to flee to her native Jafrabad just so she might scheme up what she would do with Vardhmaan's wife. Divi-bai had hoped he would tie the knot with a plain pastoral porgi who could be trained to do what she was meant to do: work till her spine gave in. Instead, she discovered that Vardhmaan had married someone who not only stemmed from one of the more illustrious families of Udaipur but, far worse, had even been to college.

And—would you believe it!—the girl spoke English!

Anuradha did not talk to Divi-bai in the first week after her arrival; they evaded each other like tigers on uncertain turf. Anuradha's closest contact, however, was with Divi-bai's much-loved African parrot Zenobia, originally bought from a three-eyed Senegalese trader who had pilfered Zenobia from a Hebrew scholar who had trained her to speak Latin and French as well as a peculiar line of Olde English now entirely out of use. However, only a few days into Divi-bai's ownership, the ashen-winged, yellow-eyed, spiky-taloned Zenobia lost all her erudition, all the poems of Shelley, all the writings of

Sappho, and in their place Divi-bai taught her how to hurl abuse like the most bitter whore in the bazaar—and that was *exactly* what Anuradha got a taste of on the morning she went up to Zenobia's cupola-topped copper cage.

'Arrè Mithoo! Sweet bird ... you like guava?' Anuradha's eyes were bright, friendly. What a beautiful bird, she thought.

'Oh, my little country cousin,' Zenobia said, in a world-weary voice, 'please wash your face before you speak with me again: you look like something even the alley cats wouldn't drag in.'

Anuradha was aghast. The fruit fell out of her hands.

When Zenobia let out an evil chuckle, it served to reassure Divi-bai that in her impossibly lonely world she had at least one faithful comrade. The old hag had been watching Anuradha in secret, marking how easily she glided through the household, cooking up delicacies, mending a missing stitch, lavishing children with affection, filling the eyes of the neighbours with awe. Rage swelled up in Divi-bai like the belly of a drowned dog. *She'll just have to go,* Divi-bai decided. *One way or another, this rustic witch has to get out of MY house.*

But then how long could they avoid each other in such close confines?

One evening, right after the grandeur of an autumnal sunset, the two women bumped into each other in the corridor of that rambling house of terrifying windows. As they faced each other for the first time, Anuradha was instantly repulsed by Divi-bai's stifling ammoniac odour, and she noted that Divi-bai had only one mustard-coloured tooth—in the very centre of her mouth—and yes, it was true: she had no eyelashes. *What is this unbearable stink around this woman?* Anuradha thought, but then decided it was too rude to cover her nose with her hands.

Divi-bai, on the other hand, was struck by Anuradha's uncanny resplendence: the succulence of her delectable youth; the freshness of her body still ringing with the sandalwood she scrubbed her skin with—and her own gaunt spine shivered with wrath at the flawless suitability of Vardhmaan's selection.

'Are you in my way?' Her tone was cold, and measured as a dram of cobra venom.

'Not at all, Divi-bai.' Anuradha, out of respect for the matriarch, sidestepped to let her pass.

'So *you* are the girl Vardhmaan has chosen?' Condescension covered Divi-bai's face.

'Yes, Divi-bai ... I am.'

'In that case, do you pray much?'

'Some,' Anuradha replied.

'Good for you, Ms Rajasthani Camel Princess,' she said, tightening her smoky eyes. 'Because there's nothing you will need here more than your prayers.' And saying that she rushed forward like an enraged tusker and shoved her, wham!, against the wall. Anuradha's forehead hit the sharp edge of a sconce. Blood leapt out of her skull. Too shocked to cry, she gripped her torn forehead with her right palm. A moment later, she looked at her hand: terrified by the tributary of blood running over it, she rushed up to her room.

But just as she neared her bedroom, Vardhmaan strode out of it and she collided with him.

'Anuradha ... my darling, what is ...'

He had never seen her this out of her depth. She did not speak a word. Seeing blood slithering down her forehead, he embraced her. Out of breath and frazzled, she melted in the carafe of his arms, its muscular reprieve. In that way, in that weeping embrace, they went into their large bedroom, where despite his numerous queries she would not tell him what had happened (how shallow to be a snitch).

After he had attended to her cut, they sat on the swing in utter silence: the wounded in an embrace. Soon enough night brought a liquid, comforting blackness over dusk: stars strode out; the mogra flowers below their balcony sent up loops of their fragrance.

They fell asleep in each other's arms.

A little after midnight, she woke him with a kiss that started inquisitively, gently, before it took full and able control of his lips and tongue. He carried her in his arms and lay her on the bed. He ran his hand over her neck and then started to yank free the knots from her hair (how appealing it was to her, that she could just hand over the recalcitrant disorder of her mane to someone else!)

'Do you think a bath would make you feel better?' he asked lovingly.

'It's not something I do well alone.'

For this, he requested her help to unbutton his linen shirt (she obliged); he requested her to pull down his mahogany emerson trousers (she obliged); he requested her to untie his white khadi draw-string underwear (she obliged). Then they washed each other with the simplicity of children exploring each other's naked bodies trembling with curiosity. In the balmy texture of the night, he poured a tumbler of cold water down the swathe of her hair; she giggled in libertine gusts. She turned to lather up his navel, the erotic tufts of black hair that led to his organ which she held confidently, inspecting its rigid attentiveness, its embarrassing will-power, and told him that this was the *other* sort of flesh one could have a ravenous appetite for: chicken club sandwiches, my beloved, were only practice. His eyebrows went up, up, up. After he cascaded water down the fullness of her breasts he pulled her to him, their wet, youthful forms closer than they had ever been.

But on some nameless erotic whim, she escaped out of his clutch.

So he chased after her.

A giggle filled the room; in the absolute darkness, Anuradha hid in one corner.

'Where are you?' he whispered, his dripping, dark body just as desirable as hers.

'Just where you need me to be'—an answer which immediately prompted him to search her out, hands reaching out into the air—oh, he almost knocked over the console—

and inside a few minutes he found her and they briefly wrestled playfully before they almost reflexively plummeted into the spaces of each other's bodies. Was it on the bed that she sat on him, her weasel-like loins clutching and unclutching his lovely, long, louche manhood, as though squeezing an orange for its juice? Or was it on the balcony swing, much later, that he buried his thirsty tongue in those thick pink lips between her legs? She loved most the lusciousness of his buttocks, their dimpled circumference, as though God had created them only so she might pull him farther into herself and then muffle her rapturous pleasure as she had, only a few hours back, muffled her anguish. *It is so strange,* she concluded after they had exhausted all the wild beasts lurking in the forest of their flesh, *that love and loathing, joy and distress, quietness and noise, all eventually blur and one is left wondering where one started and the other ended.*

6

In the next few months, Anuradha and Vardhmaan Gandharva, upon the discovery of the dissolution inside their loins, indulged it no end. Their lovemaking was unhurried and full of an animal moistness if commenced in the dewy sleepiness of dawn; swift and furtive if conducted at dusk to the compositions of the European maestros. To delay his pleasure and extend her own, she would, just before he was about to spill into her, distract him with the banality of things, and in a perfectly sensible manner, even as he was ramming her with the love in his heart, she would tell him, in her breathless, excited voice, the prices of the vegetables in Dwarika market. That the beans were more expensive than the bitter gourds, that the carrots were sweet and the tomatoes were not, that coriander had not come in weeks and the onions from Nasik were small and tasteless. In this manner she kept him going much longer than he expected, and because of this there were times when he was driving through Dwarika market and seeing its bounty of vegetables that he grew maddeningly hard at the memory of last night's deeds. It was no wonder, then, that other family members wondered why they were always holed up in their room, and to put them off the trail Anuradha fibbed: 'Oh, I was writing a letter.' Very soon, though, when Taru deciphered what 'writing a letter' really meant, she teased Anuradha, 'Isn't it time you were writing letters?' to which Anuradha rejoined, 'Actually, my dear, I am only awaiting the postman.' Some nights she ladled him into the bowl of her womb while other times she sat atop him, her knees digging into his torso, her lush black hair free, her hand clawing into his flesh as she aroused and drank up that gummy, insanely creative sap of his being. And when he submerged his fingers in her she was wicked enough to suck them in with a velocity that made him shudder down to the last fine hair on his considerable and, er ... de*licious* scrotum.

'You are making me mad!' Vardhmaan complained of the times when she resisted.

'Well, I certainly don't have to try very hard,' and she clipped her blouse back on.

In the year and a half that went by, Anuradha understood that the simplest way to keep Divi-bai content was to avoid her. So she would go into the city to spend time with Radhamashi, whose famed Spanish cook Picasso taught her how to make a sauce hollandaise without butter as well as a chocolate soufflé that was so light it had to be strapped down with thin copper chains in the oven lest it float away. Anuradha also took to reading more in her room—the novels of Tagore and Premchand—although a few breaths before dusk, her anxious heart watched for the horse carriage or the automobile returning her husband to her.

Charmingly enough, Dr Gandharva never arrived empty handed. One time he brought her a fine green bandhani sari from Bhuleshwar market. A silver betel nut chopper from Shor bazaar, shaped like a chameleon. And more often than not a delicate braid of frangipani flowers that he ceremoniously tied around the thick bun of her hair, on the swing, at night: she loved this the most, his hands touching her neck, the formal intimacy of the act. In return, she read him extracts from the letters she was writing to her mother or elocuted a poem she might have composed under the raat-rani arbour at the back of the house (unbeknown to Anuradha, Divi-bai watched her and wondered what she was writing, why her solitude was so assured, and just how she might wreck it).

The newlyweds also enjoyed taking walks on Juhu beach, only a mile or two away from the Dwarika house. Juhu beach was a long, clean strip of untainted beauty: the east side was lined with lissom coconut trees whose crevices in their ringed trunks allowed wild parrots to nest. At the other end spread out the shimmering magnificence of the Arabian Sea, its silver honour of ripples, its monsoonal fury and winter susurration.

Under the shawl of dusk, they would walk, their fingertips touching.

Now one evening, a little after seven, as they were returning to Dwarika from Juhu beach, Anuradha put her hand on her husband's shoulder and motioned him to stop outside a certain mansion that had gripped her attention, oddly enough, with its spectacular ruin.

'I wonder why we have not seen it before,' she said as they walked towards it.

'Yes.' His eyes relayed his awe.

The sandstone mansion, a royal elephant of a thing, seemed to celebrate its devastation, as a soldier sometimes boasts about how he lost his arm in a war. Tiny balconies jutted out of its numerous rooms, creepers crawled all over it, trees masked the front, like an ardent embrace of green, and a massive half-moon balcony projected out of its back (beyond which, Vardhmaan said, there was nothing but acres of marshland). Yet, in the fiery remains of this house, Anuradha saw nothing but the immaculate beauty of a teardrop. She pointed out the large, broken windows, the stately carved portal, the steep, sad driveway leading to a veranda. He was taken in by the kadam trees on either side of the carved metal gates, the spellbinding fragrance of their flowers, and they both left in agreement that the house stood in a mysteriously luminous sadness.

'One day,' she said in the car, 'I would like to live in a house by the sea.'

He nodded and gripped her hand. Although he tried his best to make things easier for her, he knew how painfully uncomfortable she was with Divi-bai around; in fact, only a few weeks back, after Divi-bai tore into pieces a poem Anuradha had been writing, he went into the ghostly darkness of her room and warned, 'If you treat my wife less than decently, it will be difficult for me to fund the flour for your chapattis.' Divi-bai was flabbergasted. Although the Gandharva family had some resources, it was Vardhmaan's generous doctor's income which kept it standing with distinction. Besides, she had never imagined her refined, unfailingly polite stepson could react in this manner. Because she dared not answer him back, her spite towards Anuradha turned more insidious.

'And in a house by the sea,' he asked as they neared the Dwarika house, 'would you sing for me?' She tilted her head and smiled. But even before she could utter the resounding *yes!* waiting inside her, she clutched her navel and muffled her mouth. She dashed indoors, slamming the car door behind her. Vardhmaan hurried after her anxiously. *Just what is wrong?* he thought. She continued running. Up the stairwell she went, down the corridor and into her bedroom, where she headed straight towards the porcelain washbasin to retch her insides out.

Nothing.

She retched some more.

Vardhmaan was behind her, panting.

'Are you OK, Anuradha … ?' She wheezed. A solemn trepidation of sweat banded her neck. After a minute, she looked up at him with tears in her eyes. He embraced her, whispering calming words. Her breath was fast; her heart beat against him with unidentified anxiety.

A week later, on the balcony, just as he was about to kiss her, she put her index finger on his lips. 'I believe I might be carrying our child.'

'What?'

At the time she tried to stop him.

When he got up on the bed and danced like a madman. When he lifted her up on his shoulder (oh yes, she thumped his back many times). When he sang some albela song so loud it woke the neighbours three houses down. *I'm going to be a father! I'm going to be a father! I'm going to be a father!* If only Anuradha had known how transient the brilliant flames of Joy are, she might even have indulged his prospective father's thrilled lunacy because, years later, when Fate altered Vardhmaan into the man she never imagined he could be, *this* night and its vivacious jubilation would surface in her mind and mock her.

7

Eight months later, as her son bawled his way out of her, the pain he employed to announce his arrival caused Anuradha to faint. But only a few minutes later, consciousness returned, and the light in the room was soft and came filtered through that terrifying window behind her bed.

'Your son is ridiculously lovely,' said Sumitra-bhabhi, whose wise, kind hands had towed the child out of her.

She handed Anuradha the baby. The new mother proceeded, very meticulously, to count his fingers and his toes, and examined other anatomical parts for fitness or shortcomings before she joined him to her tumescent teat and asked where his father was. Apparently, the midwife said, the 'slightly demented' son of Shri Purshotaam Patel had tried once again to 'fly' from the top of the house and landed himself with seven broken ribs and a smashed wrist—and Vardhmaan had had to rush there only seconds after he had delivered his own son. Anuradha lay back in silence wondering why no opera of emotions was performing inside her, and whether there was something vitally amiss because of it: she failed to comprehend that the vastness of a mother's love, if it arrives immediately inside a woman, can knock her senseless with its heft.

A week later, the three of them sat on the swing: Anuradha shored up her back on two white bolster pillows, extended her legs and lay her tightly cloth-bound mite on her thighs. Vardhmaan sat by her with only a few inches to claim as his own, keeping the swing in motion with his feet.

'What do you think of him?' She spoke coolly, as if she were asking his opinion of a new Benarasi sari. Vardhmaan lifted the rock-oil lamp over the child. The scatter of golden light, in the pitch darkness, unveiled with gratifying clarity what the couple had created: exquisitely molten eyes, that fragile incline of nose, and already, a clavicle of such elegance that lovers would expound its winged merit in letters years from now. However, it was more than his physical loveliness which overcame her: the awareness that this former tenant of her womb was the *mélange* of *their* moods and dreams and history elicited in her a love *for* Vardhmaan, which she had not anticipated childbirth—of all experiences—might forge.

'What ... what, my lovely?' Vardhmaan wrapped his arms around her when she started sobbing from the overwhelming experience of *being* a mother.

'I love you.' Her admission was thoroughly unselfconscious.

'Here is the treasure buried deep in the soil of our kismet. Thank you for bringing him up to me.'

Wiping away the single elliptical tear that came down his right cheek, she said, 'I want to call him Mohan.'

'As fine a name as your own.' He touched his fingers to her jaw—a trellis of flesh over bone. 'On the day my mother died, she begged: *Can you save me, please?* I never told that. To anyone.'

'Oh, Vardhmaan ...' A gasp in her chest.

'But don't you see? All of that seems so far away. When I hold Mohan, all things are redeemed. I'd never known salvation till I saw my baby smile. After my mother died, I studied hard. Tried to lose myself inside my books. And kept miles away from Divi-bai. Soon enough I trained to become a doctor. I got my own practice. Then one morning, Ghor-bapa walked into my house and told me about a woman who sang so beautifully that even the moon stepped out to listen.' He touched her arm. 'And now, you have brought Mohan into our life. Here he is,'

Anuradha's throat tightened. She ached to tell him that no one could save anyone: that neither God above nor the saints around, neither money nor magic, could rescue you because everyone had to bear their own cross.

'I wish I could have met your mother,' she said finally.

He nodded, and it was obvious to Anuradha that his translation from man to father had grown new skin over the old wounds, and here, now, the three of them sat in an inevitable intimacy that scented their dreams with its power.

In the next few days, relatives and neighbours and friends dropped by to see the child of mythic good looks. Wrecked widows and cruel cousins, kind aunts and lecherous grandpas, arrived by the carriage-load, walked up the hallway, up the three storeys to Anuradha's room, for just one glance at the child. And they came out, their hands behind their backs, shaking their heads in agreement: 'He is more handsome than the handsomest.'

Of course, all this hardly went well by way of Divi-bai.

Or for that matter Zenobia.

She flapped her serrated wings irritatedly and scorned respectable relatives: 'Go home now, you sons of sows! And get right back into the arses you tumbled out of!'

Divi-bai narrowed her smoky, lashless eyes and sizzled seeing the luminous regard Anuradha evoked so effortlessly, and how with the birth of Mohan she had only strengthened it further. Envy whirled through her veins like tiny cyclones she hoped to unshackle one day. But how? And when?

Divi-bai saw Mohan only when he was six months old and she remarked to Zenobia in a pensive voice: 'Did you mark his flatulence? *Unbear*able!'

'You'll have to do something about all this,' Zenobia said heinously.

'But what?'

'You have a brain, Divi-bai,' the parrot slurred. '*Use* the damn thing.'

8

Mohan was seventeen months, four weeks and six days old on the day he sang for the first time: it was a little after six, and Anuradha was in the bedroom ironing and folding his khadi nappies. The voice was but a blur, a *fata morgana* of a tune, and she stopped dead in her tracks and wondered whether she was singing (and didn't even know it?) or if some long-dead soul was trying to communicate something to her. Her queries, however, fell flat on their faces: the Song had such enchantment that her mind stood rock still and the coal iron in her hand burnt the nappy and spurned smoke into the air. In the moments that went by, she never noticed. The smoke. The crinkle of cloth burning. All she did was stand glued to the spot and listen until the song completed itself, and only then, through the stifling smoke, did she ascertain that it was, indeed, Mohan who had been singing. She gasped, not from the spirals of smoke or from overpowering emotion but at the prescience that for such depth of talent the price would be *ferocious.* At that instant Vardhmaan walked in and pulled her and the baby out of the smoky, coal-smelling room.

'Mohan was singing,' she mumbled, grabbing Vardhmaan's arm. 'He was ... singing ... the boy was ...'

At first Mohan picked up the loris Anuradha sang him to sleep with, as though the lullabies had dissolved into his rest and gushed out later. On some evenings, when his mother was working in the kitchen, the sound of the child singing, the raw, searing finesse, gripped her ears and never let go. Then he sang the songs that Pashi-ben, his massage ayah, crooned as she pummelled his back and thighs with coconut oil: Mohan reproduced the words, the arc of her melody, the hauteur in it, without a single error. Finally, by the time he was a little over two, he unfurled the songs he heard his mother sing for his father, in the evening, on the balcony, and if they stunned his mother, they released a dark treacle of admiration in his father's chest.

'The magic of your songs has come to him. even without your training,' Vardhmaan told her one night.

Mohan was at their feet, putting together a few wooden blocks.

'Did you lock the window?' she said, turning to feel whether the window above their bed was latched.

Vardhmaan felt that her response was entirely unrelated to the stream of thought he had paddled up. 'Yes—why do you ask?'

She shook her head. There was no way she could articulate the viscous terror at the base of her throat, the one she had carried like a scar of her entry into the Gandharva household from the day she had first set foot in it. 'I'm sorry ... what were you saying, Vardhmaan?'

'I was talking to you about the songs ... the ones you sing at dusk ... the ones which now Mohan sings ...'

'An aunt of mine could sing a song that lit up all the oil lamps,' Anuradha replied. 'And there was another one who knew a song that brought the monsoon on time. She sang, and a few measures into her song rain gushed down into the deep drought of Rajasthan.'

Vardhmaan was mystified. 'Are you serious?'

'The songs are a dowry of magical arias handed down in my family. Each woman came with her own tune,' she said, in a low, guarded voice. 'My mother, for instance, knew a song that made the trees flower. I remember this one time, Vardhmaan, we were at a park in Udaipur and my mother started humming her song—and there, right in front of my eyes, a grand old acacia burst into this shimmering yellow, a fever of blossoms.' She paused as she pictured the sight in her own mind. 'In our life, my mother once told me, because we cannot alter our kismet, we *must* know a way to tide through its ruthless currents. And the songs are that one device. For us, the women in my family.'

'And were *you* taught your special song?'

'Yes,' she answered, looking down. Mohan was listening intently. She wasn't sure whether he understood the import of their talk but his eyes were wide open and concentrated.

'And what is that?' Vardhmaan inched closer to her, feverishly curious to know what her song was. She was unsure whether she ought to tell him of the charmed attribute of her Song. What would he make of it? Would it overwhelm him? Maybe. Maybe not. Just as she was about to disclose its enchantment, Mohan scaled up Vardhmaan's leg, all the way to his chest, shattering, in the bargain, the poignancy of the moment.

'Violin!' he cried.

'Arrè baba!' his father exclaimed. 'What are you doing, you budmaash!' Undeterred, Mohan snaked himself around his father like an ivy, and with as much delicacy.

'I want a violin,' Mohan demanded whimsically.

'What?' Anuradha was curious as to how on earth a two-and-a-half-year-old knew about a violin, not to mention the fact that he demanded one this cavalierly.

'It's a musical instrument,' he explained, and then lifted his toy cricket bat as a makeshift violin and gestured a bow with his hands.

'I *know* what a violin is!' Anuradha restrained an urge to point out that her precocious son still wet his bed. 'But you don't even know how to play it'

'Ah,' Mohan said, closing his eyes. 'That's what *you* think.'

9

Around two months after Mohan Gandharva first made demands for a violin, he started giving impromptu musical performances of such unqualified lure that the folks of Dwarika dropped all they were doing only so they might come under the spell of his voice. The canary traders and the patrician widows, the females of flexible morals and the asexual philanthropists, upon gauging the first measure of his bizarrely sweet voice, would rush to the garden of Gandharva's Dwarika house and listen with their eyes closed, and without the slightest drift of concentration. Time and again, from the kitchen window, Anuradha would see Mohan clamber into an ancient circular bird bath, throw his legs over its mossy ledge, and then unleash a melody she didn't even know he knew.

And she was astounded by the effect it had on others.

How they stopped folding their saris (indeed, some ladies rushed out in their lace-fringed petticoats and no more!), how they stopped haggling for the crimson aubergines that cured impotency, how they forgot a century-old quarrel, overlooked a bitter grudge, glossed over a painful regret and *flew* into the firmament of Mohan's refrain. Anuradha smiled quietly at the comings and goings of people, all bound with a common love for Song and for the great healing it brought with it, and she soon grew to recognize the regulars: some came with praise, some with presents. Such as Mrs Zimmermann, the German missionary, whose husband was related to the incurably insane poet Holderin. But Mr Zimmermann had long since been burned alive by Hindu thugs when he went too far spreading the 'Word of God', and Mrs Zimmermann told Anuradha that Mohan's voice was an 'alcove of forgetting'. Vijhla, the madman, the famously failed poet, would thump his fists on the ground and wail theatrically, and it was never clear whether he was mourning the end of the recital or the fact that it reminded him of the Only One he had ever loved: a black billy goat some Mohammeden had filched from him and then butchered on Ramzan Eid.

Soft and full, Mohan's voice, like his beauty, grew and charmed, and Anuradha was astonished by just how *much* she could love.

'I never even imagined I could be this way,' she divulged to Vardhmaan.

'What do you mean?'

'It's as if all the parameters that I set in my mind—lines of discretion, borders of control, and orders of poise—have fallen away. And from my deep core rises an all-encompassing spirit that holds Mohan as he sleeps and covers him with its grace.' *He was her night's rest, and that rare, luscious laughter of the afternoon.*

It must take magic, she told her husband, to make such a being.

It was early night and Debussy's 'Arabesque' was on the swirl. Vardhmaan pulled her into his arms. 'In that case, my darling, let's make some more magic!'

Despite a firm iron leash around the neck of her emotions, Anuradha Gandharva could not believe the recklessness of her heart. Each time she sang Mohan to sleep or bathed his seamlessly soft brown body (uncreased shins; smooth pink soles) she secretly rejoiced in the arc of his eyes, the scroll of his lips, the pendant of his earlobe. Many times during the day, Mohan would rush into the room and enfold his darling arms around the column of her sari-bound form, or just before siesta, he would tumble asleep in her embrace and in doing so, he broadened the geography of her heart and extended its vocabulary. One afternoon, Mohan came running towards her, a few drops of sweat lingering over his beautiful brow. 'I want a violin for my birthday.'

The cheeky exhilaration in his voice delighted her. She remembered it was only a few weeks before his third birthday in July.

'We shall see,' came her non-committal reply.

Then, as if to attract her attention, Mohan started trouncing around on the bed, creasing up the bed sheet: he knew how much this annoyed his mother.

'And just how do *you* know it is your birthday?' she asked.

'Because I was there when it first happened.'

In spite of Anuradha's strict directive that Mohan's whims should not be taken so seriously, Vardhmaan, indulgent father that he was, went all the way up to Princess Street and bought from A. G. Nariman Traders the finest violin available that year. The trader, a Bori-Muslim with hennaed eyebrows, sold him a Guadagini-inspired Cremonese violin. Vardhmaan lifted it to admire its subtle dark radiance, its Amati arch, its gallant purfling.

'It's for my son,' he proudly told Mr Nariman.

On his way back to Dwarika, Vardhmaan stared out of his car. His eyes examined the growling sky, the opaque cloud cover, and he recalled what the levitating soothsayers of Dwarika market had been trumpeting about: that this June would herald the most brutal monsoon of the last seven decades. It could well be true: already the winds were so deliriously savage that they lifted toothless old men several feet into the air before dropping them over rooftops, and the moist, rain-heavy air provoked an intense gloominess which left the city's innumerable spurned lovers successfully suicidal. Vardhmaan, however, remained indifferent to the weather. Right now, his heart was brimming as he imagined over and over again Mohan's bright elation upon the gift's receipt.

I want my violin.

And here it is, he would say.

10

By the middle of June, Anuradha was irrevocably repulsed by the visiting herd of Divi-bai's relatives: each year the old dame imported a handful of her illiterate, hairy and fusty kin to give them a show of the life she commanded in Bombay *city*—and more importantly, to convince them that contrary to what everyone dished of her in Jafrabad, she was certainly *not* the kind of woman who would feed her own twin sister to the crocodiles.

'I have *never* in my life met such kind of people,' Anuradha told her husband one evening.

'What do you mean?'

Because Vardhmaan was out on his practice for the better part of the day he had hardly interacted with the relatives—and hence had no clue about the freak show shacking up with them.

Wasting no time, Anuradha enlightened him. One uncle, she said, was ominously silent—and according to rumour this was because his wife had caught him cheating on her and she had, in a fit of irrepressible rage, severed his appendage of urination with a tailor's rusty scissors, thereby introducing a voluntary burst of fidelity among the men of the village, who realized the women knew that man was not their enemy, only his manhood was—which, of course, required no more than a few friendly snips to keep in check. Another crank case, Veljhi-bhai, a chronic kleptomaniac, kept pilfering even the very utensils he'd been served his meals with, and so she and Taru spent many an afternoon surreptitiously relocating what he had appropriated with unrepentant virtuosity: Mohan's socks; the silver betel nut cutter; several pairs of women's undergarments.

'But out of this entire jingbang,' Anuradha said, shaking her head, 'no one quite beats Shilpa-ben.'

Of her even Vardhmaan had a slight idea: every night, barely had Shilpa-ben traipsed into sleep, than she would let out loud, breathless, erotic moans—*Aarggh ... Aargggbh ... Aaarrrhhhhhh!* This caused the neighbourhood children to stay up, not only because she was groaning like a virgin on her wedding night but because their parents were giggling like schoolgirls.

No wonder, then, that, by July, in the heart of long rains, tempers were high—and no one moved around in a viler mood than Divi-bai. In fact, everyone was secretly awaiting the day when Divi-bai's people would pack off (Taru even crossed off the dates on a calendar in the kitchen).

'Three days to go!' Taru chirped one morning. 'I tell you, I'm going to feed *all* the bloody mendicants outside the Laxmi Narayan Mandir on the very day that they get out ... Oh, has anyone seen the teapot ... or has Veljhi-bhai been at it again?'

'I don't know ... I'm tired,' Anuradha responded. She walked away with a feeling that was a curious blend of homesickness, dejection and plain exhaustion. But even in such times, glimmers of delight still found their way to her on secret, circuitous paths: in the song of the wandering flute caller; in the early morning drizzles of such incandescent lightness that you wanted to drape the sari pallo over your head and weep. None of these delights, however, came close to the pleasure that Anuradha got from reading the letters her mother wrote to her. She tore open and read Mrs Patwardhan's letters hungrily: asphyxiated as she was by Divi-bai's noxious presence, her mother's neat and tiny writing arrived like undistilled oxygen posted all the way from Udaipur.

In one of her letters Mrs Patwardhan wrote that she was well, that her grandsons were growing like tenacious weeds, and that there was now living with them an orphaned cousin. Nandini Hariharan was her name, and although no older than fourteen she was stunning any bloody way you looked at her: she scrambled around barefoot; swam naked in the Pichola at midnight; and seemed gladdened by her parents' deaths in a freakish car accident because this liberated her in a way a conventional childhood never would have. Anuradha's eyebrows knitted up as she took in the further exploits of this girl—how solitary she was; her frightening faculty for painting; how none of the other relatives wanted her—and she suddenly badly wanted to meet the mysterious Ms Nandini Hariharan and yet simultaneously stay as far away from her as possible.

Fire attracted with its luminescence: but you could get only so close before it scorched you.

'Anuradha!' Taru called out one very damp afternoon in July. 'Will you *please* help me with the khandvi? I never figured how to roll it out.' The optimism in Taru's voice, no doubt, was linked to the fact that Divi-bai's relatives were packing off after lunch.

'Your eyes tracked the rains?' Anuradha said as she walked into the kitchen.

'Pray they quell so the guests get going. A storm would be an ideal excuse for them to stay on.'

'I don't get a good feeling,' Anuradha said out of the blue.

'What do you mean?' Taru tilted her head.

'There's something about ...'

'The rains? Divi-bai's relatives?'

'I don't know ...' Overwhelmed by a dark presentiment, Anuradha lost her words. When she turned, Mohan was looking at her with a cheeky grin in his wide, liquid eyes. 'I want my violin, Maa!'

'And you'll have it, beta,' she comforted. 'On your birthday.'

'That means you don't ... love me enough.'

She looked at Taru, shaking her head at the child's emotional arm-twisting.

'If you had any idea of how much I ...' She stopped herself because at that moment Divi-bai stormed into the kitchen.

'Are we going to get some lunch out? Or shall we *all* sit down and play with the children this afternoon? Listen here, Ms Rajasthani Camel Princess ... you had better get the khandvi rolling.'

'It is better that you rest, Divi-bai,' Anuradha said coldly. 'Your guests have never gone without their meals—and I'll see to it that they won't today either.' Perhaps this was why she'd felt that trepidation a short while ago: this toxic interaction with Divi-bai was what she had intuited.

'And what are *you* doing here?' Divi-bai squatted and faced Mohan: she despised his beauty, the allure of his voice.

'Nothing!' he said, hiding behind his mother's sari pallo. 'At all.'

'See!' Divi-bai cried gleefully to Zenobia, who came flying into the kitchen. 'What did I tell you? Back-talk runs in the blood.'

Anuradha ordered Mohan, 'Go to my room, please.'

'I want my ... violin.' Divi-bai's eyelash-less face terrified him.

'Violin?' Divi-bai had never heard of such fancy things being brought into her house. 'So you can keep us up with your vile screeching as you do with your singing? *Vilein* indeed!' She was tickled with her unexpected pun.

Anuradha felt a sob accumulate in her throat. 'Just go upstairs, Mohan, please. I'll see you there in a bit.'

'Only *after* you've done the washing, my dear. Utensils in this house don't just sit up and scrub themselves clean, you know.' Divi-bai touched her one remaining mustard-coloured tooth.

'Maybe they do in Udaipur,' Zenobia trilled wickedly. 'In these small towns, all these magical things happen! Maybe if you bring in the vegetables, they'll even cook themselves. Maybe they'll even get into the serving plates and beg, EAT ME! EAT ME!'

During lunch Vardhmaan dropped by. Anuradha sighed with relief: she needed the caress of his words to recover from her ghastly encounter with Divi-bai, and as always just listening to him was solace plenty. He told her that one of his appointments in the south end of the city had been cancelled because the rains had submerged roads up there. But Anuradha, who had seen the ugly face of the Rajasthan droughts, said that she held no grievance against the monsoon in Bombay—if anything, she indulged in the dewy, dreamy temper of July. She loved how the rains announced themselves, their flamboyant entrance: the air that grew dense with storm stories; doors that bulged with moisture and refused to shut; and those mighty bullfrogs that croaked all night long.

'I found a violin teacher for Mohan. Mrs Goldsmith lives in Bandra.'

'Will she take on someone so young?' He was tying a frangipani braid around her hair; she decided there was not a lovelier feeling than this, the touch of his hand, the breathtaking aroma of the flowers.

'Ah ... well ... yes. Mrs Goldsmith sounded quite keen actually. By the way, we're all going on holiday next month. Shimla is gorgeous in late August.'

'And just *how* would you like to be thanked, Dr Gandharva?'

'I would not,' he said with a wink on his way out. 'But I'm sure you'll work around that.'

It was three in the afternoon when the guests left in the overture of a storm, and after Anuradha had cleaned up she ambled back to her room to sleep without having to worry about Shilpaben's orgasmic moaning blasting her slumber to bits. Mohan was sprawled on the bed; the cream-coloured fan whirred over them languorously. When the weak, wooden shutters behind her bed shuddered in the wind, she pulled them back, tightening them. They fell open again. A mist of rain from the leaves of the shingh tree blew in and over Mohan. She shut the windows and edged them tight with a napkin.

That afternoon, she loved her descent into her sleep, such unfathomable comfort, a plunge into dreams.

An hour and a half later, Mohan woke her. 'Maa ... may I have some milk ... please?'

He sat up on her navel, his feet to her sides, and then gently fell into her, resting his head over her shoulder. *He smells of sleep,* she thought, *and what lovely, innocent skin.* She looked up at the Seth-Thomas wall clock: it was a little past four, and now the rain was coming on like ammunition.

'I want my violin.'

'You know you can't have it till next week. Do you know how old you'll be then?' She stretched her arms and yawned; she could easily sleep for another hour.

He gave a scowl that dissolved into a grin. 'Thirty-two!'

'Close,' she said. 'But try ... say ... three?'

'I want milk.' He was certain that he was thirty-two.

'All right—but first tell me whose baby you are.'

'Pappa's!' he declared with disloyal glee.

'Then go—go ask your pappa for your milk.' She got up from bed; her back felt rested and relaxed.

'No! Oh, no!' he said, promptly reverting his allegiance. 'I'm yours! Only *yours.* One hundred and one per cent!'

'Budmaash!' She rapped him softly on his back; he giggled.

She went downstairs for his milk, the temperature of which she tested on her thumb. When she returned to the room, he was sitting on the edge of the bedstead and, seeing the milk in a bottle, he insisted: 'But I want it in a *glass,* Maa!' He started his jumping up and down.

'*Don't* do that, please.' She detested his bouncing on the bed. 'Please just sit still, Mohan, all right?'

'I want my milk in a glass.' He sat down. But a moment later, he got up again.

'You *always* spill it—drink from the bottle—I'll give you your night-time milk in my glass. And for God's sake, sit down!' Her irritation at his restlessness was rising.

'No!' he demanded. 'I *want* it in a glass. I'm going to be ... three in a week ... what will people think if they see me drinking out of a ... bottle.' He curled up his lips disgustedly; it brought out the dimples in her smile. She turned. He was jumping on the bed as she unflasked the bottle's nipple and poured milk into the glass on the teak counter.

'Here,' she said, resignedly. 'Happy now?'

But when she turned, a moist, hard wind smacked her in the face and she saw that the windows behind her bed were open. *Mohan had disappeared.* The shutter crashed back into the sill. She stood there a moment, heard time drip from the arrows of the clock, felt the lines on her palm change course, and knew that it was perfectly possible to live even if you didn't breathe for a long, long time.

11

Because she jams her entire body against the window sill, her breath is thrust out of her, but her hands are extended towards her son, wedged in the branches of the shingh tree, right outside the window: a blur of brown short pants and blue gingham.

'Maa! Maa ...' Only tiny hands are visible; the branches seem to be gulping him in. 'Please ... come for ... me ... Maa ...'

'Mohan! Mohan, *give* me your hand! Your HAND ... *give* it to me, beta!'

And he does! Throws it right up, and her fingers catch his, kissing in mid-air, her flesh against her son's. Stretching herself perilously out of the window, she is grateful for the tenacious grip of her hand over his. She starts to haul him up. He emerges slowly, hair first, then skull, then forehead, and soon his face rises up, like someone drowning, surfacing for air from the dark, mean ripples of the green tree.

'HOLD on, Mohan! Don't let go ... I'm here ... you just hold my hand ...'

'Maa! I'm scared ... *Please* don't let me ...' At that instant, the monsoonal wind smashes the wooden shutters back into the sill—against Anuradha's arm with such intensity that she loses her grip ... and he slips back into the verdure. 'NO! NO! Mohan ... Mohan! MOHAN!'

He is trying to hang on to the iridescent, slippery branches.

But they slide out of his small fingers as quickly as he gets a grip on them.

'Maa! Help me!' the sweet, terrified voice begs.

Seeing her son dangle helplessly in the tree and certain there is no way that she can get him from where she is, she turns and tears out of her room, racing over the cold corridor marble, her sari pallo billowing to the wind, hoping that her own crazed dash will, perhaps, get her to the shingh tree so that she can catch her son tumbling out of it. Downstairs the front door is hopelessly and wretchedly locked—Divi-bai has decreed it ought to be, in the afternoons, during siesta.

'Bhagwan! Hey Bhagwan!'

Slamming her wrists against the door, her evanescent, precise fury is now redirected into her feet as she considers: *back door.* Retracing her steps, she runs through the lounge, through the dim hallway with its draconian portraits, through the bare kitchen until she gets to the back door which she shoves open and charges through, suddenly aware of how precious time *really* is: every little second in life is unbelievably irreplaceable. *Mohan ... my darling ... I'm coming for you ... you just hold on ... I'm coming ...* Praying for an event out of the sweep of everyday life to occur and save her three-year-old, she sprints over damp earth and the file of earthworms, across the amaryllis patch, down the border of heavy green palms until she makes it to the front of her house. It is as if Fate has waited with held-in breath for Anuradha Gandharva to come, for her tremulous feet, for the potential hold of her arms—that occurrence out of the scope of reason—and on seeing her, Fate loosens her grip and lets go of Mohan. He comes sloping off the branches, in front of Anuradha's eyes, slowly, like an infinitely elegant tear reeling down the face of Time. Even as she rushes forward, she misses him by inches.

Falls.

To the floor.

The nastiness of gravity.

Rubbing off the mud splattered on his soft face, she lifts him up, the very shards of her life. He folds his little arms around her neck and frees the whisper that will haunt her for the rest of her life: 'I want ... my ... violin.'

'Yes, beta! Yes! You'll have your violin ... come ... let's go get it *now* ... it's yours ... I was wrong to have kept it ...' But already, the clasp of his hands around her softens, and she feels him leave as scent leaves old flowers.

She brought him into the house, laid him on the settee and called his father.

'Vardhmaan!' she cried. 'Come home *now*—your son fell from our bedroom window, and ... he's ... he's unconscious.'

'What?' Vardhmaan stood up; in the rain-bloated air he smelled something he had never wanted to smell again: cinnamon.

There was, she noted, something icky on her back, and when she touched it she found it was blood. *Mohan's blood? On my back?* By then Taru and Sumitra-bhabhi had woken, and although they had been crying in distress they somehow managed to compose themselves: Taru quickly melted pills of arnica into a cup of water and poured a teaspoon through the edge of his lips while Sumitra-bhabhi comfortingly ran her hand down Anuradha's back. 'Arrè! He'll be fine! I promise you ... just let Vardhmaan come ... now, now ... be brave ...' Sumitra-bhabhi thought back to that day in July when she had drawn Mohan out of his mother, how ridiculously attractive he had looked.

As Vardhmaan sped back home, he recalled the time he had woken at dawn and watched his mother die: how haunting her death had been, a profound, heaving occurrence that took him years and years to wrangle himself out of. Mohan had helped, no doubt: the singer of songs, performer of caprice and bringer of succour; but how was he right now? And could *anyone* survive a fall from that high—let alone a child?

As it turned out, Mohan was very much alive.

After he had examined the little boy with the motif of red earth over his right cheek—the side he had landed on—he felt that Mohan's chances of survival were unclear: he had only a small, steadily bleeding wound on his forehead; but he was senseless, in the quagmire of some heinous sleep.

So what *was* the matter?

'Hospital. I want X-rays. It is a new-fangled device that allows you to see what has happened inside the body.'

'Nanavati?'

'We'll have to make it to Harkisondas Hospital—that's the only place with the facility. I have a friend there, and he'll help, no doubt.'

It rained.

The car pushed through the silver ballast of the Indian shower, a grand dance of Kali on the chest of Shiva, and Anuradha sat with her unconscious (nearly) three-year-old in her arms, his feet extended over his father's lap. Under the dry, dramatic ivy of lightning Anuradha held back her tears, not because she was brave but she figured that she would have to be.

'Vardhmaan ... my baby is going to be ...' She needed some kind of assurance from him. But he would neither meet her gaze nor say anything. She sighed. Watching the rain gun down, the roads flood over, Anuradha wondered how they would get to Harkisondas Hospital in time. Touching the instep of Mohan's foot, the soft flesh of his earlobe, the perfectly formed nose, she realized that something inside her, without her active influence, had created his magnificent details. He was utterly vulnerable and untitled, like the work of a young artist.

It rained.

And then, the car came to a grunting, unexpected halt.

'What's the matter?' Her whole body froze. Vardhmaan started the car again. It rumbled—and then stopped. He pressed his feet on the pedal. Nothing.

'Should I get out and push?'

'No ...'

As he pressed the pedal over and over again the car would rev up and appear to start—and then just when he thought it might move forward, it would clamp down. He hit his fists against the steering wheel, in the same way that she had earlier slammed hers against the closed front door. Only a few years later, when Vardhmaan was called from work and into the arms of another tragedy, something similar would happen: then, he would give up his car and run home. But now, here, with a child in their care, that option was not open. Having no idea why, Anuradha hummed a song, in the rain, many miles from the hospital. On a grey afternoon. And over the rippling sweetness of the song, Vardhmaan turned the ignition. Song. Rain. Ignition. Song. Rain. Ignition.

Finally, this time around the danged thing started.

Grunt. Roar. Forward.

'Thank God!' *How bitter the small mercies in life are,* she thought. *How bitter and unexpected.* As the car contested its way through the rain, the density of the shower made them feel as though they were swimming underwater. Half an hour went by. They were close to the hospital now. At that moment, it struck Anuradha, that years from now, in the larger scheme of life, it would not be the evident things, or things of measure, but the impalpable, unmattering inklings which would stay with them forever: promises we ought never to have made, words that shouldn't have been spoken, glances we should not have cast.

And the legacy of her regret was a knot of four words: *I want my violin.*

In the savage rain, she wanted nothing more than to turn back, return to the Dwarika house, to her room, to the tall wooden almari above which, bound in a faded olive sari, was stored a violin—and place little Mohan in its company. When a tear rolled past her cheek she brushed it away so Vardhmaan wouldn't see it. But there was scant time for tears because only a moment later, the car broke down again—and this time, because it was evident it wasn't going to budge and because the hospital was only a short walk away, they decided to gamble it.

'We had better cut tracks, Vardhmaan.'

He nodded. 'Yes, the lane to the hospital seems flooded anyway.'

She unfurled the black umbrella as she got out. Cold water nipped at her calves. That was when she felt a knock against her heart. Seeing Vardhmaan carry Mohan in the sprawl of his arms, like a new bride being carried over the threshold.

Strides cut ripples into floodwater, and it seemed a terribly long walk.

Inside, once Mohan was placed in the care of the doctors, there was little to do but wait. Vardhmaan had found acquaintances who allowed him in as they examined Mohan's injuries. Anuradha waited outside on a wooden bench, alone. Looking out of the window at the burnt face of the sky, she thought to herself: *Is there, for such an hour in the evening, a song? A song, whose note or phrase will take me by the arm, slip its fingers into mine, or lend a space inside of which this occurrence might occur?*

A song of our time? A song of dusk?

'It's a dosed head injury.' Vardhmaan stepped out holding the surgeon's file. She felt he looked suddenly smaller, as if this day had pruned something inside him for ever.

'W/3 brain contusion.' He placed a coarse X-ray to the moth-coloured tube light above their heads. She saw the hazy shape of Mohan's brain, the halves, the grooves, the dells, the curved holder of her blood, the folds squirrelling away the memory of colour, sound, scent.

'It's a vasospasm—it occurs after a subarachnoid haemorrhage.'

She stared into the calm rage of his eyes, at his effort to delude their fears with words.

Then she asked simply: 'Is he going to make it?'

'Let us carry on with the operation, Anuradha,' he replied shortly. 'Then we shall know how things are.'

She nodded.

He returned to the operating room. She heard the click of the door behind him and saw his shadow fade. Now close to seven, completely dark, disturbingly still. Occasional lightning tore up the sky. In the calm after the storm, it came to her now, finally, the song her mother had taught her, and if she could just straighten her mind, she would remember its opening bars. *Song. Come to me, now. There be a voice that needs you most.* Cautiously, like daylight blushing on mountains, it surfaced, her mother's faint, tender voice, the bend of tune, the words—but only a few—and then the chorus she used to join in as a young girl. Mouthing the words lightly, crossing and uncrossing her fingers, she decided it was true: *we never forget.*

She had been carrying this song for all her years, for *this* evening.

An hour later, Vardhmaan returned. She stayed right where she was.

He put his hand on her shoulder. 'I'm so ... incredibly ... sorry ...'

They returned home with Mohan on her wet lap, his face covered with the pallo of her peach sari. Folks in the Dwarika home had been informed, and Taru had even cabled Anuradha's parents, who happened to be in Poona: they had already left for Bombay and were expected with sunrise. The night smelled of the frangipani braid Vardhmaan had clasped around his wife's hair that afternoon. And now, out of the corner of his eye, Vardhmaan saw her undo this braid. As he watched her pull apart the frangipani petals and sprinkle them over Mohan, an unbearable agony blinked open inside him.

With her hand over his smooth brow, she hums quietly, achingly, a lullaby for her dead son.

12

Unable to sleep that night, Anuradha oscillated between dazed anguish and hopeful disbelief. Vardhmaan, meanwhile, rested on the teak recliner, his right hand touching the floor, his sleep being the secret love child of unmitigated exhaustion and a pellet of opium. Anuradha woke at dawn and combed Mohan's hair with her fingers. She found that contrary to what others had said Death was, in fact, not deadening at all; rather, it was a dynamic creature whose black fragrance, whose concrete stillness, seeped into the wood of the furniture, the linen of the bed, the flowers in the vases: it was everywhere, as omnipresent as its only sibling, Life.

Dawn brought an orange sky and Mrs Patwardhan from Poona, all puffy-eyed and ruffled hair; Anuradha hugged her and cried without sound: the deepest wail of all.

'Damnum Fatale,' Mrs Patwardhan reasoned. 'An Act of God.'

An hour later, Radha-mashi came in a landau drawn by four Shetland ponies and told Anuradha: 'This is how life is. Makes us imagine the unimaginable. Stretches the imagination, and then our hearts with it.'

Taru and Sumitra-bhabhi were in one corner, blank-faced, bereft.

In the secrecy of her room, Divi-bai was busy glowering at that girl from Udaipur and at the way she notched up all the attention all the time.

At seven that morning, Mohan was lowered upon his bier in the lounge. Anuradha felt that his tender face was turned towards that unilluminated space mirroring life. She grew breathless from an inventory of memories: her womb remembered his restless fetal kicks; her hands remembered his gentle, flawless skin; her ears remembered his voice, bright enough to light up the night.

Twenty minutes later, they took him away from her.

When Vardhmaan lifted the bier and ledged it over his shoulder he felt as though he might smash open inside his chest. *I never once imagined I would have to put my own child to ground—wasn't it supposed to be the other way round? Why can I not speak of this sorrow? Can anyone else smell cinnamon in this wretched air?* That was when a howl thrust its whorled horns through Anuradha as she recorded it all with blistering accuracy: her husband carrying away her dead son, lilies scattered on the bier, the faint cries of a prayer, the sun resting its shafts on the quiet file of mourners, and the west wind blurring it all.

'Come along with me,' Radha-mashi counselled later that afternoon. 'This house probably has too many memories, and now they must all seem too painful.'

'I told her to come away to Udaipur,' Mrs Patwardhan added. It was an hour before the six o'clock funeral.

'I need to stay here,' Anuradha said simply. 'Because Vardhmaan will not be able to bear this loss otherwise.'

At a little before six, when she came down, she noticed that almost all the residents of Dwarika and relatives from beyond had gathered in the courtyard. Widows, young wives, children and even young men made up the convoy of mourners. An aggrandizement of tear-makers. She nodded to Mrs Zimmermann and Vijhla and all the other admirers of Mohan's singing. Through it all, Anuradha sat composed but remote: immersed in the pond of an unspeakable tragedy.

An hour later, when the full force of the respectable mourners was assembled, an unsettling moan shattered everyone's solemnity: it was Divi-bai.

'*Maari nakhyo! Maari nakhyo—maara Mohan ne maari nakhyo.* '

'Yes, yes!' Zenobia said in a theatrical tone. 'She's killed him. Killed her own son.'

It took a minute for Anuradha to ascertain that this was not some hallucination she had conjured up.

'How many times I must have told that girl to keep the window closed—but did she listen to me?' Divi-bai was shaking her head feverishly.

'No! Not once,' joined in Zenobia.

'And now I've lost him for ever. My beloved Mohan. My only son's *only* son. You tell me—could she not have been more careful? I mean, *how* could she let a three-year-old out of sight for even a single moment? And why didn't she check whether the windows in her room shut fast or not? Just you look at her, Pramitiben,' she said, addressing a startled mourner, 'she's not even let out a single tear. She must have no heart under that blouse.'

'*Besharam*!' scolded Zenobia. '*Saali suaar ni bacchi*!'

Even Taru and Sumitra-bhabhi were dazzled by this performance: for a moment, Divi-bai's convincing theatrics almost fooled them too. Vardhmaan stormed down the stairwell from the other side of the house, where the male mourners were assembled. But Anuradha motioned him with her hand to stop right where he was: the last thing she wanted was an ugly confrontation on the day her son was given to fire.

Of course, this restraint was just the fuel Divi-bai's performance needed.

'And just why would she listen to me? That girl! I am only a hapless widow in this house. And tell me who listens to widows these days?'

'These modern girls think they know everything,' Zenobia said.

'Arra-ra-ra!' Divi-bai smote her head. Then she sat back and cried, 'She *must* leave MY house!'

'What?' one of the mourners admonished. 'Please, Divi-bai. Stop! Enough said!'

Again Vardhmaan was held back by Anuradha: a single solid gaze that said it all. It bolted him in his place, even though he was shaking with fury.

'Come to think of it,' Zenobia added in a contemplative shriek, 'you're right. The woman is a murderess.'

Shock rippled through the crowds: some got up and walked away; others were shaking their heads. Mrs Patwardhan clutched her daughter's hand. 'This is *it*—I'm taking you back to Udaipur. Away from this witch. Right this instant.'

'But Vardhmaan ...'

'He's welcome to come with us as well ... but *you* are getting out of this hell.'

Anuradha went up to her room. She packed her clothes, a few photographs of her years in this house, her books of handwritten poetry, and then she stopped at Mohan's birthday present, the violin from A. G. Nariman Traders: she didn't know what to do with it. She looked out of the window: horrible, *horrible* window. She saw that Divi-bai was still at it. She smiled to herself: perhaps *this* was all the mercy in life. Where one astonishing nastiness distracted you from an agonizing sorrow. Clutching her suitcases, she walked down with her mother; at the doorway, she explained to Vardhmaan that she needed some space to mourn, an acre of cleanliness to encompass this disaster.

He agreed and was about to embrace her when Divi-bai flew to the doorway in the midst of their farewells.

'What? She's leaving the house!' As though it was an utter surprise to her. 'How can she leave you in *such* circumstances? And who'll look after you, Vardhmaan?'

'Some people will fall to *any* level,' Zenobia decided. 'Any bloody level.'

Anuradha took hold of Vardhmaan's hand because she didn't know where that fist of his might land. And because it could be the last time she would ever touch it.

'Just remember one thing,' Divi-bai screamed. 'If you leave MY house today you will NEVER EVER step foot into it again—understand? A woman like you has *no* place in my house.'

'You are absolutely right, Divi-bai.' Anuradha looked the hag right in the eye. 'A woman like me has no place in a house like yours. None whatsoever.'

PART TWO

In a House by the Sea

13

Once upon a time, a long, long while ago, when Anuradha and Vardhmaan were no more than a twitch and kick in their mother's navels, there lived, in the town of Taunton, in Somerset, the only son of Lord and Lady Beauford, Edward. A noted rememberer of the epics of Dryden, an admirer of Arabian dressage, and an inveterate loner, it was said Edward's disposition was most genteel: everyone who met him liked him. In the final chapters of the eighteenth century, to bring in Edward's twenty-first birthday, the gregarious Lady Beauford hosted a magnificent gala attended by all of the titled and the upper crust of England.

It was at this gala that Edward's eyes fell upon a dashing Indian: his heart slammed against his chest with a Desire as old as time, perhaps older. The heir to a minor princely state in Rajasthan, Raghubir Singh's gleaming black sherwani, the various sartorial accoutrements that included a bejewelled sword in his waistband, his regal, curled moustache and masculine carriage, had stimulated more than a few loins that evening. Young Edward had heard his mother mention that the prince would be lodging with them during his time in England since his kingdom had recently been 'relieved' by the Visiting Whitepeople—and he was now one of those wastrel monarchs who lived an utterly louche life, pawning away the odd diamond when bills came calling. The more Edward stole glances at Raghubir—the brown-skinned man's Byronic jaw; his rolling, rakish laughter—the more he felt his entire body tremble awake, as though every cell in his skin had eyes which were opening up and seeing for the very first time.

'So ... how long will you be here?' They were under a large oak whose dignified, dead branch arched over the two of them.

'I believe for the next two months. Then, I return to India.' Raghubir had a divine smile.

'Back to Rajasthan ... I suppose?'

'That's not on the cards, I'm afraid.' Raghubir inched towards Edward; their arms were touching. 'Bombay, Presidency of Western India that it is, will be where I hang my hat. Your mother informs me you are terribly well versed in Dryden.'

'More terrible than well versed,' Edward accepted, and a blush enflamed his cheeks. Instantly charmed by the Englishman's self-deprecation, Raghubir suggested they walk by the river, perhaps to understand what made the willows weep. But even before they were entirely out of sight of the guests, Raghubir turned and with a wild hunger in his soft black eyes he pressed Edward on his haunches and fed him the adamantine sumptuousness of his manhood: a proud, thick, succulent thing had found its home.

For the next two months, every night, no sooner had everyone gone to bed than Edward would knock on Raghubir's door. He would open it, pull his young lover in, strip him naked, fling his white body on the antique four-poster bed and then take him with the craze of his ample lust. Each night his stallion's legs shuddered as he rammed Edward again and again, such gentle violence, such refined debauchery, until all of Edward melted like the frost on the grass and he felt he was everywhere: a liquid of flesh spreading over the bed sheets, over the Indian's sweating body, over the floor.

'Does it hurt?'

'All love hurts,' Edward answered, dripping with sweat in the unreasonably cold English night.

'Well ... this one might hurt more than expected,' Raghubir said, and thrust harder.

But it doesn't, Edward wanted to say. *Don't you see? This is what I was made for. This is who I am.*

Then, one June morning, when the jays were wild but the moorhens were quiet, Raghubir packed his bags and left for the port of Dartmouth.

Two years later, the very week that Edward came into his inheritance, he grabbed his last little farthing and caught the next ship out to Bombay. He landed there on a cool Sunday morning and promptly rented a hand-rickshaw to Raghubir's abode, near Apollo Pier. But in India, the river of Edward's love took a sudden dip around an unforeseen curve: much to his consternation, he found out that not only had Raghubir, as tradition dictated, married, he had also spawned, only recently, a child with very lovely lips. Entirely unperturbed by the minor detail of his matrimony, Raghubir embraced Edward warmly—feverishly?—and suggested that his staying on in India might not be such a bad idea since they could meet often enough. Under the implication that their affair would continue, even flourish, and with the benefit of his inheritance, Edward Beauford built in Juhu a mansion modelled, in part, on the manor home in his native Taunton. Upon its completion, passers-by often stopped dead in their tracks to admire its sandstone magnificence; in fact, the first time that Raghubir dropped by, he too was astounded by Dariya Mahal's lofty ceilings, the half-moon balcony overlooking the marshes, and the elegant fantail doves pacing the circular railings of terraces like miniature noblemen.

'Promise you'll visit often?'

'I'll try my best,' Raghubir said. That evening their lovemaking was urgent and insane and, conducted to the melodic, circular cries of the black cuckoo, it was infused with a lyrical quality neither had encountered before. As he watched his lover grit his teeth with passion, Edward thought: *I am Desire's secret. And Love's pariah.*

For the next few years, Edward worked mainly on his garden, one designed on the popular model of the time—*Occidentals Verdureis,* all ficuses and. tapioca and wild bamboo: a tamed jungle, if there was such a thing. And inside such wildness, the only aspect of gentility was the pond built to house the goldfish Raghubir had given him: a gift of love. Raghubir, happily for Edward, visited frequently, and they shared a ripe companionship, a history of mutual secrets, and strolls by the sea that made everything—the horrid waiting; the even horrider hoping—worthwhile. But it was waiting for his lover which taught Edward the truth that the only thing larger than his love was his hope: he earnestly believed Raghubir would, one day, leave his wife and children, and come and live in that sandstone mansion christened Dariya Mahal.

'The Castle of the Sea, my dear. That's what Dariya Mahal means.'

'And I suppose I am the prisoner in it?' Edward's eyes were forlorn.

In this way, nearly two decades went by, and one morning Edward Beauford stood in front of his armoire mirror and saw that the boyish beauty that unravels through the upper classes of his ilk had left him without so much as the benefit of its alluring footprints: caught in the quicksands of his middle age, he felt that the only way was down.

'Leave her!' he yelled at Raghubir that winter. 'And come. Live here. Like you promised. It's been eighteen sodding years now!'

'Now, now, Edward.'

'Don't you *dare* treat me like a poodle!' Even hitting Raghubir was an act soaked in eroticism.

'You know I love you. But it'd be silly to leave her. Besides, what would they say about two men living together?' Raghubir's teacup was balanced on his naked lap; they had still not dressed.

'What *would* they say?' he argued. 'I won't live in some stupid castle. A captive to my desire. No, nothing doing.'

'Well, let's aim for next Thursday?' Raghubir placated. 'At six. Wait here. I will come for you.'

'Promise?'

'Of course!'

Even before Wednesday was up, Edward had prepared for his lover's arrival.

The stairwell was lined with a stately red rug and the curios were polished; a scrumptious meal was prepared and the table was decked with the finest linen and a china set that was once part of the dowry of an Egyptian princess. At five thirty, Thursday evening, Edward donned a spiffy linen suit, cut out a single black rose and laid it on the chaise he was sitting on. Flipping through the pages of his Dryden, he imagined how things would be once Raghubir was living with him: would they wake in the morning and prepare breakfast? Would they quarrel over little things only so they might make up with an impassioned, unhurried lovemaking?

He was giddy when the grandfather clock in the hallway struck six times.

He sat upright.

His ears pricked up: was that a carriage? Horses? The sound soon passed. He heard more clip-cloppings and airy whippings—but they too faded like some tired, roving echo. When the grandfather clock boomed seven times, Edward's body twisted with hope and rage and fatigue. The fantails refused to step into their carved wooden house; the black roses wilted; a stole of velvet darkness curled itself around the lithe neck of the twilight: and gradually, a gush of stars emerged.

It turned eight.

Nine.

Ten.

Thursday. At six.

Edward waited. On that black chaise. In a half-moon balcony overlooking the marshes. He waited until the morning of Friday passed. He bore the afternoon out. Then evening came—and left. A day later, an exquisite whiteman slumped to one side; a black rose tumbled to the floor.

The fantails fluttered agitatedly because they knew: Edward had died of waiting.

By the same evening, a breathless, crazy, deceived sadness oozed out of his flesh and seeped into Dariya Mahal: it trickled into the spaces between the flat stoning, swam into dusty corners, wove around the rafters, until the house and Edward's waiting grief were one single monument to heartbreak. A few weeks later, in the absence of its keeper, the garden, *Occidentalus Verdureis,* took over the house. The Reuses crowded in and the frangipani boughs smashed through the windows. An angry lawn invaded the marble floor, wild grass covered the dinner table, and wild, nameless birds nested in the chandeliers.

Of course, in the years that followed, several folks tried to procure and inhabit Dariya Mahal. When one family tried to raze the grass in the kitchen, a majesty of hissing cobras spat out at the children; another couple tried to paint the house: but a few hours later, the lustrous ruin of the walls emerged from *under* the paint. Another family, which had the nerve to doss in Dariya Mahal, was afflicted by the Plague of Nightmares, and they had terrifying visions about men making love and tiny closets on fire and yellow wasps feeding on newborns. When the rumours of such savagery turned into legend, Dariya Mahal was left alone, and it tended to its sadness as a gardener tends his rose garden: assiduously, kindly.

And it, too, *waited.*

For someone vast enough to understand and accept its tale of love and heartbreak. Then, rather unexpectedly, one evening, a house-hunting doctor, still reeling from his son's death and desperately missing his faraway wife, set foot in it. At that moment, Dariya Mahal bowed its head and sighed, because no matter how you looked at it, it was finally at home.

14

In the months after Anuradha left for Udaipur, Dr Vardhmaan Gandharva would spend long lonesome nights on his balcony, and the mogra flowers in the bed right below, which used to send up loops of their fragrance, wilted under the gravity of his gaze. When he looked up, the moon fled behind cloud cover: the same moon that had once looked upon the couple's lovemaking, that poem of sweat and muffled moans. It was Taru who first noticed that Quietness had spread through Vardhmaan: it wasn't merely a baffling reticence but the species of heavy silence one finds in the folded white wings of Death's seraphims. But as soon as Divibai noticed this troubling hush, she decided to remedy it: after all, if anything happened to Vardhmaan, who on earth was going to run the house?

'I'll get you married *again,'* Divi-bai assured. She had stormed into Vardhmaan's room without even the consideration of a simple knock. 'Just last night I was told of a sixteen-year-old Jafrabadi enchantress who has not eaten non-vegetarian, speaks only when you ask her to, cooks frugally, and is educated all the way to the fourth grade ...'

'The fourth grade?' Vardhmaan said with disbelief.

'Yes, yes—that's all the education a woman needs because it teaches her enough to count how much her husband earns without inciting in her the need to spend it all. Unlike *that* wife of yours.'

'I am *not* leaving Anuradha.'

'I am not asking you to leave Anuradha,' she reasoned. 'I am only asking you to marry someone else.'

He threw up his hands. He had still not forgiven Divi-bai's vile conduct on the day of Mohan's funeral, and his rage was unexpressed simply because of a puzzling quietness that had settled in him like a silverfish in a book.

'Once you will see this girl all your romantic loyalty will disappear.'

'I *love* Anuradha.'

Divi-bai paused for a minute and said to Zenobia: 'This boy has gone mad.'

Zenobia added, 'He has become like those pig-eating British. Next he will be writing poetry for her.' She tch-tched dramatically. Then they announced unanimously: 'But WE will cure you!'

Vardhmaan refused to respond. He only prayed that his stepmother and her parrot would leave as quickly as they had come: but after ten minutes more of her company, when it seemed as though she might sprout roots here if she stayed a flash longer, he ordered: 'Please get out of my room.'

'*That* girl will never step foot in this house!'

'I agree entirely,' he said as slowly as he could. 'And that's precisely why I am getting out of here.'

It was as if his words had worn boxing gloves and socked Divi-bai in the stomach: she stared at him in the bleak awareness that *this* was a defeat that defeated her. Then she drew her white sari pallo over her head and returned to her room, where she sat up on her bed, her hands cupping her face, weeping inaudibly. Who would run this house? What would the gentry of Dwarika think when they learned that the son of the Gandharva clan had left it—and that too for the love of ... of ... a *woman?* How would she cope? Only Zenobia grasped the pain of a woman who would bear the fate of a queen bee—and perish in her own chamber.

In the days after Mohan's passing and Anuradha's departure, Taru heard Vardhmaan rise along with the sun and listen to *Memories of Alhambra* or Handel's *Messiah,* which, in the raw, sweltering dawns of India, seemed like shy communications with the afterlife. Taru considered writing to Anuradha to ask her to come back because it was enough that she had lost

Mohan; she shouldn't lose her husband as well. But she felt it was not her place to do so. Instead, she decided to be even more sensitive towards Vardhmaan—although she was never sure how to approach him (not because she was afraid of what he might say but because of his devastating silence which stood up like an imposing, unyielding rampart against the World). All Taru hoped for was that Dr Vardhmaan Gandharva, frangipani braid buyer, Handel aficionado, chicken club sandwich scaredy-poo, might find his rescue in the consoling touch of his wife.

And Taru was absolutely right.

Some nights, Vardhmaan was convinced that if Anuradha didn't mysteriously rise from the darkness of his bedroom and drape her hands around him, he would break. Like a mirror. Or glass. And if she was here, and if she might hold him, he would confess what happened between him and Mohan right before he had died. *What Mohan had told him.* A simple sentence that was now a noose around his neck ... but he knew she would never return to this house.

And so, after seven months unfolded between them in a pashmina of exquisite remembrances, his sorrow calmed, his thoughts acquired resolution, and he decided to get out from the Dwarika house—away from its cruel memories and its toxic atmosphere. He had told Divi-bai. The next step was to go house hunting. And after he found that house, he would board the Marwar Express to Udaipur and woo, plead or threaten Anuradha into returning to his life, to *their* life. Would she come back? How was she right now? And where on earth was he going to find a house large enough to accommodate their sonata of lament? *Oh, Anuradha* ... he whispered one night because he suddenly remembered *just* the kind of house they might move to ... *my Anuradha* ...

... *Vardhmaan,* she said right back, *Vardhmaan, my beloved storyteller, there is blood on my back.*

Can you see it?

Those days in Udaipur, exiled out of love on many levels, Anuradha woke in the early mornings with a disturbing wetness on her back. At first she had pointed out the presence of this blood to her mother. 'Maa, can you ...'

'No, beta,' her mother said, looking down. 'There is nothing there.'

'Are you sure?'

'Are you OK, dear one?'

Anuradha stared pointedly at her mother. 'You think I am going mad, nè?' She even remembered touching it, as she had on that afternoon when she had lifted Mohan back into the house and the blood from his head stained her back.

'Well, it must have dried up by the time you showed it to me,' Mrs Patwardhan said feebly. Anuradha's throat turned to stone: why could her own mother *not* see that slippery, icky, sindoor-red slur of red? Why, only a few hours back she had felt it under her shoulder. And now her mother was saying it was not there! Unable to cope with this discrepancy between her reality and the reality of everyone else, she ran to her room because the only respite from this sensation was a long, cold bath with an infusion of eucalyptus leaves. Pouring tumbler after tumbler of water over her back, she sat naked on a three-legged wooden stool certain of one thing: that the only other soul who could also see this most mysterious blood on her back was her husband.

Because he too had it on his hands.

Because it was their son's blood.

Blood that *they* had created together, adding flesh and memory and bone and song along the way.

When life didn't seem to get any better, Anuradha feared that she might misplace her sanity on the circuitous road of mourning. Like her husband, so far away, she too would wake in the still of night and remember Mohan—the softness of his earlobe; his pink soles which she kissed after bathing him—and when she found there was no Vardhmaan here to divide the density of her recollections, she panicked that she too might break. Like a mirror. Or glass. Sensing the vulnerability of her condition, an aunt of hers, a barmy old creature, built like a ship with shadowy topaz eyes and a certain talent for melody, took things in her hands. She confronted Mrs Patwardhan and warned her that if they didn't do anything about this, Anuradha would lose herself in the labyrinth of her suffering. Mrs Patwardhan listened attentively because this aunt knew a song that made houses fly, and indeed, around half a century ago, she had lifted the Palace of Bikaner from its location and transported it thirty-four miles to the west so the princess in residence might enjoy longer twilights, unobstructed by the acacias present in the previous setting.

Narrowing her eyes, the aunt advised Mrs Patwardhan, 'You will sing to her ... and *teach* her the songs such that she will not forget ever again ... otherwise ...'

'Will you help?'

'Certainly!' she assured.

They found Anuradha in the parlour, reading. Grabbing her by the elbow, they brought her to the pergola, at the back of the estate.

'What?' She was stumped by her mother's demeanour and her aunt's presence: what *did* they want from her? It was there, under a shimmering sunset, under three hundred pelicans in flight, that the two women sang with profound sincerity, unparalleled talent, and such pathos that when, during the recital, Anuradha felt a red ickiness over her back, she let it be: a few measures into the Song, the blood dried up by itself, like gems of water drying into the hot desert soil, without a trace; for eternity. Stamping back her tears, she joined in with the chorus. The veins on three necks throbbed like land before an earthquake; their bangles lent a metallic resonance when their hands lifted into the air, an ivy of flesh that spoke to the Heavens; and their voices wove and tightened with such enchantment that villagers on the opposite side of the Pichola felt an urgent, inexplicable need to cry and grown men and adolescent women and newborns opened their mouths and thrashed their hands on the banks and wept so much that a small, steady stream of their tears flowed into the lake.

'No one can change Fate,' Mrs Patwardhan said after it was all over.

'What's for dinner?' Anuradha asked brightly.

Mrs Patwardhan beamed. Linking their hands, they went back inside, where, at the circular marble-topped dinner table, Anuradha ate with the appetite of a mud wrestler, with a boorish voracity that implied her healing was underway. Sure enough, one week later, Anuradha felt that she was *seeing* again. Once again, she was aware of the glory of the gloaming and the peacocks at dawn. A day later, she became aware of the yellow, nameless flowers whose fragrance lingered in the soul like the echo of footsteps in a cathedral. She laughed for no particular reason: the laughter of children. And when memories of Mohan gouged her chest like spears in her war against Destiny, she sat down and repicked that silken thread of the magical song her mother had taught her, and freed it from her throat and launched it into the great sky above until she was one with the blue vastness, and her own sorrow found a far larger landscape to blur into.

In this way, a speculative peace slipped on red woollen socks before it stepped into her sleep.

Then one evening, craving for her husband—his apt selection of Mendelssohn; his detailed anecdotes—she walked into the alcove of her room. Under the yawn of dusk, she ached to tell Vardhmaan of the fruits of her mourning: how the songs had leapt to her rescue; how she wanted nothing more than a frangipani braid, and the glance of his fingers on her neck. She bit her opalescent nails raw considering that she might never be with him again.

What had he done with the violin? Would he ever come for her? When?

Now, though, after so many months apart, it seemed more and more unlikely.

Maybe Divi-bai *had* succeeded in splitting them apart for ever.

Anuradha's throat felt like a live coal. She looked up and tears raced down her cheek. *Where are the small mercies?* Right then, through the tearful prisms of her gaze, she saw a most spectacular sight. There, in the distance, in a raggedy blue gown, hair cut short as a tramp's, arms bamboo-like, feet making long strides, was an adolescent girl walking over Lake Pichola. And what do you know! She was as lovely as the moonlight stuck in puddles. *No,* Anuradha argued with herself, *this cannot be. I've been asked to believe much in the last few months. But a girl walking on water? No! I won't buy that.* To confirm her doubt, she ran breathlessly down to the pergola, where she motioned to the girl. The ruffian looked up as slowly as she could: her hair was wild but secure in its wildness, and her stride was strikingly feline.

'Were you really walking on water?' Anuradha asked her when she was in earshot.

'Walking on *water*?' the girl said, entirely unflustered. 'That's nothing! You should see how I do it on land.'

15

In the next few weeks, Anuradha pieced together as much information about the walk-on-water girl as she possibly could—mainly from her mother.

'Hmm ... Nandini's an odd thing, my dear, and you might be wiser to keep out of her turf.'

'Really?'

'Everywhere she has been ...' Mrs Patwardhan lowered her neck and her voice. 'In each house, in each estate, the population of weaver birds goes down.'

'But what does *that* mean?'

'Well ...'

Cat's blood she had in her. *Cats.*

Seven generations back, on Nandini Hariharan's maternal side, a woman had coupled with a leopard in the mountains of Matheran, and to this day the family could not rid the bane of cat's blood in their veins. Blood that made the women gorgeous and selfish and recondite, and eat all sorts of things. Little mice. Sardines. Weaver birds too. Of course, Anuradha was far too modern to believe such chit-chat—until, that is, the evening she saw Nandini crouched under the neem tree, under the nests of the weaver birds: the look in the girl's eyes was unhuman, burning, troublingly concentrated. So Anuradha drew the gauzy curtain because she did not wish to know what would happen next: it was enough to see someone walk on water.

A week later, Anuradha's normally reticent father was uncharacteristically vocal about the orphan living with them. He mentioned, in a raspy voice, that not only did Nandini smoke beedis—powerful tobacco rolled loose and lit high—she also jumped at children because she had a lifelong detestation of them (although she was, at fourteen or fifteen, barely out of the talons of her own childhood).

'What's worse, she paints,' he concluded. 'And that's the scariest bit.'

When Anuradha asked him just what was so wrong with a hobby as harmless as painting, he clarified it was *what* she painted which left everyone in a duck fit. Apparently, Nandini, since the age of five, had made portraits of people that revealed them in *essence:* seeing through flesh, past bone, she recreated on her canvas a portrait of the core of her subject. For instance, when one haggard, sparrow-fingered relative sat for her hoping for an accurate, one might even say flattering, representation of her self, Nandini created, with the lick of her brush, a Medusa-like creature in a red sari with blood dribbling down her fat, voracious lips. Unfortunately, everyone who looked at this painting—a discus of imagination whirling out paint—was awed by the astonishing likeness she fashioned, and they too thought to themselves: *Why, that's exactly how I thought she really was.* And never mind if this meant that a middle-aged, God-fearing, bhajan-crooning dame with six children became, under Nandini's hand, a Medusa with blood dribbling down her lips.

She saw people for who they were.

And people hated her for it. *Hated* her.

That same week, in the month of June, as rain was glowering in the Rajasthani sky, Anuradha saw the little tramp painting under the banyan tree by the lake. The air was clear but dry and expectant of moisture, like a lover awaiting a letter from her beloved.

Anuradha approached cautiously. 'May I ask who it is that you are painting?'

'So, you too have lost what you loved?' Nandini did not even look up from her painting: her concentration was so intense it reminded Anuradha of that instant in a ballet when the dance and the dancer become one.

'Am I to assume you have as well?'

'No,' she said. 'I've been lucky enough to never love.'

'Not even ... not even your parents?'

'I was painting you,' she said after a moment; she licked the side of her lip with her tongue. 'Want to see?'

With intrigue flapping its wings in Anuradha, she peered at the canvas: she saw a woman with an uncanny resemblance to herself—possibly older—standing under a massive kadam tree. The older Anuradha was waving farewell to a child in brown half-pants, cream shirt and a camel tie standing at the opposite side of the road. At first she conjectured that maybe it was an oblique representation of Mohan's death; but after a moment she saw in it an altogether different species of sadness, and she had to stifle a sob that was as sudden as the thunder above them.

'I've been meaning to talk to you,' Nandini continued; she was used to people being overcome by her artwork. 'And tell you that all that this heart esteems will be snatched from it.'

'How wise you are!'

'Oh, not at all!' she said without any affectation of modesty. 'But I'm brighter than a comet's arse because I've been through hell a time or two.'

'I ought to have talked to you earlier ... Mother mentioned you lost your parents in an accident ...'

'I know, I know,' she said, brushing away Anuradha's concern. 'There are losses to mourn and songs to sing. Oh, look, Anuradha, the rains are here!' Indeed, startlingly silver spears of rain ambushed down, changing the topography almost instantaneously: the red earth heaved its arid chest to the liquid embrace of the mausam.

'Let's make a dash, tootsie!' Nandini grabbed her painting and easel, 'Ships ahoy!'

Parrots shrieked; peacocks quivered their flashy, blue-green plumage; and two drenched women, bonded by loss and rain and a very perplexing painting, sprinted indoors. When Mrs Patwardhan saw them from her bedroom window she sighed. But her trepidation was not without valid reason: she had, after all, known Nandini's family much better than anyone else in their house.

Nandini's father, the genius Dr Hariharan, a student of Pierre Janet, had restored the mental status of people long ascertained as incurably insane: brides abandoned at the altar, women who had lost their first-born during labour itself, as well as an assortment of useless grandmothers, ugly spinsters and aging coquettes. Upon the personal invitation of the Queen of England, he moved his practice to her quaint little isle, where he arrived in the flaming heart of the Era of Insanity: hundreds of thousands of women were losing their wits even quicker than the men. His practice in Harrow flourished and they bought a Victorian house in Harrow-on-the-Hill, with a bald viscount for a neighbour who enjoyed his four o'clock tea naked as a jay bird, carefully scanning his copy of *The Times* with a tortoiseshell magnifying glass.

In the next few months, many remarked that it was very strange, indeed, that Dr Hariharan's curative style—a mixture of charm and masochism—extended to curing *only* women. Most doubtful of this was none other than his own wife. Nandini's mother, the nearly illustrious Mrs Hariharan—who had worked with Picasso when the fella still drew cartoons for girlie magazines in Louveciennes—was ever suspicious about how her husband cured his patients, alluding more than once to the immensely restorative powers of physical love which English women, in the regrettable company of English men, were alien to. Perhaps Mrs Hariharan was not that off target. Dr Hariharan's patients snapped out of their lunacy with a smile that history showed as lasting a lifetime, and as the fame of his madness panacea grew far and wide, his relationship with his wife crumbled like a day-old peda. Before long, the couple were arguing at length—and breadth and height and width—and when they ran out of things to disagree upon, they started to beat each other out of the sheer repulsion they felt for one another. They scrapped splendidly, starting an argument over lunch and concluding it over dinner by hurling things at each other, slapping a cheek, kicking a navel until exhaustion or a wound put them to sleep in the hope that they might wake up refreshed and scuffle like famished piranhas after some hapless fish.

Nandini, in fact, was born in the midst of one such momentous argument.

Mrs Hariharan's labour pains started on an amayvas night in Harrow. So she summoned her husband from the mental hospital to help her deliver the baby. But because he arrived after the water bag burst she accused him of irresponsibility and all through the delivery abused and kicked him like a colicky mare till he left, bushed and bruised, letting her bring Nandini into the world all by herself, which she did successfully—cutting the bloody umbilical cord with her own nails, wiping away the messy placenta with her wide palms—and then putting the babe to her breast to suckle. Much later she confided to Nandini: 'You arrived during an argument I was having with your father. And thank your stars that I won—otherwise I'd have gagged you from my shame.'

Now, three or four years later, when Dr Hariharan, the insanity guru, was caught practicing his exotic Indian-style medical procedures on the pallid, prose-ridden wife of Lord Windermere of Cumbria, he was promptly banished from the country for disreputable behaviour.

'Bah!' He threw his arms in the air. 'That bloody Lord Windermere reads far too much. Does he think the world would have advanced in number if men went no further than reciting poetry at women?'

When word spread that Dr Hariharan, medicine man and Saviour of Women's Hearts, had been evicted from England, an ominous hush fell upon the island and all the women wore black for many days until one morning Lady Windermere, in a fit of uncured lunacy, killed her husband by shoving a rusted rake through his poetic chest. By that time, though, Dr Hariharan had been forced to leave the country, not only because of his dalliance with Lady Windermere, but also because he had corrupted everyone with the notion that the missionary position caused nightmares, and because he had famously declared, 'Let's do it rover-style!' And so, on a ship called *Chastity,* the Hariharans arrived in India, where the doctor and his wife soon gained the reputation as 'unarguably the most arguesome couple in Udaipur'—as a result of which, no one talked to Nandini because every mother worth her name in salt knew that contention was as contagious as clap, and if only one of their children were to realize the delight of the repartee, the Argument Pandemic would obliterate Udaipur's long-nurtured code of politesse for ever. They lived in a large house on the very outskirts of the city, and it was said that Nandini Hariharan had not spoken to a single human other than her parents in all her time there. Nandini took to painting when her parents rowed, not to cope with their fighting but to understand it better, perhaps even to immortalize their unearthly rage. It was no wonder, then, that, at the age of seven, a few days after her father had done the most Unimaginable Thing to her mother, she wisely concluded: *Life is pathetic.*

'In fact, they were rowing the time they kicked it,' Nandini told Anuradha a few days later; their intimacy was not tender but it was brutally frank. 'We were getting back from the Bazaar of Two Rupee Birds when my mother felt the need to wallop my pa because he was in the habit of speeding—and he did that only for the purposes of making her vomity. So she lashed out at his eyes with her silver purse; not unsurprisingly, my old man on the wheel lost control and hit a humongous bull chewing cud in the middle of the road. The car was totalled. I was thrown out.'

'And then?' Anuradha cupped her mouth.

'Then they were history. Old hat. Dust to dust ... and the rest of that bollocks.' She lit herself another beedi. 'Then I was moved around like the luggage no one wants. Not nice. But worse came when I was sent to live with an uncle from my mother's side.' Because her smile was chillingly bitter, Anuradha wanted to ask her what had happened there—but Nandini's shroud of reticence prevented any further probing: all she knew was that something awful must have happened to Nandini during her time with her uncle.

'Anyway, enough about me. What's your story been like?'

With an unsentimental memory and meticulous details, Anuradha told her about how she and Vardhmaan had met for the first time at Radha-mashi's house, the whole chicken sandwich tamasha, and Divi-bai's wickedness, and Mohan's prodigious singing, his tragic passing... ending her account with the simple words: 'The man taught me the waltz.' Anuradha's tone was perfumed with longing. 'There was a time, Nandini, when I wrote poems. Not that they were anything to speak of. But we would sit out on the balcony, on the swing. He was my most intimate listener.'

'You reckon you'll ever scald your fingers flipping chapattis for him again?'

'It seems unlikely,' Anuradha said. She had given up on seeing Vardhmaan now. 'It's all over.' She would not return to the Dwarika house; he had not come for her. Her heart sank back a few inches; the sun went down; no stars came up.

None at all.

Of course, Anuradha Gandharva was only deceived by her pessimism as she would be later deceived by her optimism. Because only a few evenings later, as she was coming back from the pergola, she saw a man in a natty dove-grey suit, his head held up straight, a metal travelling case in his right hand, walking solemnly towards the house.

'Vardhmaan!' Her panting whisper reached him as though her voice had risen from inside *him:* and, in some ways, it had.

'I have come for you.'

'Not a single night has gone by when I haven't thought of you.' She embraced him, tightly, vehemently, something in her flesh burning to dissolve into his. 'He was much too large for his own life. Mohan was.'

Although she could not weep, she sensed that *he* wanted to: she felt a rush of pity for the hearts of men, for they did not have a language to translate its most aching secrets.

'Come back to Bombay. With me. *To* me.' He looked leaner, but just as luscious.

'I told you, Vardhmaan,' she said as she walked him to a stone bench under the guava tree. 'I will *never* step foot in the Dwarika house. Not after what Divi-bai did.'

'Who said I was taking you back there?'

'Then where to?' Her eyes were puzzled. He explained that he'd taken up a new house, by the sea, that it was so large he still hadn't seen—and probably never would see—all of it: but the bedrooms had high ceilings and curved balconies and a large, somewhat feral garden with fruit trees and a circular moss-bank pond in which the goldfish never died. Was this the house they had stopped outside several years back, when they were returning from Juhu beach? That house of radiant ruin. She listened sincerely, enchanted as she was by the prospects of returning to the sonnet of their marriage.

'We could start over again.' He took her hand in his. 'We may even be safe. This time.'

'But someone might come along with us—is that all right?'

'Who would that be?'

The same night, as Vardhmaan was washing away the sweet, iridescent beads of Udaipur perspiration off his back, Anuradha ankled it to Nandini's room. She sat by the little orphan, who was already in bed and reading by the light of a hurricane lamp. She suggested, asked and finally insisted that Nandini come to Bombay. Anuradha's fear for Nandini was that because no one wanted her, sooner or later her extended family would marry her off to some blind, leaky man with one foot on his pyre.

'So come! Free yourself from this little town. Discover how a big city might fête your genius!'

'Golly, Anuradha, I couldn't do that.' But her eyes brightened up: diamonds in her pupils.

'And why not?'

'Because Vardhmaan and you are ... are ... starting anew ... I'd only be the bone in the kheema.'

'You're the last person to intrude, Nandini. Come. We'll cut a few laughs.'

'Do you suppose that if a baby's buried alive, it dies soon? Does mud go into its mouth? And that must surely make it choke, right?'

'Nandini ... !' Anuradha stood up in revulsion; she couldn't even picture an infant buried alive, suffocating from mud slipping down its throat and nose. 'Where did *that* come from?'

'I'll come.' Nandini sighed. 'I'll come but I'll come as a friend—*not* family. Neither Vardhmaan nor you will question what I do because what I do will provoke questioning. And by the way, did I mention? Your husband's all velvet. Smooth little charmer—but a bit on the silent side, nè?'

'How sweet of you, Nandini!' Just what did she mean, *quiet?* If anything. Vardhmaan was Mr Anecdote himself; Nandini was off target, she decided. 'You'll love Bombay, and I know this much is true. That ... we shall ... be ... all right.'

'I sunk that painting I made of you. And the child at the other side of the road.'

'Why?'

'Too much blue,' Nandini said. 'Had to go ... down into the Pichola waters ... with all the other things thrown in there.'

'What "other things"?' Anuradha wondered whether that was why Nandini had been walking on the Pichola the first time she had seen her. But the girl would entertain no more curiosity: 'By the way, when do we leave for Bombay?'

'Next Friday!' came Anuradha's upbeat reply. 'Where we will live in a house by the sea.'

16

On Sunday of the following week, a rusty Panhard Levassor came to a grunting halt outside Dariya Mahal. Three individuals disembarked from it, pushed open the lofty black gates and walked up the steep, narrow drive. They swung open the main door and walked in: Anuradha was instantly electrified by the damaged rafters, the exquisite ornamentation of the flooring, the dining table on which a mongoose was sitting with one gold eye open, the teardrop chandeliers of atavistic glamour, the whorled wooden stairwell, which, in a few years from now, would do something *awful* to Nandini.

'It's *something* else!' Nandini said in an awed voice. 'How many storeys?'

'Three. But the last one is only a terrace. So one might enjoy the sea at dusk.'

'And you spoke to me of a balcony.' Anuradha touched his elbow.

'Come ...' Taking her arm, he led her up the stairwell, up its three vertiginous spirals, before they came to a landing that led to the half-moon balcony. Fantails burst out in a sputter of white. The railing of tiny stone pillars doubled as a trellis for the black roses, and past this, in the distance, the thick marshes spread out endless and rebounding—like the vast space a lover finds in love.

Anuradha sat on the black chaise. 'The house is so beautiful. Tell me, now, what endless sorrow has made it so?'

With words carefully chosen, with no needless sentiment, Vardhmaan told her and Nandini the exquisite and unusual love story of Edward and Raghubir. Details and poems. Goldfish and promises. Isolation and betrayal. What struck Anuradha, however, was the way that Vardhmaan was telling the tale: it was entirely different from the way in which he had told her stories in the past. Where was the enthralling tone in which he had described his childhood triumph in the chilli-eating competition? And where was the wry compassion that accompanied his account of Ramu-aunty, the three-breasted quack searching for a Cure for the Broken Heart? They hadn't just been stories he had told her, she decided, they were the very narrative of their marriage. Vardhmaan continued with the story, mentioning heartbreaking minutiae in a detached voice, never once wincing as he spoke of Edward's venomous loneliness: and his gorgeous, molten eyes, Anuradha noticed, conveyed neither interest nor indifference. She sighed. And some nameless part in her reached out for those long nights on the swing, in the Dwarika house, nights brimming with parables and intimacy and sonatas: and slowly, those nights surfaced in her heart like the half-remembered splashes of a dream.

Those memories, however, could not reduce the anxiety she felt upon glimpsing the flickers of Quietness in him.

Something inside her tightened.

Luckily, though, her attentions were snared again when he concluded his lingually economic account with a single, stunning sentence: 'And so, that evening, Edward died of waiting.'

'He died!' Anuradha's eyes misted over.

'Here, actually.' Vardhmaan put his palm next to Anuradha. 'On this same chaise. In your house.'

'My house?' she asked again, unsurely. And unbeknownst to her, her words echoed and bounced off the windows and steps, and with this utterance Dariya Mahal's bricks and stones had woken, like cursed princesses in fairy tales, and received her: she whose anklets would cover the impenetrable silence, whose child's glee would resound in time, whose gaze would emboss a permanent mark on the history of the house.

Early next morning, Anuradha and Vardhmaan's bodies lay over each other: knees crossed, hair careless, skin rested, arms embroiled with each other, like copulating kraits. With the sparrows jabbering in the madhumati, Anuradha's hand reached for his chest, tugging at the hair around his brown-red nipple: it grew erect. Then her fingers circled around his belly button, and he smiled, eyes still shut. Slowly the fingers slithered down to his polished firm flesh: Vardhmaan stirred in lazy upward strokes to her pull and slide.

His fingers touched her neck, tracing its length, feeling her thick, black hair.

She, on the wings of an ancient, formidable instinct, rose up and draped her body over his, slipping him into herself with uncanny gentleness so as not to wake him completely and destroy the dreamlike sensation of the act, but to amplify it further, into a deeper realm of mischief. Their forms, brown, young and taut, moved silently, as people move in their sleep: their breathing changed measure, their skin leapt to greet its counterpart eagerly like a schoolchild returning home, their scents wove through and melted, and the amatory sounds of muscle slapping over each other with gentle vigour quieted all else: the entire world, it seemed, had paused to absorb their rhythms. His hands grasped her breasts in slow rolling movements and, reaching up slightly, his tongue flicked at the red tip: a faint mark of saliva remained on her skin, a tribute of his erotic pull for her. Anuradha's hands cupped his shoulders, touched his neck and jaw, and she leaned to kiss him, twisting her tongue over his, and spilling all of herself into him. When she closed her eyes and tightened herself around him, he gasped and she chewed on her lower lip till it bled.

His thumb was there: at the base of her spine, where it dimpled.

That's where she liked it.

17

'It's not important to have good neighbours,' Nandini announced at the breakfast table. 'But it *is* crucial to have interesting ones.'

The marble-topped dinner table was sparsely laid out: two glasses of milk, a chopped banana, and an indigo ceramic plate of almonds and raisins. Vardhmaan was upstairs, bathing, readying for work, while Anuradha was chalking up a list of culinary essentials.

'When do you reckon we'll get to meet the neighbours?'

'I have no idea,' Anuradha said uninterestedly; the task of furnishing the kitchen was on her mind. Right then, she heard footsteps. Vardhmaan was sporting a smart cambric shirt and twill trousers, hair oiled back, his doctor's tan attaché in his right hand.

'Arrè ... Nandini was asking about our neighbours. I thought you'd know more about them.'

Vardhmaan pulled back the chair and sat down. He was grateful for the bowl of fruits Anuradha had kept ready for him. 'Juhu is bubbling with people,' he said impersonally, without even looking up. 'Lots of them.'

Nandini waited for an elaboration: her eyebrows hiked in interest. Even Anuradha stared at him. What kind of people? she wanted to know. Who were their new neighbours, for starters? But Vardhmaan only picked up his bowl of papaya and ate away methodically, slowly.

That was helpful, Nandini thought. *Good morning, Mr Wordy.*

Vardhmaan was secretly flustered by Nandini's flamboyant off-shoulder white crêpe dress with a plunging décolletage (although Anuradha had warned him that Nandini had nicked outrageous dresses from the collection in her mother's antique dowry chest).

'And there's a school and a market nearby?' Anuradha probed.

He nodded. Suddenly conscious that both women wanted more details out of him, he wrapped up breakfast and stood up to leave for work.

'Because I was planning to stock up on supplies for the kitchen ... how far is the nearest bazaar?'

He gave her precise directions to Church Maarkit, the local bazaar, roughly half a mile from the house, and discreetly handed her money for the shopping.

At the doorway Anuradha reached for his wrist. 'The beach is so near ... if you get home early, we could go for a walk.'

He took a deep breath. 'One of these days ... besides, you might be too tired from the shopping.'

'Is everything OK?' Anuradha felt swamped by a painful isolation in this huge house by the sea.

'Of course ...'

'Well ...' She just didn't know how to tell him that she found him still the same—yet en*tire*ly different. Where were the tales that he brought home for her like ripe, freshly picked fruits from the orchard of his observations? And where were the braids of frangipani?

Because Nandini would not come to Church Maarkit, Anuradha went alone, three camel-bone circlets around her arm, all pretty in a coriander-green sari. A shamelessly blue sky arched over her and the trees lining the broad, clean main street whispered to each other. The houses in her new neighbourhood were well-built and constructed out of brick or stone; the gates were distinguished by aristocratic fretwork; and the balconies had stone railings. *What an enchanting place to live,* she thought gratefully.

Anuradha found Church Maarkit sober yet colourfully alive, like an out-of-work courtesan: the shops were square and small and lined up beside each other with the names of their owners emblazoned on them in Hindi. Pulling out her list, she started hunting ... sugar, flour, daals, spices, oils, vegetables ... the shopkeepers were both warm and welcoming and fair in their dealings. She heard old hags bargain for green chillies and toriya and beans; a cycle wallah was greasing the chain of an upturned bicycle; in one corner, vagrant children amused themselves with a madman by dropping his cap or pulling his pyjamas. Before her shopping was wound up, she had picked up on local gossip—including the rumour that the baker, Mrs D'Souza, had, years ago, flung her haggard, unforgivably dull husband into the baguette oven and then married a much younger assistant with whom she now ran the D'Souza Bakery and Biscuits. When someone sped down the opposite side of the road, honking up a racket, a woman selling raw turmeric root told Anuradha that it was none other than that dastardly Joseph, a former maths teacher who now worked as a chauffeur after he was fired for forcing brandy down the students of standard seven when they forgot Pythagoras's Theorem. Joseph and his wife Mary lived in Juhu Gaotan and had a son called Jesus. Whenever he was sloshed to his gills, Joseph would hurl the car on to the wrong side of the road, screaming, 'Oye, there! Look at ME! Not only did I give birth to God, I even slept with His mother!'

On her way back to Dariya Mahal, because she had bought far too much to be carried by hand, Anuradha decided it wasn't clever to walk. But she didn't see a single horse carriage in Church Maarkit. Outside the market, at the crossroads, on spotting one, she promptly signalled out to the driver. He turned and trotted the horse up to her side. As Anuradha climbed aboard she noticed, on the other side of the road, a woman who had obviously been trying to nail the attention of the same tanga. Not wishing to upset her, Anuradha asked the driver to stop near her. 'I'm sorry ... were you also hunting for a ride?'

'Never enough rickshaws around here, you know ... don't worry ... I'll hoof it.'

'Listen, I'm not going very far. I live on Juhu Road—may I drop you where there might be more rickshaws?'

'Juhu Road? Ah ... I live there as well ...' The woman was around the same age as Anuradha, neither unsightly nor pretty, yet appealingly plain with short black hair, tamarind-brown skin and a kind smile. 'I'll get off where you do ... normally I walk back but I suddenly got so out of breath I just needed ... ah, yes, I'll come. Thank you.'

After she boarded, Anuradha helped her adjust her bags and then motioned the tanga wallah to start.

'I'm Anuradha,' she said, extending her hand.

'What a lovely sari, Anuradha,' the woman admired, touching the vibrantly green hem. 'I'm Pallavi ... so strange that we live on the same street and we've never met before.'

'That's probably because we just moved in.'

When Anuradha told her that she and her husband and a cousin were the new occupants of Dariya Mahal, Pallavi's affectionate face sported disbelief. 'It's just that for years no one ever could live there. Folks tried, of course. But they never lasted. So I guess no one ever expected to see someone rooming up there. I'm sure you've caught the gupshup about the house. Didn't someone die inside of it? Of heartbreak, as I recall.'

'Ah well ...' Anuradha shrugged her shoulders. 'It's home now.'

'Of course.' Pallavi reached forward and touched Anuradha's hand. 'Welcome to your new home! I hope you find only gladness here. Juhu's full of adorable oddbats—which my husband and I, unfortunately, are not. We're horribly plebeian. He teaches English Literature at the local university.'

'How wonderful! My cousin Nandini would love to pick his brain on Byron. Would he know of libraries in the vicinity?'

As Pallavi gave her directions to the nearest library, the tanga wallah, a straw-thin man with a handlebar moustache, was somewhat surprised by the informality that had swept in between the two women: it appeared that they'd taken an immediate, unqualified shine to each other. In the course of their talk Anuradha revealed more about herself and Nandini and Vardhmaan.

'Doctor, huh ... in that case, I might end up visiting your house more often than you'd like!' She grinned. Anuradha was tempted to dig into that remark but restrained herself. She noticed that Pallavi did have a somewhat worn-out face, with rings under her bright oval eyes and slowly emerging crow's-feet at the ends of her resplendent smile.

'Have you met any of your neighbours yet?'

'None—only you.'

Pallavi rolled up her eyes for a moment. Then she told her, in an animated, absorbing voice, about the folks who lived on the street, starting with Kamini-devi, the local madwoman, all wild white hair and spidery hands, who spent her nights on people's verandas ('But she's quite harmless, and she sells tragic love stories for the odd torn sari or for leftover chapattis').

'Oh, and the house next to yours—who lives there? Of course! The Millers! Well, Mrs Miller and her son Sherman. They're Irish—and watch out, for they have this irritating turtle dove who sings arias at dawn ... a real pain ... but Sherman is an out-and-out charmer ... Arrè, *bas,* tanga wallah! Stop here, huh, this house.' She stepped down, smoothly wrapping her sari's damaan around herself. She drew out her shopping bags and went on to open her tiny green purse, 'We must share the ...'

'Oh, please, *no.*' Anuradha waved her hand. 'Next time I go to the market, I'll ask you along. What a lovely place you have!'

'Come over some time ... In fact, drop by for tea the day after tomorrow—if you don't have much on your plate. But don't count on anything special: I can't cook to save my life.'

'I'd love to,' Anuradha said simply (although, later that night, she scolded herself for accepting so easily). 'I'll get some chakris, if you like. Maa's recipe, and mind-blowing to the last crumb ... I'm planning to fry a batch this afternoon.'

'Hmmm ... mouth's watering already ... see you Thursday. Around five.'

Back home, no sooner had Anuradha settled the essentials into bottles and jars and canisters than Nandini, in a show of uncharacteristic domesticity, made her a tall, cool glass of nimbu-paani, and as they sat out on the wooden swing on the shady veranda, she detailed all that she had discovered in her morning exploring the house. The champa tree in the back yard was ninety-seven years old, as the date carved into its knurled foot showed, its long green leaves were woven into nests by tailor birds whose eggs, when they didn't hatch, turned to gold with grief, as grief does to many things. A large, elaborately carved dovecote at the south side of the house was home to thirty-six milky fantails that preened haughtily on the balcony wall, like a collection of brides before the altar. Now the stone fountain in the little pond at the front of the lawn—which had even caught Anuradha's interest—was, the inscription at its base revealed, acquired from the derelict monastery of Lorezo Monaco, in Salerno, and in its waters swam the goldfish which, ages ago, had been a gift from Raghubir to Edward. (The first golden pair had been carried back from Xian, frozen in a pewter pot and gently placed in the pond, where they defrosted overnight, and much to Edward's surprise not two but a whole school of them surfaced: that they had mated and produced their offspring in glacial conditions acted as a well-meaning if utterly deceiving omen for Edward that *love triumphs over all.*) Now, though, the goldfish, as they had for so many years, lived and bred with discretion, careful as clans, elegant in structure as in movement, never rippling the skin of the pool by rising up for air but merely swimming under the translucent epidermis like scattered jewels. What Nandini kept from Anuradha was that she had also unearthed a formidable stack of love letters written and never posted, tied with jute, smelling of lavender and sadness, because she feared that Anuradha might only have them burnt or thrown into the sea.

'That's quite a lot to get out of one morning.'

'That's almost everything.'

'Meaning?' Anuradha asked.

'Meaning what'll I do here *now?* Meaning, I'm in Bombay—but I don't know a pauper from a prince in this place, and Hail Mary!, tell me just how am I going to get a start in the art world if I don't?'

'Your talent will be enough.' Anuradha remembered the painting she had made of her in Udaipur, with herself standing at the door bidding farewell to a child on the opposite side of a road. The one that Nandini had so mysteriously drowned. 'You'll glow.'

'We're all worms,' Nandini said whimsically. 'But some of us are glow-worms.'

'I have an idea. Remember that aunt of mine—to whom even you're vaguely related—Radha-mashi? Now she knows *every* trendy twit worth knowing in Bombay. Even the reclusive painter Khalil Muratta is a friend of hers. Once I get things sorted here, I'll take you to see her. How about that?'

'My mother was an admirer of Khalil Muratta.' Nandini smiled: the prospect of meeting Radha-mashi, the apsara of the art world, shot cheer into her. 'Didn't he stop painting after his wife died?'

'How awful!' Anuradha felt pity for the man whose heart could not sustain the loss of love.

'Exactly!' Nandini said sharply. 'She had *no* business just dying like that.'

Later that night, once dinner—baigaan ka bharta and rotis dusted off a coal fire—was wound up, Nandini excused herself and retired to her room. Anuradha suggested that they go up to the balcony, and when Vardhmaan asked whether it was OK to bring the gramophone along, she was thrilled at his offer. Perhaps things would be as they had always been? As Handel unreeled into the smoky, irrefutably black night, she leaned her head on his shoulder: they were sitting on the chaise Edward had died on. Above them, stars arrived in radiant finery and under the stars midnight herons wheeled towards the marshes, their eerie flapping barely audible as the tune of *Messiah* collected strength. Without asking one another they were, all of a sudden, dancing, gliding: her hand around his back, his chin pressing against hers—not quite a waltz, just a perfumed but nebulous togetherness.

'I met someone called Pallavi today ... she lives only a few houses away from us. I don't know why I took to her. She might make a decent friend, I think.'

'Good ... I'm sure she will ...' He changed the subject abruptly. 'Were you ... all right in Udaipur?' He pressed her closer.

'I learned the old songs and when some evenings were unbearable, I sang them. Saved myself. Measure for measure. Note by note. How do *you* think of Mohan?'

'Intensely.' He needed to tell her what Mohan had told him only seconds before he died. That noose of a sentence choking him even now. That was when Anuradha saw it again. The Quietness. The sapling of a silence in his grave eyes: it'd taken root, perhaps opened a first tendril, pushed out a leaf, and gently but vehemently it would extend in him, unravel through his memory, twist over his thoughts and influence his actions for ever—it chilled her to the bone.

'For some things there are no songs,' he said after a long pause.

'Never again do I want to miss you, Vardhmaan. And *never* when my breath is bouncing off yours.'

Hearing that, Dariya Mahal threw its head back and let out a bitter, hollow laugh no one heard: Mrs Gandharva's hopes were *so* cute.

18

On Friday evening the same week, around half past five, when Anuradha answered the hesitant knocking on her portal, the last thing she expected to see was an endearing white lad on her threshold, his hands behind his back, a flick of blond hair flopping over his right eyebrow. He introduced himself as their neighbour, Sherman Miller, and explained that the kite he had been flying high into the sky was now, embarrassingly enough, stuck in the branches of a tree in their back yard. Could he, he requested, rescue it from their balcony? Anuradha immediately took to his hesitant poise, his stammer of brogue. She said that because she was busy rolling out parathas for dinner she could not come with him. 'But my cousin will be glad to help ... Nandini! Oh, Nandini!' she hollered.

Upstairs, on the balcony, as she lay sprawled out on the black chaise, the depth of Nandini's concentration in a play by Ibsen shattered like pottery shards: *Now what? Is there no solitude in this world?* Putting out her beedi, she rose, stuck her thumb between the pages of the Ibsen and arrived down the whorled stairwell. That was the first time he saw her: lazy evening sunlight gave her an uncertain halo, an Ibsen drama betwixt her hands, arms all bony and head at an annoyed tilt.

'Nandini ... meet Sherman Miller ... Sherman lives next door—and he's got a kite stuck in the trees in our back yard ... he wanted to use our balcony to see if he could untangle it.'

She nodded, turned around and walked back up the stairwell: slowly, silently.

'Follow her,' Anuradha ushered him. But the cold, mysterious demeanour of the girl made Sherman Miller want only to turn and scuttle home as fast as he could. Why had he even bothered to come here? Aw, dash the kite! But Anuradha encouraged, 'Now *go*!' Grinning uncertainly, he ran up to the balcony where he saw Nandini standing with her back to him, her elbows on the stone railing, staring into the vastness of the marshes, green and gorgeous and full of cattle egrets with delicate crests.

'Won't stay a minute,' he apologized as he tried to unwedge his cobalt paper kite from the tree. Pulling at the spiky Surati string, he gave it a yank or two before it lifted out of the branches and swooped gently back to him. Putting the kite under his arm, he gave her another glance—but she still remained distant. He started balling up the string around his fist.

'So long, then,' he mumbled before he turned to scoot. 'Sorry to bother you ...' He stopped dead in his tracks when she turned and interrupted him with the lustrous audaciousness of her gaze, which convinced him of the human body's remarkable capacity to turn, most rapidly, into jelly.

'Are you Irish?' That hint of drawl had her antenna up and whirring.

'Only when asked.' He chuckled.

'Because your accent is ... How should one say? ... *most* appealing ... your single redeeming virtue. I've been to Dublin with my father, y'know. Ages back. Marvellously depressing! Death everywhere. Gloom spreading out wide and far, like a black rainbow.'

He didn't know what to say; her speech left him speechless. Besides, her sindoor-red cotton gown had an intimidatingly glamorous train that swept the ground as she walked over to his side. 'Say something, my li'l' potato picker!' she teased.

'Er ... I'm not one ... I even go to school.' He hastened to add: '*And* I play cricket. For St Joseph's School. It's only a few minutes from here. Do you go to school?'

'Education destroys the mind.' She folded her arms and looked stern. 'I couldn't take it, those frigid nuns hovering over me, those dictums of Wrong and Right, those inane school texts, and ... and for heaven's sake, they teach you embroidery! Can you imagine me sitting doe-eyed, threading a needle and then ringing a square rag with neat, elaborate stitches for six hours a week? And then go off rushing to some sad spinster once it's over and have her congratulate me on my pathetic efforts?'

He grinned sheepishly.

Although she had been keen to write him off as only another pedestrian kite flyer, she was, admittedly, quite riveted by his looks. Was it his tanned skin, its divinely polished brown lustre? Or the imminent muscles in his arms, such as one might associate with a gondolier? Those blue eyes, dreamy pools to wade inside, to never emerge out of. She leaned forward and corrected that errant slip of his dusty-gold hair; her touch unleashed a tremble down his back.

'There!' she said with a smug smile. 'I've restored you. Into a human being.'

'Are you and your family going to live here for ever now?'

'Family?' She sounded shocked. 'My old people checked out ages back. The woman you spoke to was my cousin. Anuradha. And she's more like a friend than a relative. But I'm putting up with her and her husband only until wicked and wonderful things happen to me.'

'Meaning?'

'I am Nandini Hariharan!' she announced. 'Soon to be the beedi-smoking beloved of the art world. The darling of the *demi-monde.* And the *belle de Bombay!*' Then she laughed at her own histrionics, and as if accepting her affectations, took a bow. 'By the way, how old are you, lad?'

He told her he'd turned sixteen that year, and when he asked her her age she frowned. 'Me? I'm timeless!' A moment later, she admitted she was fourteen 'give or take a decade'. That was when Sherman decided that she was entirely unlike anyone else he had ever known.

'*That* is where you're holed?' She pointed to a small cottage only a few hundred yards from where they were standing.

'With my mother. Isabel Miller.'

'What does she do?'

'She ... she is ...' Now he was *really* stumped.

'Come on now,' she urged. 'You can tell me. I've taken on every deviance in the book.'

'Er ... she's quiet after my father left. *Very* quiet.'

'Ah!'

'She's quiet and sad and broken,' he blurted; later that evening, he repented his clumsy confession. 'Actually, it runs in her family. Her mother had it and *her* mother had it.'

'What're you on about?' Exasperation tinged her voice.

'*Triste incurabilis*,' he whispered.

She thought over the phrase, translating it, twirling it with her tongue: incurable sadness. 'How fantastic! Do enlighten me, my darling Mr Miller ... what exactly is *triste incurabilis?*'

'A condition of the heart. They say the heart can break. That someone can dent it. Or gouge it. And then, it is never the same. Some of us recover. And some, like my mother, never do. But that's what I want to change,' he said, and zest flashed into his blue, blue eyes. 'I'll train to be a doctor and then I'll study *triste incurabilis* ... and then ... I'll find a cure for it.'

'Hah!' she said, suddenly angry. 'A pesky little pinthead like *you* will find a cure for the broken heart! Didn't they ever tell you? There is none!'

'But there *is* ... it's just that no one's found it ... and after I train to be a doctor, I'll be the one to find it.'

'I should have known,' she said. 'As soon as I save you, you want to go forth and become a doctor ... for Chrissake, Sherman, that's so un*forgiv*ably bourgeois!'

'But ... what do you do here all day?' He switched the topic; he didn't want to lose the single thread of attention she'd thrown his way.

'I read. I think. I correct my prejudices if they're in danger of becoming boring. And Miss God,' she said, pointing her finger skywards, 'put me down here to bring joy and sunshine into the lives of millions.' She giggled. Then sobered up: 'And I paint. So I may become the artist I am.'

'Can I swing by some time ... ?' he asked. 'I mean ... I mean, I don't have many friends and ... and ... roundabouts here is plenty lonesome.'

She asked him whether he would get her novels; he put his hand on his heart and promised he would. Then she felt she had been far too lenient with him. 'And do you know any of the verses of Yeats?'

'No!' Only sissies knew poems, right?

'You vulgar little schoolboy!' she ticked him off. The warmth on her face made way for frustration. 'Let me be, then. And no, I'll *never* let you in here.'

How could he *not* know Yeats, she thought, and if that were the case, why was he even alive?

Knowing there was nothing left to say, he turned to head home. Now it was certain he would never get to be with her again. Oh, blast! He wanted to kick himself. Just then, at the balcony door, he remembered the few lines he had heard his marmie quote after her evening whisky (or two). He clicked his tongue to his throat.

'Wine comes in at the mouth,
And love comes in at the eye,

Nandini swung around, gripped by his voice.

'And that is all we shall know for truth,
Before we grow old and die.
I lift my glass to my mouth,
I look at you and I sigh,'

'Come back on Monday.' She waved. 'After school. I need a subject. To paint. And get some more Yeats, please.'

19

It was at Nandini's tactful, but unrelenting urging that Anuradha was travelling all the way to Radha-mashi's mansion on Altamont Road: after Nandini had read in the *Bombay Gazetteer* that Radha-mashi was the sort of lady who put the *demi* in *demi-monde,* she wanted to check for herself whether Radha-mashi really did know her Rembrandts from her Rodins.

'What's she *really* like?' Nandini's louche linen gown was torn at the edges, a bundle of beedis was ensconced in her pocket, and her straw hat was not removed even in their hired black buggy, but merely adjusted at a haughty angle.

'Well ... Radha-mashi lives a large, free life. Her coterie is all artists and writers and pianists ... a bon vivant in the truest sense, and her parties are *the* must-attend events of our city ...

Oh, and she breeds Yorkshire terriers,' Anuradha filled her in. 'She shows them at the Bombay Presidency Kennel Club, and they are—and I'll lynch you if you tell on me!—all addicted. To gin and tonic!'

'Gosh! How awful!' Nandini exclaimed. 'I mean, hasn't *anyone* heard of tequila in this town?'

'I'm afraid they're only waiting for you to enlighten them,' Anuradha said as they were coming up the drive of Radha-mashi's house.

A few minutes into their introductions, charmed by Nandini's absurd humour, her epigrammatic savoir-faire, her reckless gung-ho, Radha-mashi stood up and clasped Nandini's cheeks in a billow of affection which she herself had not anticipated this early into their acquaintanceship: what was it about this girl that just made you fall in love with her?

'You're a buried treasure, my rose petal!'

'In that case, feel free to unearth me!' Nandini unleashed a savage gale of laughter that left the Yorkshire terriers hot and bothered.

'Well, da*rrr*ling, I'll bet my zardosi silk that one day you'll be an outstanding artist,' Radha-mashi said after she learned more about Nandini's interest in painting. Over the years, she'd encountered innumerable prodigies, and could easily sort out the pearls from the pellets.

'Nandini's fiercely talented,' Anuradha affirmed; she was sitting on the davenport opposite them. 'Maybe you should see some of her works. You should come to Juhu. To Dariya Mahal.'

'Better still,' Radha-mashi suggested, 'why don't you bring your artworks to one of my Thursday salons? That way I can even introduce you to my dear friend Khalil Muratta. I'm sure you've heard of him ... ?'

'In bits and pieces.'

Although Nandini was fully aware of Khalil Muratta's standing—the *International Art Herald* had dubbed him 'the world's greatest living painter'—she feigned a sophisticated indifference, as if Radha-mashi had merely mentioned a talented dhobi who could beat every stain out of a filthy kurta. 'But I suppose it wouldn't hurt to say hello to him,' she added cunningly.

'It wouldn't hurt at all!' Radha-mashi agreed. She was convinced that the members of her salon would adore this wild and wonderful vagabond.

While Nandini and Radha-mashi were animatedly discussing the latest novels of Paris, the bohemian fashions of Romania and the peculiar bedroom afflictions of the colonials, Anuradha closed her eyes and harked back to that day, only a few years back, when she had come to this same house and seen Vardhmaan from the window of her room for the first time as he had stepped out of his black buggy. She grimaced, recalling the chicken sandwich gotala ... her own disappointment when she never heard back from him ... and then how he had come careening up the driveway to ask her hand in marriage (and yes, she did have the right side of the bed). It had all seemed so perfect, so impossibly romantic when, during her honeymoon, he had, for the first time, tied a braid of frangipani around her chignon. But the honeymoon was long over, and now, when she gazed upon all that had happened *afterward,* she was overwhelmed by the realization that the only purpose of innocence was that it had to be lost, and the most defining characteristic of love was that it must be longed for.

'Ready to go?' Nandini said, breaking Anuradha's reverie.

'My dear, you have only just arrived,' she said with a smile.

'Actually,' Nandini said, narrowing her eyes, 'that doesn't happen till Thursday next.'

Seeing Nandini grin wickedly, Anuradha wondered what havoc this girl would stir up in Bombay. Who would end up as a helpless little weaver bird in her devious hands? And would Nandini ever sink into the water she had long walked upon?

On the day before she was scheduled to attend Radha-mashi's famous Thursday salon, Nandini excitedly spooled off a list of all the celebrity artists and the notably idle with whom she would be brushing shoulders. Anuradha, sitting cross-legged as she sewed tiny peacocks into the hem of a yellow blouse, listened with pricked-up ears.

'But I'm *really* keen to meet Lady Annabel Worthington. And her son. Percival.' The exuberance in Nandini's voice was unmistakable, like the sweetness in a jalebi. Radha-mashi had told her that Lady Worthington, and her husband Lord Benedict, the Governor of Bombay, were heads of the wealthiest clans of England (oh, what a fortune they had cut out of slavery!). Additionally, they were also politically powerful, and their only son, heir apparent, art aficionado, the peculiarly pallid Percival, was a regular visitor at Radhamashi's Thursday salon—he secretly worshipped the artist Khalil Muratta. Percival's father Benedict, on the other hand, was notorious for saying, after watching a famous murder mystery play in the West End, 'Never mind if the butler did it, but I'll certainly do the butler!'

'And just *why* are you so keen to see the Worthingtons of all people?'

'Just because!'

'Stay clear of the whites,' Anuradha said, although she had no idea why such conviction laced her tone.

'No worries, ducky! I was born in England. I chalked up enough know-how about the whites out there.'

'It's when they leave their country that you've got to watch them.'

20

She arrived barefoot.

With a lit beedi in her right hand, and a cream, gauzy gown with its back ripped until the very last alphabet of her tailbone was visible to the gasping eyes of the salonites. Her skin shone and her hair was like a cultured tramp's, and when Nandini laughed, a ripple ran through her body suggesting that some divine goddess inside her had just achieved sexual climax. Only a few minutes into her entrance on the sprawling, manicured lawns, Virginia Woolf, an upcoming novelist of the Western world, marched towards her and scolded her, declaring that someone so little and impressionable had *no* place in such artistic echelons, and that she would be better off at home playing hopscotch or stitching smocks for her dolls.

'You're *reely* too young to be here!'

'Age is only a number,' she contested politely. But when Woolf refused to put a lid on it and continued bullying her, Nandini spat out like a hungry civet, 'Maybe I'm too young, but you, you cream puff, ought to be in your kitchen, knitting away at your diamond print cardigans.'

'How dare you! You little ...'

'Oh, jump in the river or something,' Nandini suggested, and walked off. The gorgeously green lawns were dotted with gulmohar trees, Grecian marble statues, a small burbling fountain, and a generous scattering of the city's bigwigs, togged up in saris and cloches and sacque suits. To her right, under a bevy of dense ficuses, in a small, serious circle, Nandini came across the self-appointed representatives of the Great Indian Cattle Classes: depressed revolutionaries, ambitious freedom fighters, and a single, striking chap she identified correctly as one Mr M. K. Gandhi, now increasingly famous for hurling sand into the colonial inferno. Hearing them yak on about salt taxes and celibacy and the swadeshi movement, her momentary interest suddenly curdled into unfathomable boredom and she leaned over to the all-ribs-and-dhoti Gandhi and said duskily: 'I hope you don't take this personally, but I think your loin cloth is *unbelievably* sexy.'

'I am *not* wearing this,' fumed Gandhi, touching his holy hand-woven loin cloth, 'because it's ... it's ... sexy ...'

'You're not?' Nandini batted her eyes like a doe in heat. 'Maybe *that's* what makes you great, and me merely adorable.'

Even Gandhi could not stop himself: he laughed loudly and warm heartedly. As she was leaving him, she kissed both his cheeks: 'Oh, and don't trust that Mountbatten on *any*thing: the man swings.'

Before nightfall, and after several glasses of the newly introduced pleasures of an utterly heady spirit called absinthe, Nandini heard a tantalising trombone tune and she immediately perched on an empty table and before you knew it, Oh Lord, the girl was dancing! Rocking her hips from side to side, shaking her shoulders as if she were a cobra under the charmer's spell, wiggling her darling derrière for all the world to see. Men clapped; some whistled; catcalls galore: but she remained wholly indifferent to these wolves. Catching sight of her, Lady Worthington huffed to her son Percival, 'It seems as if the Devil himself has possessed *that* girl.'

'And what a delightful possession the Devil has made!' her son responded. In his pigeon-grey button-down suit and a pink tie with the print of small daggers, Percival Worthington looked seriously deficient of any passion: lanky, the first shade of chicken fat, creepy red hair wrinkling over an elliptical skull, he was precisely the kind of bloke who put the *duh* in de rigueur. Irritated by his reply, Lady Worthington slapped his dandy wrist. 'I'll haul you home and rinse your eyeballs out if you look at her a moment longer!'

Percival immediately looked in the other direction; his mother's wrath, he knew from experience, was as horrifying as it could be vindictive.

'They're savages at the core of them,' she whispered, her eyes widening as far as they would stretch. A long time ago, Lady Worthington had come to the conclusion that inside all Indians lived something feral and fearful. A jungle waiting to happen. A beast eager to jump out. And although she might agree to meet the odd native or two—at such soirées, for instance—real prudence lay in keeping miles away from them. When Nandini Hariharan stole a glance at Percival—after all, she'd been *waiting* to see the Worthington heir—she thought he looked like one of those Boarding School Sods who took a week off to recover from a shaving cut.

She waved at him; he blushed.

Now a little away from this elegant dhamaal, up in one corner of Radha-mashi's garden, robed in a bright pink sari with lilies in her hair and gold circlets around her wrists, the infamous patron of the arts, Libya Dass, was inclined in a bathtub filled with icy cold water. For years she had hauled along her alabaster bathtub to parties, where it was brought up like a palanquin, by her seven hatta-gatta Bihari servants, whose tight, plump rears could easily double as bookshelves (throw in the odd Chaucer, some Premchand, and you had a library). Khalil Muratta sat next to her, on a huge cane Cochin chair that evoked solariums and ferns, and he had that faraway, devdas gaze everyone associated with him. But the instant he saw Nandini gyrating her devious hips on the table, his scrotum tightened, his full-bodied organ whooshed up with blood, and the need to ram this thin, bony girl with every fibre of his body woke him with a jolt.

He patted Libya Dass's shoulder. 'Her. *Please.*'

She had never seen him this captivated by anyone. 'That girl?'

He nodded. So she stood up from her bathtub, dripping in her bright pink sari, looking like one of those rare Asiatic mermaids, and promptly went after Nandini Hariharan.

'The painter Khalil Muratta would like to say hello,' she said.

'Does he have a tongue?' Nandini was immediately impressed by Libya Dass's monumental breasts (of which Malcolm Hailey, the Governor of Punjab, had quite fittingly commented: 'A few inches larger, and blimey, you could even colonise them!')

'Er ... yes! Yes, he does.'

'Well, then ask him to *use* it.'

Neither easily affronted nor quickly dissuaded, Libya Dass convinced the artist to speak to the tramp in her torn gown. He marched towards Nandini and flattered, 'You *must* be in the trade of fascinating people.'

'Golly! I'd never be so big headed as to believe that,' Nandini said, and wrapped her arm around his. 'Besides, truth is, everyone else was put down only to be fascinated by me ... now tell me your favourite vice, and I'll tell you mine.'

'Melancholy,' he admitted.

'Resilience,' she said in return. 'I've often tried to die, but failed miserably at it.'

Before Libya Dass might feel out of place, Nandini slipped her other, bamboo-like arm around the waist of Bombay's most notorious art benefactor and they started to walk towards the banyan trees. Just then, Radha-mashi spotted them: 'Ah, three of my finest guests … a more pleasing trio I could not ask for. Khalil … I don't know if the quite fabulous Nandini has told you,' Radha-mashi gushed, 'that she's a gifted painter. In time to come, she'll give everyone here a run for their money.'

'How wonderful! And what do you like to paint?'

'People,' Nandini replied after a puff from her beedi. 'I like to see them for what they really are.'

'And just how do you see yourself for who *you* are?' Khalil Muratta was tall and well built, with meaty buns that begged to be squeezed.

'Well, if you teach me how to paint better than I do already,' she said in a throaty whisper, 'then I might even tell you.'

The moment suddenly became as tense as a drawn bow string: would Khalil Muratta agree to take under his wing an adolescent who, until a few minutes back, was dancing like a wild wind to the trombone tune of a blackman? And what pluck to ask *this* brazenly! Libya Dass looked skywards; Radha-mashi pretended someone was calling her and left the scene.

After a moment he leaned forward and touched Nandini's delicate jaw. 'Yes. Yes, I'll teach you how a brush sways over canvas. I know how to paint because I know how to fall in love.'

'That explains the bruised shins,' she responded. 'So I'll teach you something even better. How to fall *out* of love. It's a gift I got, honey, and I'm planning to ticket the act.'

'Now just *what* makes you such a master in this?' Libya Dass's skin sizzled: what would it be like to pour cold, cold milk over the girl's navel and then lap it up hungrily?

'Legend goes, one of the women on my mother's side loved a leopard,' Nandini informed them. 'They shacked up for years.'

'Was he any good in bed?' Libya Dass had the glimmer of a laugh in her eyes.

'Oh, lousy!' she said, shaking her head. 'But he was *terrific* in the forest.'

They looked at one another gravely, and then, after a pregnant, sober pause, they roared aloud till their eyes were wet and their stomachs hurt, as if they had a rotten case of the Delhi belly. Everyone at the salon wondered where they had disappeared to but Radha-mashi, when she went searching for Nandini, saw the three of them under an ancient banyan tree: Nandini was sprawled between the painter and the patron of the arts. Naturally, Radha-mashi assumed that Nandini—little child!—was only knackered, and had hence decided to catch a few winks on the laps of such august company. Poor Radha-mashi never once suspected that although the tableau was so laden with innocence, Nandini Hariharan's mouth was, in reality, playing with the painter's fly and the tumescent, torrid baton behind it while her curious hands were snaking into Libya Dass's navel, stroking flesh where it ached to be tickled. Of course, neither adult in question imagined, even in their wildest dreams, at the time, that a fourteen-year-old might be in possession of talents that left them breathless and clammy, and they chose, instead, to believe that it was the fantastic discovery of absinthe which had reduced their loins to liquid and that the child lying between them was merely a lotus over the pond of their lust. It was only much later that either would grasp, much too late alas, that under all the lotus flowers that ever bloomed were the anacondas that could wring you alive, not because they were evil or preferred to suffocate their wretched victims but only because that was who they *really* were.

21

Barely had December opened its drowsy eyes and invited winter in when Anuradha Gandharva was woken from her siesta by the travelling flute-seller rendering, with flawless accord, a love song of Meerabai's. Lying in bed, she let the undulating refrain caress her for many moments until, quite unexpectedly, a gasp and retch held her by the navel and yanked her right up to the copper washbasin. She heaved once, gently. Sweat gathered on her clavicle. She had experienced this kind of sudden nausea only once before: and she hadn't forgotten it.

'It cannot be,' she said, half smiling and half crying, 'it cannot be.'

For the rest of her life she would think of that Meerabai hymn when she saw her baby child, and remember that someone had been singing to God when his arrival in her—as an amorphous, safety-pin-sized clot of blood and cell—was announced.

He came on the wings of a song.

The last time she had told Vardhmaan that he was going to be a father, hardly a few years back, he had danced in the room, carried her on his shoulders, and sung a mad song that woke the neighbours three houses down: she'd been red-cheek-mortified by his glee at the time. This time, though, when she told him the same news, he looked at her for a long time, stoically, before he strode out of the house without once looking back at his wife, who was standing at the threshold, watching, waiting.

The shoreline was his only succour in a joy that was too big for him now.

His heart was bubbling with anticipation—and also with guilt: maybe he should have been more responsive to Anuradha. Held her—or whispered a few words. And he certainly shouldn't have walked away like that. But maybe, he figured, she was growing used to him now. Vardhmaan was fully aware that, in the story of his own life, he had slipped off the pages, taken refuge in the parenthesis of oblivion, become a minor character (albeit one whose vanishing left a deeper impact than someone else's presence). However, it wasn't that he had vanished from his own life as much as that he had simply stopped appearing in the lives of others: an altogether different species of vanishing. As the waves slapped against his ankles, he wanted to know just how Anuradha had recovered from the blood on her back. What song had leapt to her rescue? And why didn't men have a similar reprieve? Men were supposed to be brave, he thought. They had to drive cars in maddening rain. They had to wake to dying mothers. Their shoulders would carry biers. Biers bearing their own children. And yet, men had no songs: they had only a shield of valour.

And of silence.

Where, now, lay *their* language, the language to articulate what their hearts were unable to swallow? Had their language become obsolete? Disturbed by such questions, and panicky because he had no clear answers, Dr Vardhmaan Gandharva, Handel lover and chicken club sandwich scaredy-poo, returned home. He admitted to his waiting wife that the news was, indeed, wonderful, and that the next morning they would go and pray for the well-being of her health and their conceived, at the Mahadev Mandir, at the tail-end of Church Maarkit.

She remained unconvinced: 'Are you *really* happy, Vardhmaan?' Her eyes hunted him out even as he stood in front of her.

I'm sorry, he wanted to say, *I don't know who I've become, Anuradha.*

'We will be all right,' she said with a sigh. 'I promise you.'

That same week she told Nandini about her condition—in the hope that at least *someone* might be happy for her in this house. The girl took two quick puffs from her beedi before she stood up. 'I don't have anything personal against children. Except that they make their parents insufferable.'

Anuradha knew better than to be annoyed with Nandini's tart response; but when she went to the kitchen, and as she was stirring the kadhi, tears, quite unstoppably, came wobbling down her lean, lovely face. She remembered that even in Udaipur Nandini had a bit of a reputation as a child-basher—and now, as then, Anuradha just couldn't understand why the walk-on-water girl was so hostile towards such innocent beings.

The truth of the matter was that Nandini—being Nandini—had such over-the-top, often piercingly sharp responses to most things: and Anuradha's pregnancy was no different. Rather dramatically and quite baselessly, Nandini believed that the bawling of a baby and the stench of its nappy would somehow interfere with her painting. In fact, she was so worried that she could not channel her art with the dextrous candour with which she had done so previously, as a result of which her faithful subject, that Irish lad smitten with even the dust on her soles, was also rather disturbed. At first, Nandini was surprised that he had taken her worries to his heart, and wondered why he even bothered; if the situation were reversed, she certainly would not take *his* load on her back. That was when it became obvious: the boy was irrefutably, dangerously and insanely besotted with her. She smote her head in the awareness that she had no small hand to play in this love-locha. In the short spell that she'd known him, she had used every guile in the book to make Sherman Miller bring books from his father's library with the proviso that if he ever brought her either Jane Austen or Charlotte Brontë, she would lower his bottom on a blistering brazier as castigation for introducing into Dariya Mahal the prose of hags whose only ambition in life had been to marry well. She also directed him to pomade his dishy dusty-gold hair so that he might appear a child of breeding (as opposed to his present condition, where people might mistake him for an inordinately fair Kashmiri servant boy). And yes, she had him mug up so much Yeats that his mind was crammed with verses, and so jumbled and criss-crossed were the pining phrases that he even said them aloud in his sleep, prompting Mrs Isabel Miller to believe their ancestral ailment—*triste incurabilis*—had, alas, infected her son. But crowning the litany of his favours for that walk-on-water vagrant was the fact that he agreed to sit for her.

A painter's model.

After she'd attended a few destiny-enhancing, talent-honing classes from Khalil Muratta, she returned to Dariya Mahal with the electrifying compulsion to practise her craft—and who else but Sherman Miller would so willingly sit for her?

But then he had his own agenda.

Aware that he might get to talk to her during those sittings, he endured the awkwardness of posing without his shirt, and later he even sat through the exciting mortification of a whole afternoon with only a towel on the bursting hose of his manhood (which Nandini decided was so luscious that it required no interpretation: it was *Das ding an sich)*.

Every week, on Friday, after six, he came to her.

And she painted him.

With a dogged eye and a steady hand, she captured the almost edible plums of his buttocks; the solitude of his earlobe; the musky pink of his aureole with its sunburst of hair.

But after she heard of Anuradha's pregnancy, Nandini's concentration was irreparably diluted. She sketched over sheet after sheet, thoroughly dissatisfied with every result, and frantically tore off the papers in a gesture of melodramatic frustration that left Sherman in knots: what *was* the matter with her? Finally, she threw away her sharpened pencil and sat on the grass next to him. 'I'm sorry, but magnificent as I am, I just can't get my act together—not today ...'

'Something on your mind?' He was nearly naked, posing for her only in the taut dignity of his tight white underpants.

'Well, I suppose I ought tell you, Sherman ... the cousin's ... argh! ... Anuradha's pregnant.' She gave a shudder, as though poor Anuradha had been diagnosed with a carnally transmitted condition whose name might not be publicly said.

'What? That's super news! They must be hopping.' He was unsure why her hand was moving up and down his thigh; maybe she did it to calm herself?

'I'm sure *they* are,' she cried, flailing her hands. 'But let's get back to *me*! I'll perish in the company of a child. Do you really want to come here on Friday evening and discover me dead from ... from ... *childitis*? And then there'll be no one to paint you ... ever again ... Oh, rescue me from this trauma ... my precious little potato picker!'

'Trauma!' he repeated. '*Trauma?* It's only a child, for Chrissake! And it's your cousin at that—you ought to be tickled for her. Instead, all you do is drama-queen.'

'I'm *supposed* to; I'm an artist. If I don't cultivate affectations then who will? Housebloodywives?' She took a long, contemplative breath, as if reconciling herself to the brazen fecundity of others. 'Oh, I don't know, Sherman! Perhaps the baby might not be such a bad idea. Might even haul happiness's arse into this god-forsaken house. Besides, Anuradha and Vardhmaan are good people: I might even trust what they produce. For the most part anyway.'

'Well, if it all gets too much ... then you know you can always come live with us, can't you?' She couldn't explain why her heart beat so hard. Maybe because she was overcome with the simple nobility of his affections? She clasped his face and leaned closer—until her lips were only half an inch away from his. 'Ah! See how my company has altered you into a creature of many charms?'

'What'll become of you?' His gaze was enquiring but baffled.

'Paris. That's my real destination. Where I belong. With all the other artists. But before that, I'll marry well. Into some properly pedigreed family. With pots and pots of money!'

'You'll marry?' Sherman looked puzzled as he recalled her hatred of Jane Austen. 'But I thought you despised women whose only ambition was to find a husband?'

'D'you think this world would be half as interesting if we were all obvious?' A wry glint brightened her eyes. 'I mean, sure I'd love to do the whole Struggling Artist thingie ... but let's face it, ducky, me and penury don't tango too well.'

Stunned by the confidence in her voice, Sherman wondered what wickedness was curled up her sleeve now. Why did she sound so sure about marrying someone rich? Had she found a future husband at one of those outrageous salons she went to? Heaven forbid it should be that dastardly Khalil Muratta! Old enough to be her father—and then some. The rattlesnakes of confusion and despair and envy stirred awake in Sherman because he had never even once thought that she would consider anyone other than him (just *how* he was so sure that she would settle her easel and insanity with him, he never knew).

'No, no,' he contested her designs on Paris. 'One day, *we* shall be married. And you'll live with me in Dublin.'

She tightened her grip over his crotch. 'It wouldn't be clever to mess with me when your bits are in my hands, Sherman.'

But Nandini wasn't the only one disconcerted by the news. In the months before it grew even more resentful, Dariya Mahal found itself overwhelmed by the happiness Anuradha Gandharva was reflecting—like a mirror shining in the noonday sun: lucidly, dazzlingly. As news of her pregnancy, over the next few weeks, was confirmed, she unfurled heart-gripping melodies for no particular reason; at dusk, she lit up tiny terracotta lamps all over the balcony railing until the entire house was vibrantly and vivaciously alive. If anything, all this left Dariya Mahal feeling as though it'd been reduced to some kind of a four-penny circus with falling-over clowns: after living with someone who had died of waiting, this sweet, sweet tintinnabulation of someone's anklets was ... was ... oh ... *bugger* ...

... and so, during the times Anuradha was out, Dariya Mahal would snatch up the solitude to mull over Edward: his devoted study of Dryden; his thoughtful contribution to the garden; but most of all, the desolation of a life spent waiting for his lover. *He died, you know. On my balcony. On a chaise. With a black rose by his side. What's your defence*? Right then, even before Dariya Mahal might fold away its sepia-coloured reflections, Anuradha would return from wherever she had gone and her luminous gaiety would demolish the sacred morbidity of the moment. No wonder, then, that Dariya Mahal started thinking Certain Thoughts. About ways to drive it away. That vulgar happiness of hers.

But how? Would it be after the child was out of her?

Or *before?*

22

Under the bold, blue sky, in a twilight-orange sari, two slender circular gold earrings reflecting the burnish of the early evening sun, Anuradha was on her way to meet Pallavi, who, in a short while, had gone on to become a good friend. Their unexpected closeness, pure as it was wide, was forged over cooking lessons: Pallavi accepted that because her mother had died when she was four, her culinary skills were pretty weedy. Anuradha, on the other hand, rolled out kachories that many a dying man in Udaipur asked for as his last wish and a vegetable biryani that had caused three men to have a spontaneous orgasm (they had shuddered at the dinner table, coiled up their eyes and bucked their hips until they fell wham! face forward into the maakhi daal). So every so often, she went over to Pallavi's place, just down the road, where they'd cook up gatté-ka-saag and makai-ki-roti and various sweets that Pallavi's husband, Krishnan, had quite a hankering for, all the time talking the talk of women: profound; rumorous; wise; and inordinately compassionate at the heart of all its irreverence.

Every time Anuradha met Pallavi's husband, she was swayed by his quiet dignity. Krishnan was concise yet eloquent; his movements were controlled but fluid; and his thoughtful pauses only enhanced his speech. Pallavi had told her that Krishnan had been orphaned early on: his father had died before his birth; two years later his mother perished from cholera. Until she met Anuradha, Pallavi had never found a friend in her locality; aside from being socially inferior to the moneyed of Juhu, she was far too genuine for their company. Ostentation of any kind bored her, and a strong rapport with Krishnan allowed her to alternate between seclusion and companionship with great facility. As a couple, few were as matched as Pallavi and Krishnan: they could keep secrets from each other, and neither would wonder what they were; she could reduce him to chortles of glee by mimicking his academic colleagues—exact and biting to the last inflection; and he could astound her with his gathered insight and philosophies, which, if they didn't render life easier, certainly positioned it in clearer light.

They talked a lot, and shared several silences.

That evening, Krishnan hadn't yet left for his lecture when Anuradha showed up: under the shaded arm of the veranda, seated around a trestle table, they were enjoying their evening chai.

'May I pour you a cup?' Krishnan asked Anuradha, who had pulled up a chair opposite them. 'By the way, I spoke to Nandini the other day ... she'd come to return a few novels. My God! What an unusual child!'

Anuradha laughed. 'If you call her a child, oh, Krishnan, she'd be *very* rattled.'

'Not that I would blame her. She's pure prodigy, if you ask me,' interjected Pallavi. Around a month back, she'd read in the *Bombay Gazetteer* that Khalil Muratta had taken the girl under his wing because he believed she had a talent that might be honed into something exceptional.

'Why doesn't she go to school?' Krishnan asked. 'She'd excel.'

'I've told her plenty; but she says she would rather read at home.'

'Women *should* be educated,' Krishnan insisted.

'But women *are* educated,' corrected Anuradha. 'We're still hunting for a university that can cope with our intellect.'

Pallavi laughed. She poured Anuradha some more tea. Ten minutes later, Krishnan looked at his watch. 'I'd better be headed for college ... I'm conducting a debate on Middleton at six ... I'm sure my students are waiting with *bated* breath.' His eyes rolled up sarcastically. Pallavi escorted him to the square lounge. Through the grilles of the window, Anuradha watched them. Pallavi patted out a crease on his shirt; he touched her cheek with the back of his hand. She laughed, and when he bent into the creek of her neck, she pushed him away. To her, their actions were a symphony, a falling-into, an accord ... but mostly it was the way they spoke, *that they spoke*—half-laughed words, unfinished sentences, cosy rhetoric—which gripped Anuradha.

What it would be, she thought, *to love a man of many words.*

'I'll leave you alone,' Krishnan said before he left. 'It was lovely to see you.'

'You as well. But you still haven't met Vardhmaan ... I keep telling Pallavi one of these days we must have a meal together.'

'Oh, certainly ... maybe we'll meet this Sunday? In fact, I was going to come over last night—on self-serving grounds, might I admit—Pallavi was completely down and I was sure it was her ...'

'It was nothing,' Pallavi cut in hastily. 'Just one of my headaches. Balm drew it out.'

She threw a furtive glance at Krishnan. 'My husband worries too much.'

Anuradha didn't know where to look until Krishnan waved and went on his way.

A minute later, Pallavi returned. 'Shall we turn to the kitchen?'

Grey shadows coloured the dim kitchen walls. Pallavi energetically pumped up the kerosene stove and it soon threw out a spitting cerulean flame. After preparing the puran for the chakris, Anuradha poured it into the pipette from which she churned out the swirls of chakri into the bubbling sunflower oil. 'The secret is aniseed.'

'Aniseed? For chakris? Ah!' Pallavi always relished the nuggets of information Anuradha brought with each round of her cooking, and she wondered whether this was what it was like to have an older sister.

A short while later, having fried around a dozen or so, they decided to reward their efforts. 'Shall we eat, then?'

'It's terribly inauspicious to reject food!' Pallavi said with a serious look. 'I read that all your hair could fall off if you ever refuse food.'

'I'm not very sure where you get your beliefs,' Anuradha said, clicking her tongue to the roof of her mouth. 'But I'll *happily* fly with them!' But on the veranda, barely had Anuradha put the first, warm, khasta chakri into her mouth than she felt queasy and she rose up and hurriedly spat it out in one corner of the lawn. 'I'm sorry ... I'll clean it ...'

'Are you all right?' Pallavi was right by her side.

'It's nothing ...'

'Shall I get you some water? Or some ...'

'Pallavi ...' Anuradha could no longer keep it inside of her. 'I'm pregnant ... I found out a month ago ...'

'Gosh!'

'It was a surprise to Vardhmaan and me too.'

'Oh, Anuradha! I'm so happy for you ... this is the most amazing piece of news I've heard in ages ... have you told anyone else? Nandini, surely? Your mother-in-law?'

'Nandini knows. But my mother-in-law … Vardhmaan and I *never* talk about Divi-bai. It's best that she shouldn't surface in our lives in any way.'

'Well, you wait here … such good news deserves something sweet on the tongue.' She raced back to the kitchen and scoured the cabinet for the laddoos Krishnan got from Suleman Halwai in Mahim. 'Here!' she said, chucking one into Anuradha's mouth. 'This'll take care of *everything*!'

'Even my nausea?'

'Even that!' Pallavi laughed. 'Now you don't fret a thought, OK? I've looked after a cousin of mine during three of her deliveries … I know which poultice will take care of cramps and which herbs will hoist up your moods … the ghee and clove raabs, and the langots you'll need cut, the … Oh, Anuradha, I'm so delighted for you!' Her cheeks were shining; her eyes had filmed over.

'I knew you would be … that's why I told you. I haven't even told my mother. Only Vardhmaan and Nandini … and now you … know. It's so odd carrying. All over again, and such a different feeling this time.'

'And why's that?' Pallavi figured that if anything a second child would only lower the tension of childbirth because she had been through the ring once already. They sat back on the chairs and Anuradha thought for a moment, her finger at the end of her lips. 'With Mohan there was this restlessness and hope and trust—I was so sure that nothing could *ever* go wrong. And of course, you know what happened …' She closed her eyes. 'But this time, Pallavi, I'm happy—but I know I've got to watch it. That's the gamble with happiness. You step over a certain line, take one breath too many, and it'll all be snatched up. *Like it was before.*' Her mind raced to the sight of Vardhmaan carrying Mohan in his arms, in the hammering rain, just like a bride being carried into her new house. She didn't know whether she was ready to tell Pallavi about the distance that had come about between her and Vardhmaan: besides, she was not sure that *she* had the words to flesh out *his* wordlessness.

'Everything will end up just fine!' Pallavi refused to sully the moment with a speck of despondency. 'I'll look after it all. I still can't get over it. It's just brilliant! I know I'm going on and on about it ... but I absolutely *adore* children.'

'Well, in that case, you and Krishnan ought to plan one too, nè?'

'Oh, we'd *love* to ... But ... but ... I mean, we've thought about it ... and then, well, you know ...'

Anuradha lifted her palm in the air questioningly. 'Know *what*?'

Pallavi didn't respond. All of a sudden, everything seemed awkward: Anuradha's throwing up; Pallavi's merriment; this silence sitting between them, nudging its elbows into their unspoken pasts. After a moment Pallavi sighed. 'Well, while we're swapping secrets ... do folks with holes in their hearts live long? I know my mother didn't. Why plant a garden that you'll never see flower?' Pallavi looked down; it felt so clumsy to speak of something so awful. The plainness of death.

It took Anuradha a minute to grasp the ailment. And its consequences. She had had a friend back in Udaipur who never made it past her twenty-sixth year. That was pretty much the norm. You could stretch life from the late twenties to your mid-thirties—no more. Was that all Pallavi had too? A few years. Was that why Pallavi didn't want any children?

'Some days I wake with bubbling rage. And know that if I might unfree the holler inside me, why, I could change the course of rivers.'

'Rage? Because you're ... dying ...' Anuradha couldn't believe how easily the word slipped out of her. A quizzical look came over Pallavi; then she slapped her hand to her forehead: 'Arrè ... no ... no ... that plagues me by a hair's breadth ... it's Krishnan ... he has no blood family ... and because we're so close we don't even have many friends ... what will *he* do after I ...' She could not finish; despite her bravery, a weep outdid her and warm, delicate tears reeled down her cheeks.

'Oh, Pallavi ... my dear Pallavi ... we'll make a good time in what we've got ... I know we will ... just hand me your faith, lay down your worries, and I know we will cut a good time ...' Although Anuradha didn't know whether she believed what she had said she was sure that, right now, it was all she had to believe in. As she was caressing her hand over Pallavi's back, an instinct older than time pushed a melody out of her, a lullaby of sorts, and this, a sweet, slow, consoling song, changed not the inevitability of things but helped them receive joy as sorrow in one glorious breath of utter detachment.

'What a time we'll make, Pallavi, what a time.'

An hour later, Anuradha returned to Dariya Mahal, in a dusk of indigo light, and the house received her with dark familiarity. The brooding structure, curating sadnesses, took her by the arm, led her up to the balcony, and seated her on the iron chaise. Sitting there, under the fading light, Anuradha wanted nothing more than Vardhmaan. To verify the existence of love. To tell him that her world was full of those always leaving. And remind him that she was *starving* for his kept-carefully anecdotes. That was when she noticed a single black rose lying on the floor, and bent to pick it up. Dariya Mahal winced. Could she *ever* know the depth of Edward's waiting? In a clap and shudder, white doves soared over her, and night came all at once: thick and black as molasses. Ten minutes later, hunting solace from the sandstorm of grief she'd rambled into, Anuradha trundled down to the kitchen where cooking for her husband and the painter-girl, she thought, might mellow the intensity of the evening. With scant time before Vardhmaan would be back she thought it best to make sukhi bhaji and chapattis—with a little cucumber raita if she could squeeze that in. But barely had she bound the dough for the chapattis when she heard Nandini call.

She stepped out. 'What is it?'

'Very soon, I'll abandon India,' Nandini said mischievously. She was making her way down the stairwell with a beeswax candle in her fist. 'Khalil and Libya also think I'll never snap up the value I deserve out here. They'd sooner write me off as three annas short of a rupee and Christ! I'll have to scramble *again* ...' Here, Nandini paused—around ten steps from the floor. Her body trembled. Anuradha gasped. Because at that moment, Nandini fell on the stair, stayed there for a horrifyingly remote moment, and then, like an undulating ribbon, came rolling down to the ground. In the wink of an eyelid that it took Anuradha to wing it to Nandini's side, it was already too late: Nandini had smashed her green glass bangles and the shards had torn right through her skin. Her jaw had split open and was bleeding profusely.

'NANDINI! Oh, Nandini! What happened ... Oh my God ... it's your ...'

It wasn't the fall itself which shook the living daylights out of Anuradha; rather, it was the ugly, unbearable fit that had besieged Nandini: her pupils were dilating, her hands were twitching like the freshly severed head of a drake, and her eyes blinked rapidly but paused intermittently to stare vacantly at the ceiling, as though she were seeing a great and wild view privy only to her. Cradling the orphan in her arms, Anuradha hoped, prayed—oh, hell, *demanded*—for Vardhmaan to be here.

With her. Right now.

And for ever.

23

A few months after that horrible evening when Nandini fainted, Vardhmaan woke in the moist, insouciant dawn of June and sat up next to his wife—his face exactly parallel to her navel—and saw that she was showing. Beneath that graceful brown mound of her belly, someone was breathing, perhaps even kicking, someone who would come out in the next five or six weeks.

Who was it?

And would this one stay? And sing?

And laugh, but never leave?

When an applause of thunder roused Anuradha, her eyes opened to the sight of Vardhmaan gazing at her navel; she was secretly convinced that if *this* child came into the world safe, she might have her husband back. And maybe, just maybe, even a braid of frangipani. Swimming in such hope, the two of them were bound by the presence of the absence of the unborn: the only other creature awake to this was Dariya Mahal. Perturbed that her annoying optimism might infect Vardhmaan, it had decided to take things into its hands.

Bitter hands. Cold hands. Hands that held a whiteman waiting for the brown one.

Who never came.

'Vardhmaan ... what're you looking at?'

'Would you like to go down?' He seemed startled at being discovered in such a vulnerable position.

They woke, dressed and went out to sit on the veranda. Nearly seven and a half months into her condition, and oh, how lovely she looked! Gleaming skin; laughing hair. And what was more, even the monsoon was here! Red earth sighed to the pouring tempest; black scrawny crows sat on the combs of coconuts, periodically shaking their heads.

'Tea?' He didn't look at her when he asked the question.

'No ... I'm fine ... thanks ... Do you remember, Vardhmaan? I used to write poems. Back in the Dwarika house. I'm sure they were quite bunkum. But I liked writing them.'

He touched her hand. She wondered whether talking about the old things might somehow remind him of who he used to be. 'Isn't it strange? If Divi-bai hadn't done what she did, we'd never be here. Together.'

'Yes.' Sometimes he thought of Divi-bai and how she had orchestrated their departure from the house. He never told

Anuradha that although they were living here now, a small cut of his earnings went to the Dwarika house secretly. It arrived in a brown envelope, slipped into the postbox each month—without any details of the sender: he didn't wish to damage his heinous stepmother's monumental pride any further, although Divi-bai knew perfectly well that it wasn't just some stranger off the street sending her the money she needed to run her life. Not that Divi-bai had responded to this subtle kindness with either humility or gratitude; in fact she had given strict directives to both Taru and Sumitra-bhabhi never to contact Anuradha and Vardhmaan in their new house: she hoped this would further isolate them.

'And I would never have met Nandini, I suppose ... what do you think of ... Nandini ... isn't it dreadful, what happened?'

Anuradha wrapped her hands around her stomach and arched her neck back.

The night that Nandini had her fit was agonizingly clear in Vardhmaan's memory.

He had been returning after treating a patient called Savitri Shah, a notoriously ugly spinster who years later, when the Famine of Suitable Boys struck Bombay, would have the audacity to wed her own father. In the absence of street lights he was walking home with a flare. But only a few breaths before Dariya Mahal, he heard an eerie flapping right above. When he pointed the torch upwards, the flame showcased three white crows.

Now, he hurried.

He opened the gate. He saw Anuradha crouched on the floor. So he started running up the drive. A goldfish pond lit up by moonlight. Closer to the doorway, he saw Nandini cradled in her arms. Hearing him, Anuradha looked up, frazzled. 'Vardhmaan ... save her ... for God's sake, Vardhmaan, *please* do something ... she fainted.'

'Get me a pillow ...' He flipped open his medicine case. 'And don't worry a thread ... she'll be fine.'

When she returned, Vardhmaan requested a cut lime and then opened a vial and administered Nandini three white pills which seemed to calm her.

'I'm sorry,' Anuradha said, her heart beating through her chest like a drum around a wildfire. 'I should've told you that she used to have fits. But she made me promise not to.'

'How long has she had it?'

'Since she was a child ... tell me she'll be OK ...' Just then Nandini's cold, sweaty hands tightened their grip over Anuradha's wrist. 'Yes, Nandini ... I'm here ... Vardhmaan's here too ... you'll be fine, little one ... you'll be OK ...'

She wiped dry the blood gushing out of Nandini's nose. Vardhmaan opened a bottle of mercurochrome and set to work: he drew out splinters of bangle glass gouged into her arm; some skin had been ripped open in the tumult of the fall.

'I'm holding you, Nandini ... not letting go ... oh, Vardhmaan ... Pallavi is dying ...' Their eyes met briefly, a small, invisible bridge, and much later she was dazzled to learn how his gaze could convey a solace his words, alas, never would. She couldn't understand why her need to share this information was so desperate. Love, she believed, divided the density of loss—and maybe *this* was the mercy in life which her mother had said there never was. That was when Nandini regained her senses. She stared at the ceiling blankly and started screaming ... *WHY ME ... WHY ME ... WHY ME ... WHY ME ... WHY ME ... WHY ME ...*

Only Vardhmaan noticed it wasn't a question.

24

That July, it never stopped raining.

Water arrived in all its manifestations: from that no-good drizzle that reminded colonials of the pitter-patter of their own island to storms that lifted little children from their mothers' arms and flung them into the cesspit right off the Thana Creek. And rain infused mad life into Dariya Mahal: tapioca wheeled its way around the dusty circumference of haggard columns like soggy green armlets; Himalayan balsam set up shop by the pond and an immodesty of purple burst forth each day. Three stoically white crows waited on a calloused bough of the kadam while newts appeared like rapid, black glimmers over the moist earth. Although Anuradha tried to rein in such a sensational takeover, she soon gave up because in the past, when she'd tried taking on the garden—cleaning patches, cutting hedges, trimming bushes—there had been only so much you could do before Dariya Mahal reacted crossly, before it spat out a soundless obscenity that made you yelp with shame, and before it reassigned itself to its destitution. In any case, she had scarce energy left from the heft of the child inside her and her time was simple but sweet, for she read and sewed and read and indulged her whimsical palate.

Now one grey afternoon, gripped with the caprice common to pregnant women, Anuradha wanted a tamarind. When neither the kitchen nor the storeroom revealed a supply, she asked Nandini whether she'd go across to Church Maarkit

'You need anything else?' Nandini pulled a black hooded cloak over her off-shoulder cream dress.

Anuradha nodded in refusal.

'I'll be back in half an hour. Maybe I'll ask Sherman to tag along. If the cad's even home.'

As Nandini trundled down the drive, isolation whooshed in, and Dariya Mahal thought, *Got to do something ... she's alone ... for a while.*

Alone.

Now's the chance!

After Anuradha saw Nandini walk away with her Irish deewana in tow, she lay down on the divan for a nap. But roughly ten minutes later, her siesta was shattered by a growl of thunder that so shifted her balance she decided that a cup of chai might soothe her edgy nerves. So she went to the back yard where, by a parade of banana trees, there grew the lemongrass she considered essential for her brew (along with cardamoms, a few leaves of mint, a smashed coin of ginger). Hardly had she bent and knifed away the lemongrass sheaves than she suddenly felt speared. With rain. It was as if her skin would split open to this torrent, so entirely violent was its ballast. She turned and made tracks for shelter. Lightning splashed over her. She continued running; Dariya Mahal thought: *Do it! Now's the time. She's alone!*

That was when it happened.

Nandini pulled Sherman under the canvas of the lime-seller's pushcart, under an enormous almond tree in Church Maarkit. When a puddle gathered around them, she started walking on the rainwater; he was dumbfounded.

'It's like any other blessing,' she explained. 'Because it doubles as a curse.'

Dr Vardhmaan Gandharva looked out of his clinic window, paralysed by the ferocity of the downpour, convinced that some havoc lay hidden in the whip of the lightning that lashed over him. He sighed, although he had no foreseeable reason for a sigh of such desolation.

As of yet.

For as long as she lived, Anuradha Gandharva was never sure whether the tile under her foot actually rose and made her fall on her navel or whether something, someone, somehow caught the tip of her sari and pulled so hard that she landed smack on the floor. Her hands curled over her stomach; her tears competed with the rain (and almost won); and her ears tried to figure out whether it was she who had screamed—or whether the impact of the fall had caused her baby to cry out prematurely but prodigiously. Jolted inside its mother, it was now awake. Blinking its translucent eyelids. Struggling. For air. For life. Where was it? In a pool of some sort. With this tube. Fluid. Darkness. But just what had slammed *against* it? Was it a wall? Or the ground? And had something inside or around it burst open?

The unborn had worries: because there she was, its mother, wham on her face, senseless and bloody as something newly slaughtered.

'We should do a gypsy,' Nandini hissed.

'Let's wait it out. I'm enjoying this downpour.'

'Hush the mush!' She was keen to get back home. Anuradha was alone. And God knew what could happen in that macabre house. But hardly had she taken a step and unfurled her umbrella than the wind yanked it out of her grip, and there it was, a cloth raven flying into the soaker.

In the lurid blackness of her unconsciousness, Anuradha dreamed of the time her mother had bade her farewell in

Udaipur with the words: *'In this life, my darling, there is no mercy.'* She dreamed of a man living in a cage and a man waiting outside it who perished just from watching this locked-up being. A single black rose also came in a dream, the kind that mysteriously appeared on the day Pallavi told her about the hole in her heart. In her last vision, a girl was suckling a leopard cub at her breast. Then her eyes opened under the ballast of water, and she thought she was still dreaming.

Actually, try *nightmaring.*

She struggled to get back on her feet—but her limbs just wouldn't budge. So she hollered for Nandini. Why wasn't she back? Could Vardhmaan be home? Who would hear in this mad tumult? Her screaming rapidly turned to silence when she saw a rivulet of red around herself. The pretty little rill, which she tried to disclaim as a peculiar kind of rain that was rust-brown in colour and icky in texture, was actually the harbinger of a news that jerked her every molecule: her water bag had burst, and this was blood of her loins. Blood that came from the place Vardhmaan had, eight months ago, thrust into and helped make a child she might have heard scream already. Blood from a holy, horrified place. When she lay back, the house seemed to crowd over her, as though she were the freak show in a travelling circus—a seven-legged hag or a woman with giraffe's spotting—and Dariya Mahal was her sole, fascinated audience. Grasping what'd occurred, she whispered, with that rill of red around her, *Dariya Mahal ... please ... let my child live ... I know not what harm you have seen but let my child be and ... and I'll send the child away ... from you ... from all of this ... To a place of safety ... let be my child ... or I swear I'll bring you down to dust and haul you to hell with me ...*

If it had had legs, the house would have slipped on its dancing shoes, clicked its knees, and done a hurrah! number to a song louder than the thunder above: *Joy, sweet joy!*

Vardhmaan pressed the phone receiver closer to his ear to fathom what Nandini was shouting. 'It's an *emergency*! Drop everything and just come this instance!'

'Who is it?' he asked.

'Your wife. HURRY.'

When the car broke down in the rain he didn't even attempt to restart it. He just got out and ran. As fast as he could. But as he was running, Vardhmaan realized that he wasn't even thinking about Anuradha or, for that matter, the child inside her—he was thinking of Mohan. Of that time they had driven him to Harkisondas Hospital, and the car had stalled and Anuradha had hummed a song and Mohan was senseless and then they had eventually got there and then ... he felt as though he were running head on into *that* day and its outcome, and his legs slowed some. That was the awful thing about words: they allowed you to remember. The map of the experience. The flesh of the feeling.

Dariya Mahal spotted him from a distance. *Oh, fuck.* What'd that bitch on the ground said? Maybe it should take her up on her promise: let her keep the baby but trade later!

Roses are black and blood is red.

Hack yourself; it's time I was fed.

Nandini swung open the door. Told him. Together, they lifted Anuradha inside. When the steady stream of red flowing out of her showed no signs of abating, he rolled old saris into her insides to absorb the blood. By the end of that evening, Nandini and he had moistened some nine white saris that were now a solemn, solid russet.

'I'm sorry,' Anuradha whispered. 'I did it again, didn't I?'

'*You* need to rest. That is all I know.'

'Vardhmaan, there are only so many saris we ought to use. After that, save the baby.'

She grasped his hand before abruptly plummeting into sleep. And in her vast, mysterious sleep, the emergency elapsed. The bleeding abated. The swelling over her ankles subsided. But her instinct that the water bag had ruptured was right; the only way to keep her safe in this condition was for her feet to be hoisted up in the air, tied with silken twine to the wooden rods that supported the mosquito netting: in the hope that the baby wouldn't fall out prematurely.

He slept next to her, on the cane recliner.

'I feel clumsy,' she complained at dawn.

'The child is all right. You are all right. Elegance is not everything.'

The succinctness of his explanation caused her more grief than the entire accident had.

25

For a month after the evening of Anuradha's accident, it rained.

Lightning burnt down the Telegraph Office. Power went off. Four feet of water on the streets. One morning, the damn Arabian Sea lifted her hem and came rushing right into Juhu. Bright pink octopuses on the veranda chair. Seven-foot squids ate up pet cocker spaniels. On the day the rain showed *some* sign of ebbing, Anuradha felt that her baby could no longer endure its captivity, and she woke her husband in the night. 'Hasn't it chosen the perfect time to be born?'

'I'll go and get Nandini,' he said. After all, two minds and two pairs of hands were better than one. But she was out. At Libya's? Or with Khalil Muratta? With both, probably.

'I might have to call Pallavi ...' he told his wife. 'Nandini ... is not in ...'

'Yes, do so,' Anuradha urged. 'I want her here ...'

Ten minutes later, clutching a hurricane lamp in her right hand, a half-wet, frazzle-haired Pallavi stepped into the unnatural, molten darkness of Dariya Mahal.

'I'm here, Anuradha.' Her voice had the warmth of sunlit rooms, of old, unforgettable poems. 'How can I help?' But she had done already what Anuradha needed most: she had bent down and embraced her.

'Don't ever leave ...' Anuradha said, a catch in her voice.

'No matter what ... I know you will be out of harm's way.' Pallavi brushed off the rainwater lingering on the edges of her jawbone. For Anuradha, the mere presence of her dear friend had brought infinite relief: only a woman, after all, could fully understand the exquisite, mind-boggling agony of childbirth.

'Are you OK?' Pallavi asked when she saw a puzzled expression on her best friend's face.

Anuradha sensed a peculiar sogginess on the inside of her thighs and she caught Vardhmaan's arm. 'What's this *thing* running out of ...' Because her voice had the hesitant enquiry of a lover's first kiss, he gently pulled back her sari—only to see that she was bleeding so profusely that her shadow on the wall seemed to melt in shape and size. It was dawn now, and Vardhmaan opened the windows: although the rains had calmed somewhat, the roads were flooded hip high: taking Anuradha to a hospital was out of the question.

'It's simple, then, isn't it?' she said. 'We'll just have to have the child in the house.'

He lit the naphtha lamp in their room. A bright flare; three spectral shadows on the walls. Trepidation quivered down Pallavi's back: how would Anuradha survive this? After all, she had lost so much blood already—what if there were complications during childbirth? How on earth would they get her to the hospital if it came to be absolutely crucial?

'It's not the child that worries me,' Vardhmaan accepted. 'It is you, Anuradha: you could die.'

'Silly man!' she scolded affectionately. 'Hasn't that happened many times before?'

Before anything else, it was vital to stop her bleeding. Vardhmaan told Pallavi that the only recourse in these circumstances was the newly introduced Harvill's snake venom injections. The only reason they hadn't been fully accepted into contemporary medical practice, he said, was because they were deemed too dangerous: a single surplus drop killed instantly; a drop less, and it was useless. Professor Harvill had concocted these injections in his laboratory in Coorg, at a coffee plantation, where a cobra bite was a notorious ender of destinies. The scrupulously extracted snake venom clogged blood vessels, froze their flow, temporarily drying them upon the interior of the patient's veins—*exactly* what Anuradha needed right now. Vardhmaan decided to use the injection; it was not as if he had too many other options at hand. He drew the milky liquid from the ampoule into the copper-needle syringe, secretly fretting about whether it would save life—or snatch it away. Whispering a prayer, he delicately pierced Anuradha's frail arm; she winced slightly.

'It'll be just fine,' Pallavi comforted. 'This should take care of everything.'

'I wouldn't go *that* far,' Anuradha said with a wry smile; Pallavi was amazed at how in order Anuradha's wits were—even under such circumstances. It was Vardhmaan however, who was most tense: because the venom was in the habit of clotting so rapidly—in the syringe itself—a single dilatory' motion could result in one being left holding the solidified cobra venom in the plunger. Luckily, though, the venom had travelled just fine—and was gradually inking its way through Anuradha's veins.

'Worry not, my dear,' she reassured her husband, her voice drowsy. 'You did the right thing. I can feel it.'

'But what if ...'

'Then it'd be a perfect way to die.'

Thankfully, the pain eased. Blood froze, and her body turned as cold as ice. In this state, it was essential to examine the position of the unborn. He bowed and inserted his hands into her: his fingers exploring the nebulous architecture of their child, its soggy contour, that steady smote of heart. He gasped.

'What's the matter?' Pallavi asked as softly as she could.

There was something horrendously wrong. But how could he explain to Pallavi that the umbilical cord was looped around the baby's head? It was like a lasso, and if it made the slightest error of movement as it came into the world it could die being born.

'Vardhmaan—is it time the child came out?' Anuradha was getting impatient.

'Is it pushing? Do you feel your muscles contract and relax?'

'All that is too fashionable for me,' she panted. 'Tell me when we should have him out, and we will.'

'Now is a good time,' Vardhmaan affirmed. 'Start pushing.'

Drawing in a breath, she thrust herself inside out as he encouraged her with another shove or another breath or another count of one to ten, and before long it came to the point where it wasn't her alone who was birthing the child but the two of them, because Vardhmaan felt his own stomach clench and release, his own muscles tighten and relax, his own breathing hasten or drop in synchronization with his instructions to her: a single sweat bound them with an intimacy that she had *ached* for in saner times. Pallavi drank in the incandescent screams and the spit-balloon gasps, vaguely aware that in this life of hers, this was about as close as she would come to childbirth: this, perhaps, was the dearest present Anuradha could have given her without even knowing it.

'It's coming!' Vardhmaan's voice was shaking. 'It's here! Anuradha ... the child ...'

And out it flew! With a cord around its neck, dangling like a hangman's rope. Vardhmaan feverishly ripped it off. Tore off the placenta too. Wet, bloody. At first, he thought the baby was dead because the customary cry of infants was never emitted; but in truth, he—yes, *he*—was alive, staring at the edges of the room, observing his father's face, the shadows that the lamp was flinging over the ceiling. When the wind put the lantern out, Vardhmaan struck a match over his son's face and the shivering flame revealed the child's glossy wheatish skin, his elegantly red lips, his almondine eyes with a hint of green, and a palm over which the Line of Fate was ominously criss-crossed. Pallavi marked the precise time of his birth (later, it was ascertained that he was born under the constellation of Putrada Eka Dushi).

'It's a boy again,' he told her.

'Call him Shloka if I don't wake to see him.'

While Anuradha slept for the next twenty-seven hours, well into the evening after the Storm of Nine Days, her newborn refused to shut its eyes. Glaze faced, without complaint: impeccably resigned. *Should my heart awake? To this one?* Vardhmaan steepled his fingers. *Silent-so as me. Born with a noose around his neck ... Shloka* ... he floated the name over the infant's face ... *my lovely Shloka* ... and then his hands started to shiver and sweat glossed his forehead. Why wasn't the child crying? Or moving? If he didn't suckle or cry or show any other signs of life Vardhmaan would consider burying him under the plumeria tree since death was better before they grew to covet him than after: and his symptoms, after all, seemed to hint at a gradual perishing.

There were only so many sons you could lose before going mad.

'Are you OK?' Pallavi was practically dozing off; her health didn't afford her too much stamina.

'I'm fine ... but you should go if you need to,' he said. Pallavi ran her hand over the baby's brow and got up to depart: even though she didn't want to leave Anuradha's side there was only so much exertion she could shoulder. She asked him whether she should send Krishnan over; Vardhmaan turned down her offer, saying that all that needed to be done had been effected already.

'Remind her that she will be safe, please. Tell her I said so.' Although the conviction in Pallavi's words was an unexpected succour, for now at least, Vardhmaan couldn't quite yank free his attention from his son—and his disturbing stillness.

Hours later, Anuradha awoke, in the murmur of the fading rain, to the bouquet of wild flowers, and pulled the infant to her side. She ran her fingers over his cheek, over the incline of his nose, the promontory of his chin.

'He hasn't slept since he was born,' Vardhmaan informed her. 'He doesn't seem right, Anuradha.'

'It's only the cobra venom.' There were dark rings under her beautiful eyes. 'When it dries, he'll sleep.'

But Vardhmaan pointed out that the baby didn't cry or move his limbs. In her heart she was terrified that the uproar surrounding Shloka's birth might have forced Vardhmaan deeper into the cave of his Quietness: the birth of this child could end up taking away more than she had expected to lose.

'Do you have any idea how *much* I miss you?' She pressed her palm against his right ear. He looked down and told her that Pallavi had gone because she was very exhausted. Anuradha drew back her tousled hair; she took a deep breath.

Then, she got up.

And her scalloped gold bangles slid off her arms, so thin had they grown, her cream nursing gown felt oversized, and she yelped out in pain for her feet ached with every step she took forward. As *if she were walking on nails.* With the child in the arch of her folded arms, she made it out to the balcony.

Now the drizzle is at its barest. Tumescent, faded purple water tulips bloom over the marshes that Anuradha's gaze grazes on; coming down, in leisurely flight, white geese: behind them, a persimmon sky opens flat and far. She sits on Edward's chaise, her hand over the infant's face, protecting him from the mist. And she sings to him. A lullaby. Tender. Unhurried, as though she is inventing the tune even as she is singing it:

Nahni kali,
Sone chali,
Hava dhere ana.

A fragile petal
Turns to rest,
O' wind, blow softly.

Even before the song is wound up and put back in a box in her heart, the supple creases on Shloka's forehead overlap and then even out. His eyes widen; his lips smack open and shut. As she notices his pure red tongue for the first time, a thrill careens up her spine: cell by cell, she is dissolving into the uncanny gentleness of the experience.

'This, little one, is a song for you. When you grow up, you too will find the songs that will bring your heart its rest. But for now, here is mine for you this evening.'

She puts the child to her breast, and Shloka suckles hungrily, and it is only a matter of minutes before the milk mixes with the songs and the venom and the stories flowing through his fragile, fine veins.

PART THREE

Matheran Madness

26

On the sheer green manicured lawns of an elegant villa at the very top of Malabar Hill, a girl with infinitely beautiful collar bones sits atop a naked supine artist: two hawks, reeling hundreds of feet above them, watch. Also included among this august audience are other bedazzled birds and bees, and a woman in an alabaster bathtub under a dusty almond tree: she balances a goblet of red wine on the rim of the bathtub; her left hand is plunging in and out of herself. Losing no momentum yet applying no vigour, the girl's shins straddle his chest, her hands grab his elbows, and she bounces up and down him with the fluid, symmetrical grace perfectly befitting someone with just that odd dash of feline ancestry.

Her upper teeth bite into her lower lip.

That wet, desultory, holy sound of muscle slapping over muscle.

The man under her is striking in the manner of an old poem: all melancholy and ambiguity, with a penis she fits into herself as though *this* were the saddle she needs right now, as though if it weren't inside her, firing her loins and rousing the scorpion of destiny curled inside her, then, alas, the poor vagrant might slip off the edge of the Earth and vanish for ever. The more he moans, the more she bucks up with that peculiar, feverish vitality of maidens around a tribal fire, and then, without any warning, she squishes down and grinds her hips into him as if she wishes to take the firm roundness of his almost hairless testicles within her: perhaps as a memento of this evening. The woman in the alabaster bathtub, with rose petals over her bathwater, is amazed at how the ruffian takes him deep inside herself, how she alternates between the riotously carnal and the quietly compassionate, how she mops up the wetness of the other, heals, comforts and maddens, as though wild cats were roaring inside her flesh.

'I'm going to die,' Khalil Muratta murmurs. Sweat erupts on his torso. His tackle tenses up. 'I am ... about ... to die.'

'You have to wait until I kill you.' She bends herself and grips his neck with her sharp, flawless teeth, which immediately hampers the flow of air to his brain and intensifies his pleasure to such levels that, as he spends himself in her, he is convinced that the world has only just been born, that he has seen the first few stars whizz by, that light arrived barely three minutes ago. Seeing the lithe girl, the exemplary talents of her biology, the diabolical grace with which she curls over the man and bites his neck, Libya Dass shudders because the slurping juices of her loins detonate in bathwater: the rose petals quiver, and the wineglass falls to the ground.

How lions mate, she thinks.

For over an hour afterwards, they lay tangled under the gloaming: heads meeting torsos meeting hands meeting legs, the jumbled noodles of their anatomy drying itself from the tender, gooey ointments of an afternoon of hectic lovemaking. But while Khalil and Libya were in that blank space where no thoughts might be entertained, Ms Hariharan was already busy planning an escape route. In the past few weeks, she'd figured out that all she needed from the Afghani had been taken; now it was time for the ta-tas and I'll-write-soons.

It was over. Or was it?

'I want to ...' Khalil Muratta's eyes were closed; his lashes were long licks of brown hair.

'Hmm?' Libya Dass was unsure who was being addressed.

'... paint you.'

Every living fibre in Nandini shuddered, as if thunder were echoing through her veins. '*What* did you say?'

She had, in all her years with him, expected to learn art—not *become* it.

'I've decided to paint ... again.'

Libya Dass sat up: her best friend, who had not so much as lifted an easel, who had nearly forgotten that smarting, hollow smell of turpentine, wanted to paint *again?* 'Are you sure, Khalil … I mean, you haven't …'

'Will you sit for me? Hmm … ?'

Nandini threw her head back and unleashed her haint's high hoot to celebrate the news that she had, this evening, on her path of life, walked into an event of immortality.

'If it's half as fun as sitting on you,' she said, 'then I'll do it in the name of art, Mr K.'

Later, on her way back to Dariya Mahal, she wondered whether Khalil Muratta had picked up that she was soon going to wave *ta-ra, tootsie*—in which case the only way to make her stay on was by offering to paint her: the unrefusable bribe of permanence. When Nandini had asked when he planned to begin, he had said he'd do it over the summer, at Libya Dass's place in Matheran, because he was of the belief that Matheran's intoxicating air, its definitive solitude and jungle dreams, would yank art out of his veins and splash it over the canvas. Libya went on to explain that they summered in Matheran, a resort in the mountains, where the well-heeled vodkarati flocked to skirt Bombay's swelter *and* partake in Matheran's scandalous night life, which included parties where clothes were frowned upon ('How lower class of you!') and mingle with resident eccentrics—such as Roxanne Mistry, who bred every kind of snake there was. Nandini knew a trifle about Matheran because Radha-mashi owned a Manglorean-style house—the Owl's Retreat—there, on Upper Louisa Road. Nandini told them that she was going to be there over summer anyway since Radha-mashi had invited her and Anuradha to vacation in the highlands.

The first thing Nandini saw when she flung open the gates of Dariya Mahal, past the mad green of the garden, past the headless Greek statues and their mossy elbows, was Shloka. She loved the four-year-old's ascetic, disengaged air, as if he had an amazing genius for melancholy. As always, he was sitting by the pond and watching the goldfish. (Every now and then, he saw the blurry reflection of a whiteman, in a linen suit, with beseeching eyes, looking up at him from the pond. Did anyone else see him? *And who was he*?)

'Shloka!' Nandini waved excitedly; Muratta's electrifying request had put gaiety into her step. Not that she expected Shloka to say anything: he hadn't spoken a word since the day of his birth. Four monsoons ago.

'What're you doing ... itty-bitty li'l' thing?'

Then she answered for him: 'Ah, the goldfish. Of course. Mind if I join you?'

He smiled shyly. She cleaned the stone edge of the pond and sat next to him. Lowering her head, she gazed down intently, causing the goldfish to turn vigilant first, jittery next, and in a breath most had vanished under the flat, glossy lotus leaves. The serenity of the moment was ruined when her hand smacked into the water and plucked out a single, scaled goldfish with a glazed, petrified eye. Shloka gasped: would she throw it back in? Why was she studying it with that burning glint in her eyes? She threw it on the grass, where it writhed away.

'Think how much the crows will thank us.' She laughed. She tousled his hair and went in, humming some ditty to her mad, mad self.

Anuradha, who was watching all this from behind the French windows, saw Shloka struggle to pick up the goldfish and dunk it back into the waters. She considered helping—but the boy managed just fine. *My silent child,* she thought. *The only one.* Out of the parlour and through the shaded veranda, Anuradha shuffled her way into the garden and to Edward's pond, to be with her son. In many ways, he reminded her of Mohan, the same smooth skin, the perfect nose, those clever eyes and curled lashes—and yet, the two boys could not be more different. Shloka didn't have Mohan's confidence, his genius for music, his startling good looks—but he engaged you with his humility, his magnificent demureness, his solicitous gazes.

'Shloka ...' Her hand touched his head. 'We're going to Matheran. Next Friday. For a few months. You know that ache in my feet, huh? Well, Radha-mashi feels mountain air will suit me tidy. Nandini will come too. With us.'

He nodded and looked up at her quizzically. So she confirmed, 'No ... no ... your father has work to do ...'

He looked at his tiny feet. Anuradha heard the gates creak—it alerted both of them that Vardhmaan was home. With the sudden swiftness of an impala, Shloka raced up to the front of the house.

Even before his father could fully disembark from the car, Shloka circled his arms around Vardhmaan's leg. Vardhmaan gazed briefly into those impossibly lovely eyes before scooping the boy into his arms. Shloka, thrilled but quiet, wanted his father to know about the envy-green grasshopper that had landed on a novel in the library. About the goldfish he had rescued a short while ago.

What is this emptiness, Vardhmaan worried, *that lives in this child's eyes? Look too deep and you might tumble right in.*

He felt Shloka tighten his hold around his neck: he seemed to be fiddling with his tie, a gorgeous burgundy silk looped around with perfect efficiency. Vardhmaan smiled, knowing that this lad had quite a thing for ties: more than once he had seen Shloka peer secretly as he put on his tie before work each morning. His suspicion, of course, was absolutely true: Shloka was fascinated by this mundane, obligatory ritual, and the facility with which his father turned a piece of fabric into such a dignified sartorial adjunct.

Would his father teach him how to knot a tie? Shloka wondered. Was it easy? How would he look with a tie? Did his pappa have *any* idea how madly, how secretly he was adored?

'And are you well?'

To Anuradha's ears, this question, coming from her husband had the same ambivalent, faraway beauty of foghorns. 'I could not be better,' she replied. 'Come to me, Shloka ... come ...'

She sighed when he sat on the ground, cross-legged, unreservedly vulnerable, and looked at her.

'I had an aunt, Shloka, whose singing lit up all the lamps of the house. I wish I could take you to Udaipur. But my feet. One day, somehow, I'll take you. Show you the pergola by the lake where I learned by songs. Show you how I fed the peacocks. Do you have any idea *how* happy I was there?'

He stood up and touched her thin, scalloped gold bangles.

She continued, 'But 1 am all right here too. One has to rip open the chest to know how to love well—and that's *only* the beginning. A few months into my marriage, I fell in love with your father; now, I learn what it is to deepen *that* love. Weld it for eternity. Remember, baby child, there are songs inside you that will surface in your dreams. In evenings of disquieting grief and in the arms of a lover. You will remember my song of the dusk ... the last one there is ...'

27

After Nandini had settled into her train compartment, she chatted with Sherman through the bars of the window and over the sound of the announcements and the coolies haggling for business and the rancorous Singing Widows of Ratnagiri performing Marathi nautch-girl ditties from another era.

'Now there you go ...' she accused wrongly. 'Deserting me to some feral land.'

In a blue check shirt and tan trousers folded on the ends, Sherman Miller, now in his early twenties, was entirely edible. Strapping, you could call him, with large, graceful hands and a masculine tenor whose charm roused the sleeping fantails of the heart. 'You won't forget me, will you?'

'I couldn't if I tried,' she teased. 'But I promise I'll try harder!'

'I'll write. And stay away from Libya Dass. Please.'

'What?' After she'd told him that her friend Libya Dass had scant use for men in the bedroom, Sherman secretly started loathing her.

'I mean ... let her not try to lure you into something or the other ... best to keep a foot's distance. I mean, I'm not running her down or anything ... but if she's a lady-lover, then I'd appreciate it if *you* just keep away from her.'

'And I'd appreciate it if you'd take a five-foot bamboo and ram it up your rear, my darling.' She said that she found no one more crooked than someone all straight because they were the folks who could hate large and wide. And did.

'But *how* can a woman ... love a woman ...' Merely the thought of Libya Dass curled in bed with a member of the same sex made him queasy.

'Look up, harp-boy. What d'you see?'

'The sun,' he said.

'Now who told you?'

'I know that much, for Chrissake! You must think I don't have my oars in the water.'

'Ah, but does the sun know it's the sun? Ever asked the sun, "Hey, you, mister, what's your name?" Uh-uh! Someone long before you woke one fine day and decided, "Now *that's* the sun." And so it grew to become *your* truth too. Same goes for folks like Libya Dass who get all oiled up for the kitties. Of course, ages back, someone told her she ought to be all hopped for men—but she found that blokes couldn't get her tit up to save its life. Why settle for someone else's *version* of the truth? Besides, my beautiful barmbrack, truth is only what we make up ... by the way, seen where my ol' cousin is?'

He looked around and saw Anuradha next to the peanut-seller, talking with Vardhmaan; Nandini wished that she would board soon since the initial boarding whistle had already been sounded.

'You'll come back. No?' He memorized the matured beauty of her face, its veiled nuance of suffering under its sassy panache.

'Will I come home to Yeats?'

He threw a crumple of paper in her lap and ran off. She flattened out the sheet.

... I will find out where she has gone,
And kiss her lips and take her hands;

And walk among long dappled grass,
And pluck till time and times are done
The silver apples of the moon,
The golden apples of the sun.

A single immaculately cream pearl looped with a thread of silver.

There, by the peanut-seller, Shloka stood in the vast propinquity between his father and his mother. His mother, in a sky blue sari, sported large hoop earrings and had extended her hands to Vardhmaan: it was astonishing, this intimacy, this embrace of fingertips, in a place as bustling as a train station. 'Don't worry ... Radha-mashi's there ... call Pallavi or Krishnan if you need something, hmm?'

'I will.'

When Anuradha's eyes fell on the grand old railway clock it reminded her of the time they had all landed on this same platform at Victoria Terminus when he brought her back from Udaipur.

'Vardhmaan ... I've wanted to ask you ... for the longest time ... the frangipani braids. Remember? Why don't you ever bring them for me any more?'

'I can never forget them.' Did *she* remember, he thought, that the last time he brought her a frangipani braid she had untied it from her hair and sprinkled its blossoms over their dead son?

'No ... *tell* me something more ... talk to me ... like we used to, Vardhmaan ...'

'I love you, Anuradha.' Vardhmaan pulled her closer with her fingers.

'But don't you see?' she said, shaking her head. 'Love is not enough ...'

He let go of her hands.

At once she wanted to hit herself. And her regret ran deep. So deep that it took a shovel and dug up that other sentence buried in her heart: *I want my violin.* Pulling her sari over her head, gripping Shloka's wrist, she turned and hurried to the train, as the stationmaster, in his navy blue livery with gold epaulets, waved a flag to signal the train's departure.

Dr Vardhmaan Gandharva stood there, on the station, for a long, long while, unfailingly erect, arms crossed, till the train was no longer in sight.

As the train rolled into motion, the dusty city started to fade like the ellipsis points in a plaintive verse, and soon they were immersed into the blurs of countryside vignettes: white Brahma bulls tilling loamy black earth; crested egrets in the rice fields. Nandini thought that Anuradha looked somewhat disturbed, as if she were holding back tears. So she said, with the hope of opening a conversation, 'The last time I was on the train was from Udaipur. Do you remember the evenings we spent under the pergola?'

Anuradha shut her eyes. 'It's not possible to forget, is it?'

'That's true,' Nandini responded. 'Why do you ask that?'

But Anuradha didn't say a word further; she knew that if she did, she would break down. Thoughtfully enough, Nandini didn't egg her on. She lit a beedi and decided to leave Anuradha in the whorled seashell of her solitude. An hour later, as Nandini traced the path of her life, she was overwhelmed with gratitude. What a long way she had come! From her harrowing years in Harrow ... to her lonely orphan's adolescence in Rajasthan ... to this evening, when she was on her way to Matheran, a poised young artist who was not only the student of one of the most extraordinary painters in the world but expected, very soon, to also be his muse. What a marvellous and maddening route she had taken! Then she thought again about what Anuradha had asked her, and wondered whether it were possible for the present to wrestle the past. And vanquish its heinous archives to the ground, like a matador plunging a sword through the red heart of the bull?

Would she ever forget what had happened to her in Udaipur? Was it even possible?

Nandini's life in Udaipur, like her life in London, was a carefully recorded palette of smudges, not because she had a bad memory but because she had a terribly clever one: it was tutored to forget. Not that it ever really learned how. For instance, when she ran her thumb under her chin, the mark, that monstrous, minute gash, was still there: Udaipur's brutal, secret dowry for her. When she'd fainted in Dariya Mahal, she had recovered under Anuradha's care: the soups and herbal ointments and quiet walks helped no end. But when she'd fallen down in her parents' home, in Udaipur, when she was around seven years old, her chin had smashed against the edge of a corner table and gouged a dent so deep even time could never mend it. It happened on the night her father did the most Unimaginable Thing to her mother. And over the years, the gash served as a subtle reminder of a life she had almost forgotten. Well, *almost.* Because, more than a decade later, all Nandini had to do was trace her finger over the tiny, unhealed, chin-under gash—and she could clearly summon to her mind its vicious, entirely unforgettable arrival into her kismet and over her body.

The Hariharans had had a huge house with intricate cantilevers and Spanish-style balconies, on the peripheries of Udaipur, at the foot of the same lake that flowed outside Anuradha's house as well. Their life had followed a routine: Nandini's father, the genius doctor, left for work in the mental hospital at seven each morning; her mother awoke at nine, had her camomile tea and set to work on her paintings in a makeshift studio near the end of the square garden; somewhere inside all this was Nandini. Watching. Listening. Memorizing. Dr Hariharan returned at lunchtime only to recommence an argument with his wife that he had abandoned the night before, and they opened with the very words they had broken off at, ending over lunch at the point when each felt that they no longer had the inventive, vicious edge in their battles necessary to keep their interests in place. So they resumed work and met again at the dinner table, at eight, where they ate in an eerie hush since they were still brooding over their hastily concluded noonday argument. As always, the meal was fairly inedible, because a grotty meal—a charred roti; a daal that tasted like a salt-pan—doubled as the gracious harbinger of a quarrel that could rise now and continue well into the night and be consummated at noon the following day.

Every night, no sooner had one of them thrown a dish off the table or upturned a bowl of sabzi, they would ask Nandini to go to her room, claiming that the chimes announcing her bedtime had struck on the antique grandfather clock in the study. And hardly had Nandini stepped into her room than her parents would start one of their arguments. The irony was that even though the couple were of undisputed brilliance, they had not the ordinary insight of the golden rule: children are *never* sleeping in their room. In her wretched wakeful restlessness, young Nandini was hounded by a doubt that *she* had brought about this fight, for on more than one occasion she'd heard her mother shriek, 'If it wasn't for Nandini, you harami, I'd have left you two days into our marriage ...', to which her father cruelly rejoined, 'If it wasn't for Nandini, I'd never have married you in the first place, you filthy sewer-cleaner's daughter!', establishing that indeed it was she who was to blame.

For the broken ceramics. The amateur dramatics.

And especially for the dismal, frustrated sadness two people sense when the anger over curdled love has faded.

Then one night as they were fighting, Nandini stepped out of her room and into the awkward silence her presence had commissioned, and she fainted in the lounge. That same old dilating and salivating and perspiring. For the next few days, concerns over her health took a vague precedence over their rowing. Perhaps, she naively believed, she had solved the dilemma she had brought about. Now, they would stop fighting. Now, no more dishes would fly from one end of the lounge to the other. A bigger buddhuu there never lived! Because no sooner had the test results proved that she was quite all right, that such convulsions affected one in every ten persons, that even great men like Alexander the Great suffered from them, than they resumed their rowing: their voices high pitched, their brows feverish, their eyes red, their necks strained, their insides emptied of all meaning.

As for that gash under Nandini's chin.

Well, now *that* was instituted in astonishing circumstances: during a fight that started in the withering heat of April, on the day that her mother announced that she was pregnant. Well into her eighth month at that. Her rounded stomach, it was now clear, was not the fat from over-indulgence but the flesh and heartbeat of another living creature. Hey Bhagwan! Dr Hariharan was knocked for six: a woman—*my bloody wife*—was pregnant. And eight months, no less. What had he been thinking? Were his eyes hanging with his balls?

Nandini, hiding in her room, could hear her father yelling so that the glass panes shivered to his masculine timbre, which insulted his wife three generations back, describing her father as a castrated pig, her mother as a cheap village whore, her grandmother as a lower-caste drain-cleaner and so on until their invectives were overlapping and redundant and, in despair that they might run out of things to say, Dr Hariharan started to beat his wife, first with a soup ladle he picked up absent-mindedly from the table, then with the back of his hand. This went on with merciless delight—thrash, thrash, thrash, thrash, thrash thrash, thrash—until with a pregnant woman's ferocious instinct for survival, Mrs Hariharan fought back. Kicking, biting, clawing, kicking, biting, clawing, kicking, biting, clawing, kicking, biting, clawing, kicking, biting, clawing, kicking, biting, clawing, kicking, biting, clawing, kicking, biting, clawing: as much as a woman with an infant stored in her womb could. Displeased with the reception that his beating had provoked ('How dare she!'), his fist rose up in a tempest of rage and knocked her over.

She crumpled to the floor with a holler that etched shivers down Nandini's back.

In the darkness of her room, Nandini hurried up to her door and pressed her ear to it: what now? Who was being pulled? What *caused* those screams? Animalesque. Unearthly. Well, actually, there was a perfectly logical reason for those shrieks: right outside her bedroom door, her father was dragging her mother by her lush black hair—like a raggedy li'l' doll—down the teak landing, over the polished staircase, through the lounge and on to the porch where the nearly illustrious Mrs

Hariharan, clad in a loose, pregnant woman's peach flower-print gown, was boxed on her head ('That'll knock some sense into you!'). She caught his boot the first time he aimed for the navel ('Let's get rid of that sailor's baby, you filthy bitch ...'), although the second, third and fourth wham-phut of his shoe in her stomach let loose a river of blood out of her cunt.

Nandini opened her door. Gingerly stepped out. Red footprints on the teak landing. Clumps of loose black hair. Where was Mother? Should she go down? Ah. Music. How odd. Why was her father playing a suite of Mendelssohn? Even as Nandini diddled with her queries, her mother, sensing that the blood gushing out of her was the premature arrival of her baby, started groaning.

A maddening groan that ran around and shook everything in its path.

Nandini dashed back to her room. She hid behind the curtains, thoroughly petrified that the Hand that had knocked her mother down was also waiting for her.

But no. Oh no, no, no! It was *far* worse.

When Nandini looked out of her hiding place, she saw, through the window, the dry Rajasthani earth basted with moonlight, and under this swathe of light, Mrs Hariharan was on all fours. Like a dog. Crawling towards the trees. Panting. She rested back on the tree trunk. Crying. Reddishblackblue. Peach flower-print gown. Nandini pushed her face against the window pane. Her mother caught a glimpse of her. So she started calling out to her. Hysterically. Flailing her battered arms. Oh, hush, in the name of Shiva, hush! Scared witless that her father would hear this and grow mad at her, Nandini ducked below the window. But she could still hear her mother howling under moonlight, *Nandini ... help me, please ... save me from your father ... for God's sake, I'm a pregnant woman ... and the baby is here ... it's here, Nandini ... your little sibling ...*

Ten minutes later, the music downstairs changed: now, Rachmaninov. Outside, under the tree, Mrs Hariharan, convinced that her daughter too had abandoned her, was back on all fours, digging with her hands, like an Olive Ridley turtle digging up a nest. Intrigued by her mother's sudden silence, a sweaty little Nandini peeped up to watch. And she saw her mother spit out a child. Tear away the placenta. Rip out the cord. Small and dirty it was, but it was lifting up its soppy arms and wailing forcefully. *Breathing.* Kicked *aargh* out of the stomach it'd rented from Fate. Nandini saw her mother lean down and kiss the bloody baby before she ... she ... why! ... she chucked it into the hole she had dug to the tune of Rachmaninov (the small mercies in life: *good music to bury your baby to).* Fistfuls of earth after fistfuls of earth she hurled over the newborn that was bawling and begging not to be buried alive but only little Nandini, clad in a white summer shift, watching intently, understood that her mother had done the right thing. That night, Nandini felt this could not be, that this was not the life a seven-year-old child should have to encounter (and decided: *never* be a child), that her life, no matter how mesmeric the violence had once seemed, never mind its decrepit glamour, was now truly terrifying, and all she wanted was some relief: the capacity of dying stars to forget that they ever bore light. At that instance, her feet melted and she fell and smashed her chin on the marble-topped table whose sharp carved edge indented into her, for ever, the memory of the night when her mother was left out howling for her to *help me please* right before she buried her infant brother with her hands, and all Nandini did was faint, to fade like the echo of a wail that rises from the deep gut of the Earth itself.

She put out her beedi before they reached Matheran.

28

Radha-mashi's summer house, the Owl's Retreat, was spread long and built low and sported a red slate roof that trembled to the boisterous packs of rhesus monkeys that frolicked and fought on it, emitting a sound so raspish it altered the very texture of human skin. Since the house stood in the dip of the valley it was entirely invisible to the world beyond, and the opaque parade of trees around it only further curtained it from inquisitive eyes.

'What a *char*ming spread!' Nandini took an instant shine to the Owl's Retreat, its wide, airy rooms with graceful Palladian windows overlooking the tennis court at the east side and the monsoon pond, Walkers Tank, at the far end. The limestone flooring lapped up the petulant noon heat, the intricate entablature housed mourning doves, and the shady porch was ideal for writing letters.

'Yes, indeed,' Anuradha agreed, sitting on a wrought-iron bench. 'I think the pond at the back must be lovely to sit by at dusk, nè?' Her feet already felt better here.

'Got to watch for panthers, though,' Radha-mashi warned. 'And for rabid dogs. Other than that, I've had more than a few champagne soirées around it.'

'Panthers!' Radiance spread over Nandini's face. 'Oh ... how awful. I suppose.'

Anuradha looked at her archly. She turned to Radha-mashi and said, 'But rabies too?'

'Hmm.' Radha-mashi shook her head grimly. 'In fact, Anuradha, you'd better keep Shloka clear of the stray pups and the mongooses and the other what nots round abouts here. Madness comes calling in ways you can never even imagine ... ah, now did *any of* you try the jamuns? Hm*mmm*! Picked fresh from the orchard, they are, and if they were any more tart I'd be accused of running a bordello ...' She promptly lifted a succulent black jamun and plunked it into her mouth: a bluish, dissolutely runny juice tainted the corner of her lips.

The next morning, Anuradha decided to stay back at the house while Radha-mashi took Nandini for a walk through Matheran. The air was clear and distilled and the white langurs in the trees were motionless: they seemed like tiny Grecian statues suspended high up in space. On their way out, Radha-mashi pointed out the moist panther tracks around the pond. Nandini crouched to inspect them with immense interest.

Snake skins on their path. Thin dirt tracks flanked with black, mossy boulders. Red earth. Dewy morning.

'Now *that* place,' Radha-mashi pointed to a brooding building with a shingled roof and wicker furniture on its veranda, 'is where Freny Dastur lives ... an old chum, she's been here for ever ... but she's *very* strange. She has these nine dolls, y'know, all named after the Muses, and they're like her children. No one else in her life. Must get damn lonesome here, I bet.'

Freny Dastur was a milky-skinned Parsee, tall, scrawny, with bony fingers and ankles so thin her gold anklets were the size one might order for a newborn. She had had the dolls from her childhood days, and she lived her world around them: each doll had its own bedroom in her grand old house, complete with beds, wardrobes, books and paintings, and each evening she sat with them at the circular teak dining table and taught them freehand drawing or needlepoint. Many years ago, Freny had arranged to have one of her dolls, her beloved Terpsichore, married. An elaborate wedding was planned and a guest list comprising royalty and gentry was compiled. But on the evening before the doll's nuptials, the Princess of Hyderabad, one of the guests, had the nerve to kidnap Terpsichore. Freny, in her rage, summoned the police. They inspected the rooms and luggage of every one of the guests—all of whom were mortified at being treated like petty bazaar thieves. When Freny realized it had only been a prank played by the princess, she never spoke to her again—and after that humiliating debacle, poor Terpsichore never did marry.

A little ways up, Radha-mashi pointed to the bungalow of Roxanne Mistry, who owned and bred every type of snake under the sun. When they saw her sunning herself with her beautiful boa constrictor, they went in and said hello.

'Churchill's moulting,' Roxanne Mistry informed them in her sing-song voice. Short and round, she was clad in a red polka-dot dress. 'He's been *so* moody the last few days. I make him listen to Bach in the mornings. Calms him no end, I tell you!'

'What's with the name?' Nandini was enchanted by the boa's soft, somnolent eyes.

'Oh, his intestines are *always* jammed. And he too likes to strut around without his clothes! But I love him to bits ... gentle as a baby, he is.' When she lowered Churchill around Nandini's shoulders, the boa settled there without complaint, looking like a fat, speckled stole.

'You're right,' Nandini cooed. 'He's really the bee's knees!'

'Actually, my dear, that was only his breakfast.'

Before long, they came to Charlotte Lake: a spherical liquid pool flanked on three sides by the forest. The deep rustling green all around them was embellished by the hypnotic ascending scale of the brain-fever bird. 'Now this here, *darr*ling, is *the* most stylish end of Matheran,' Radha-mashi said. 'See that mansion? Barr House. Why, that's the Worthington summer abode. They'll be here shortly.'

'Really?' Nandini had long been wanting to know Percival better. But at the Thursday salons, Lady Worthington made a point of keeping her son away from that dance-on-the-table vagrant enchantress. Perhaps she would get her chance here, in the gregariously debauched Matheran?

'They're planning a huge party in a few weeks—and they're even bringing in a band from this city called New Orleans, where people are enjoying a new type of music. Jazz, they call it.'

'And to what do we owe this honour?'

'I thought you must have heard.' Radha-mashi's brow creased up. 'Percival is to be engaged.'

'Oh ... really? To whom?' Nandini's face remained tight, skilfully unrevealing of her disappointment.

'Lucinda Cummings ... you know, the Cummings of Dorset. Splendid old family with mills in Lancashire. Grapevine goes, Lucinda looks like a pickled white onion with a parasol.'

'In that case,' Nandini said without blinking her eyes, 'it's a perfect match, isn't it?'

'You seem edgy.' Radha-mashi faced her. 'Is something wrong?'

'Oh no! Not at all!' Nandini struck her tongue to her palate, producing a defiant cluck. *Nothing's wrong,* she wanted to tell Radha-mashi, *except everything. But how would you understand, darrrling?* Right then, though, they saw coming their way, down the same hill, two very familiar figures.

'Are there *any* rules in the Game of Love?' Nandini asked with a wicked smile.

'Love is *not* a game!'

'But why didn't someone tell me that *before*?' Nandini said in a shocked voice. 'Hell, honey, I'd *never* have worked on my handicap.'

'What d'you mean?' Uneasiness was splashed all over Radha-mashi's face.

But Nandini did not oblige her with an answer. Instead, she hurriedly kissed Radha-mashi on either cheek and raced up the hill and into the wide-open waiting arms of Libya Dass and Khalil Muratta. The trio linked arms and vanished behind the imposing iron gates of Dass's mansion—and into the landscape of Nandini's impending eternity.

29

Nearly a century later, when the Museum of Modern Art, in New York, held a retrospective of the works of the celebrated Afghani artist Khalil Muratta, his most famous painting was featured on the cover of the catalogue: *The Hand*. Bought by a private collector for in excess of seven million dollars, it was on loan to the museum, and its visitors were reduced to hot tears or fired with unconquerable lust as soon as they looked at it: how uncanny it was that the same painting evoked so polar a response! Rendered in dark but muted hues of brown and green and dusty blue, *The Hand* showed a girl—from the torso up, lusciously bare—sitting at a circular table, by a window, looking out, a face of full-bodied anguish. Her collar bones were disturbingly elegant, and there was a hand—not her own—grasping her right breast.

Few ever knew the story behind the painting.

Painted that summer in Matheran, *The Hand* caught Nandini Hariharan at her sincerest: erotic, sad. The painting, like most great art, occurred by itself; the artist was merely the medium. In keeping with his intention to return to his craft, Khalil Muratta painted Nandini in Matheran, in the anteroom of Libya Dass's grand house which looked down on the Valley of Black Panthers. During the painting sessions, they often talked long into the persimmon evening: was it the cool mountain air or the cicadas at nightfall that loosened their tongues? Khalil Muratta told them about his wife, how her intuitions had been unflinchingly correct, her innate flair for lovemaking, and how she was the first one to teach him that two lovers really unite not during the act but after they are past the breathless tempo of lust: in that hushed dawn chit-chat about absolutely nothing at all. When it was Libya Dass's turn, she lay back in her alabaster bathtub and spoke eloquently of the loneliness of a life conducted on its own terms, of the lovelessness of folks who love their own sex. One afternoon, though, both of them concurred that they had gone on and on without bothering to learn more about Nandini. She tried to put them off, saying she had nothing to tell because she was 'just another small-town girl'. They laughed at the travesty of her proclamation—and they remained insistent about their request.

'Tell us something ... from a time when you were little ... from when innocence reigned.'

'Innocence never reigned,' she corrected. 'Ignorance did. But not for long.'

That evening, unable to combat the heat, she was sitting nude on a cane chair by a circular table, and her body had that lucid shine of a woman who has dedicated her body to loin-shattering, calf-tightening, teeth-gritting lovemaking: which, of course, she had. Through the open window she saw the deep, dark vale, the joyous hawks reeling inside it, the spine-tingling roars of wild cats waking in the jungle. Finally Nandini said she would tell them about a man. Uncle. Her face turned inward; her beauty now daubed with remembering. Suddenly, gripped by the capricious incisors of inspiration, Khalil Muratta started, very discreetly, to move his brush over his canvas. Dying sunlight bounced on Nandini's solitary face as she spoke. 'So after they died, I was moved around. Home to home. No one wanting me—not that I blamed them. What I never understood was how they'd happily shoot a weaver bird but never catch them. What *was* their logic? Now one day, I landed up at the house of an uncle I'd heard my mother speak shoddily about. His wife had jumped in the well, and now that all his four daughters were married, he lived alone, in a bungalow with custard-apple trees in the back yard.

'I don't know why I was so suddenly gutless around him. He was grotesque, fat in a loose, oily way. A beached whale with a moustache. Each night, I heard Uncle fiddle with the radio downstairs. I'd hear him pace outside my room. One night, he knocked on my door. I pretended I was sleeping. But he walked in anyway. Then he sat next to me; his smell of rose oil was vile.

'He started stroking my hair, his fat, scabby hand touching my nape.

'He did this several times over the next week. Finally, a few days later, he "woke" me and asked if my mother had ever read me nursery rhymes at bedtime. I said she hadn't. He said maybe *he* ought to. I told him I was nearly ten, and slept perfectly well by myself. But he came in the next night anyway. He recited me old nursery rhymes which he read out of a book. His English was shaky, and the rhymes, in the humid darkness of Udaipur, sounded like incantations. *Baa! Baa! Black sheep! Have you any wool?* Spells. Curses. I don't remember the first time he slid under my bed covers, but over the course of the next few days, I understood why his wife had jumped into the well. I couldn't even imagine what his four daughters had been through. The morning after the first time, I nailed my first weaver bird; it didn't let out so much as a shriek when its yellow wings were ripped apart. The first time I walked on water was in England. The pond in St James's Park. Where the spiteful pelicans tried to peck me. I was a little under four. My father was "curing" Lady Windermere that summer.'

'You ever known what it is to have a train run over your body? I was so smooth at the time. Not a hair, you know.' She opened her legs and looked down. How beautiful and tumescent and life-giving it looked. 'I was tight then. But Uncle said his fingers would take care of that. Gross, greasy fingers that loosened everything inside me. I don't know why someone recites Yeats to me today, and I don't know why the sky is so blue, but I do remember the first time he rammed me. He was reciting a nursery rhyme as he did it. Did he muffle my mouth? I guess he had to because I sure was screaming like some haint. Would have woken up half of Udaipur with a holler that high. I tore. Leaked. His sweat fell on me drop by drop, like how water drifts off some leaf after a storm. Looking up, I saw black spiders on the ceiling. *Aw, hell.* When Life cuts a joke at your cost, the bitch sure goes all the way. Because no matter how far away I am from Udaipur, I know that one day he'll find me. Uncle. He'll come back for me. With his hands and his sweat. Leaves my head spinning and then my body too.' That was when Libya Dass could no longer restrain herself and she skimmed over to Nandini's side, tears veering down her oval, kind face. Nandini continued gazing out of the window, into the valley, miles outside the geography of consolation. Libya Dass's right hand held on to Nandini's breast, as though pulling her out of everything, as though reminding her that she was still alive because she experienced both desire and agony: the undaunted hallmarks of Life.

And Khalil Muratta captured that moment of interrupted solitude.

It was there. *Always.*

The Hand.

And so, during those days in Matheran, he painted her.

Whenever his attention scattered, she yanked down his cotton trousers and enveloped his banished rod with her hungry, slurpy mouth, drawing out the very life force Khalil Muratta was born out of. Sipping on the roof of it, her tongue musing on the *v* below, in the same way that some student might diligently study the work of his favourite poet, relishing the creamy core of him: so hot, so tormented, so mystical. Those summer mornings, Libya Dass would occasionally wake with a tiny, wild-haired head nestled inside her thighs: it reminded her of those forlorn marketplace kittens that lap up a bowl of milk with a hunger heightened by their destitution. Fireflies lit up the darkness, a racket-tailed drongo called out from the valley, and when Nandini Hariharan slept under the night, the sky was softer, the stars inside it nearer.

The beauty of this world, if you gave it your heart, would break it.

30

Although a month had gone by since she had left for Matheran, there were still times when he woke inches after dawn and reached for her—to touch the reef of her shoulder; the sighing tousle of her hair—only to find an emptiness. An emptiness he could drown in (and years later she too, owing to the nastiness of circumstance that would befall her, would also go under: but no one ever saw *that* coming). After breakfast, mostly seera or pava-bateta, which the part-time maid Ramli faithfully whipped up for him, Vardhmaan would sit out for a few minutes by the pond. Thinking of his wife. Her habit of humming as she went about her tasks, how she sculpted an utterly spellbinding melody from very few words. Missing her, Vardhmaan felt, had become a physical sensation—as if his kneecap had slipped off during sleep or a finger had fallen off his hand. Did she miss him as well? And just what had she meant: Love is not enough. That sentence was still spiralling inside him. *I wish you were here, Anuradha,* he sighed. *One day, maybe I can be the man you expect me to be.*

Seeing him so rapt in his desolation, Dariya Mahal recalled that saffron cupola of dusk under which Edward, that most charming of Englishmen, had also reflected by the pond, feeding goldfish, picking out twigs, waiting, waiting, *waiting.*

Now, it appeared, Vardhmaan too was waiting.

Driving to work one morning, a little after nine, he remembered that he had to check on Pallavi on his way back; she'd spent a week in hospital, nursing her faulty heart. He decided to look her up when Krishnan would also be at home, after seven. At the traffic lights, near Dwarika, three flower-women were selling frangipani braids; he bought a single braid with that sweet, haunting scent he, like Anuradha, had almost forgotten. It was after visiting Pallavi, after his lonesome dinner, that he came to the conclusion that the scent of frangipani didn't remind him of Anuradha, but more accurately of who he used to be around her: how lovers alter in the glance of each other, that space where their moods are accepted and their surrender is never taken advantage of. Two days later, when the braid started to tan some, he flung it out, and that same evening a thin, neatly addressed envelope lay tucked under the portal.

Postmarked from Matheran.

My dearest Vardhmaan,

Matheran is full of cool shadows and breezes that blow with leisure, as if they were going no place at all. I am enchanted by the names of houses here: Petit Tour, Eden Hall, and the Pallonjis' massive Cairnmore, where I saw the gardener forcefeed their pet flamingo carrot juice so it wouldn't lose its colour! This is the best that I have felt since Shloka's birth, and I am walking a lot more, mostly around the forest bordering the Owl's Retreat. I only wish you were here, and that we might take a stroll down to Malet Spring or shop for kolapuri chappals in the bazaar. Even Shloka is doing the smiles here. Light and breezy our boy is. But I must tell you the main reason for his happiness. Since the day he came here, he'd been playing with a stray pup. But then Radha-mashi advised against this; apparently Matheran has a troublingly high incidence of rabies. Shloka was very disconsolate, and lost his appetite. So Radha-mashi, lovely as she is, surprised him and got him a puppy! The deer-red boxer pup has a pug-like face, with a fine black muzzle and a white flash right on her heart; around her, Shloka is full of high, shining laughter. Nandini named her Tia, a name that fits her like a glove.

And speaking of Nandini, she has enamoured the many faces of Matheran. In fact, just yesterday I was woken from my sleep by a sonata of Beethoven that one of her admirers had arranged for her to rise to! A Steinway in the jungle! However, I don't get to see her much. She spends a lot of time with her friends Libya and Khalil, and every now and then I see the three of them. Nandini is also keen to attend, in a fortnight, a party to celebrate the engagement of Percival Worthington to Lucinda Cummings. To be honest, Vardhmaan, I am over the moon that Percival is affianced—not for his sake but Nandini's. You see, I felt that she had set her eyes on him simply because she wanted to be part of the Worthington clan. Now, though, it will be unlikely. The only time I met Lady Annabel Worthington, at one of Radha-mashi's salons, I thought her snake-like. Vile to her last cell. How many of us have been tricked by these whitepeople's medals and badges? Perhaps someday we shall look back on what happened and smite our heads for letting them in, them and their speeches and their arrogant rifles.

Today, I remembered that the first time I ever saw Dariya Mahal, I'd promised you something. In a house by the sea, I would sing for you. It has been a while since I have, and upon my return I would like to do just that. Now that I see more of how we love in ways we never even thought it possible, I remember you from my deep heart.

Yours,
Anuradha

When he woke at dawn the next day, Vardhmaan thought of the sound of Anuradha's feet: the silver anklets that prefaced her. He pictured her striking, learned face of many solemnities, the small lines at the edges of her eyes which one might not associate with a woman in her thirties—but they were there, and left her looking timeless. All of a sudden, he was glaringly conscious of how Anuradha felt around him: he brought to her in their times together what she brought to him in their time apart—chilling loneliness. Unable to withstand the sheer absurdity of how things had turned out, he got up with a start, unlocked his wardrobe and yanked out all his clothes. Shirts, trousers, lehnga, kurtas, the odd blazer or two. After piling them up in neat heaps, he attacked the mahogany chest of drawers, and took out his socks, the white undergarments stitched by Natwar-bhai, the effeminate tailor of Dwarika, and the banians with their ignoble moth holes. With that task wound up, with puddles of sweat on his back, he started to bunch together his footwear, the elegant Rajasthani mojahdees, the moccasins from Poona, and slowly, one cluster at a time, he took them to a room directly above theirs, where, very slowly and diligently, he settled his belongings into what he felt was, from now, his *new* room. Commendable restraint was employed to not imagine her blank-faced disbelief the day she would return with vigour in her ankles, from Matheran, step into Dariya Mahal and enter a room emptied of his things. Of his particulars. Of *him*. When he sat on the single bed of his new room he felt neither regret nor frustration but the calm awareness that here, today, they were two individuals who could not be any closer. Because now they were no longer bound by love. Nor its memory. But something deeper, something whose real nature would take them many years of gathered courage and unscattered wisdom to correctly establish and then absorb into the vivid red of their blood.

Back in Matheran, in the week of their leaving, Anuradha was somewhat clutched up over Radha-mashi. Nightmares had been keeping her up. She appeared out of her element, was occasionally short, and her aloofness from Nandini was marked. After she had treated Nandini almost like a daughter for this long, and mentored her through Bombay's artistic echelons, why on earth was she refusing to share a meal with her, take a walk with her, or even hold up a no-frills, the-weather-is-so-lovely conversation? Of course, Anuradha tried to probe discreetly, but all Radha-mashi said was, 'She does not know the rules. That's her biggest problem.' Anuradha was taken aback that someone in such bohemian circles subscribed to the notion of 'rules'.

'I'll brew you some camomile tea ... it'll help with the nightmares,' Anuradha offered.

'The trouble is. They might not be nightmares,' Radha-mashi said somewhat cryptically.

To give her credit, Radha-mashi had, at first, tried to write it off as a dream, as one of those weird visions only the stimulating air of the mountains might provoke. An apparition. Maybe ... a hallucination? A few days earlier, as she was enjoying a midnight panatella, her elbows on the window pane of her room, Radha-mashi saw a naked girl with a courting lantern hooped around her right hand. Skipping along the thin dirt track leading to Walkers Tank, the girl's toned body gleamed despite the darkness. Like the high polish of an orange in ripeness. Barely had the girl sat by the pond, her feet drawn up to her chest, than, from the other side, through the ringal bushes, a panther stepped out.

Black. Liquid. Soft.

Monkeys started shrieking. Shaking branches. The panatella Radha-mashi was smoking fell out of her fingers.

When he crept up near her legs, the girl's bony brown arms flew straight up, as if unleashing her bliss through her fingertips. Although his tongue lapped eagerly, he sat at a distance from her legs, in an air of reserve, as if this intimacy was without its introduction. The formality of a courtship. *Then, did what happened happen?* Why didn't she graze her shins, abrade her palms? Why didn't she buckle under his weight? The pearl around her neck bobbed back and forth. Who else heard his snarl of release? That moment when the infinite solitude of his being rested inside her. After the creature left, she shook her hips, swiped clean the juice from her thighs and walked into the emeraldgreen consolation of the pond.

One

step

at

a

time.

31

'It is womankind's capacity to accessorize,' she told Radha-mashi on their way to the Worthingtons', 'that separates us from the world of men and other animals.' Because Nandini was sporting a fearlessly see-through sepia off-shoulder evening dress with an elegant—one might even say roguish—train, she thought it was basic courtesy to veil the succulent fruits of her flesh. For this reason alone, she had borrowed Roxanne Mistry's darling boa, Churchill, whom she had stylishly draped around her shoulders so his flesh might cover her own.

In response to her comment, Radha-mashi only shrugged her shoulder. They boarded the rickshaw: the trip to Barr House, near Charlotte Lake, would take, in the overpowering darkness of Matheran, under half an hour. Through the entire journey, Radha-mashi remained stoically quiet. But just before Barr House, she pleaded: 'Let them down easy. *Please.* For MY sake.'

'Whom are you talking about?' Nandini asked innocently.

'You know *exactly* what I mean.'

'I never meant to hurt you.' She pressed Radha-mashi's hand, then vanished into the shindig. Nandini decided that she could do nothing about what Radha-mashi had requested and chose to focus her energies on the evening.

Taking one look at Barr House, Nandini was promptly enchanted by the one hundred and one storm lanterns hanging from tree branches; by the manicured lawns which Lady Worthington had ordered to be cut at precisely half an inch and no more ('like at Windsor!'); and by the fleet of waiters flying around with platters of hors d'oeuvres, refilling chalices even before they were really empty. This same rakish glamour infected the guests: toned, towering women provoked a fever with their backless dresses of wide rambunctious hems that rose up in the slightest wind—dissolute ballerinas with silver string purses and ivory cigarette pipettes. The men in attendance were wholly consumable in their tidy custom-cut suits, bow ties, polished shoes, all strong arms and packed crotches, freeing at the slightest provocation a depraved, rolling laughter which suggested only how wonderful it might be to lie with them in a warm pool of perspiration that only their endless lovemaking might create. Barely had she walked under the regal stone arches covered with raat-rani creepers than Nandini saw a band strumming it from a sisal platform on the lawns, a little away from the heart of the gathering. The music instantly put a prance in her step: that Ooh!-touch-me-*here*-and-there-and-*every*where! trumpet of New Orleans. Out of the corner of her eye, she spied Stella Dimm, England's first ever Tit Girl, who was shacking up at the Bella Vista, near Maldunga Point, with Sudipto Buttacharya, author of the international bestseller *The Mating Habits of the Hindoos,* an updated version of the *Kama Sutra,* for which he had been awarded the prestigious Hooker Prize.

'Do they ever get too heavy?' Nandini asked with concern.

Blonde and breathless, Stella Dimm didn't look like a fallen woman but merely one who couldn't be bothered to rise very much. 'I 'ave to air them now and then,' she enlightened. 'Otherwise, in this tropical 'eat, I fear they might shrivel up and drop. One's called Asia. The left 'un.' The bosom was scarcely contained in the low cup of her mauve silk gown. 'And the right 'un is Africa.'

She giggled when Nandini prodded them. 'May I know what sort of government you practice in such vast acres?'

'Communism naturally.' Stella beamed. 'So everyone may get a share of what's not really theirs!'

'And what's even better ... Oh, sorry about this, Stella ... but I've spotted a dear friend I've long been wanting to talk to ... we'll catch up on politics over pudding ...'

Having seen Percival Worthington, momentarily alone, she slid up to him; as always, the son of the Governor of Bombay looked like the most pathetic Etonian shipwreck shored up this side of the Atlantic.

'Well! Well! Congratulations, Percy ... I'll bet all my canaryyellow, polka-dot knickers you're hopped about the wedding.' She winked.

'Yes ... er ... thanks ... we're planning a reception at the Billingdon grounds ... ah, does your snake ... bite at all?'

'Never!' she promised, her eyes widening. 'He merely swallows.'

'Oh, of course ...' Percival had never seen a snake used as a sartorial embellishment. 'Have you been long in Matheran?'

'A few weeks now ... but I've been holed up indoors for the most part. Tied hands down to painting ...'

'Ah, brilliant! And what're you painting these days?' He'd heard about her artwork from Libya Dass, among others. Heard it was all monsoon and misery.

'I'm afraid, Percy, I've been so busy *being* painted that there's been scant time to do it myself.'

He looked puzzled. She sighed. 'Can I trust you with a secret? It's a cross-your-heart-and-hope-to-die kind of deal, ducky.'

He nodded and inched closer to her; she told him.

'*You're* his muse?' Stumped that a twenty-one-year-old hellcat of no proper pedigree might be the reason for someone of Khalil. Muratta's stature to emerge out of a self-imposed retirement, his eyebrows rose up: now what was *she* cooked from?

'He's done four. *Only* four. You have to see them to believe them. The last seventeen years of his life are in every stroke. But he says he still needs a year to work on them. The finishing, I suppose. By the way, what does your Lucinda do?'

'Lucinda?' Percival Worthington was not too familiar with the woman he was going to marry; all he knew was that she had an annoying snigger, a large vanity case made of zebra skin, and a posterior that looked as if two gigantic astrolabes had been glued together. 'Why ... Lucinda does watercolours. Of the Lake District. The Sedbergh Hills ... oh, and she crochets these ... *cracking* little cardigans.'

'Crochet!' Nandini said in an awed voice. 'Gosh! How amazing! Must keep the joints lubricated. Saves from rheumatism.' And she flexed and unflexed her fingers as if performing the commendable exercise his fiancée took on so valiantly.

After a whisky or two, she spotted an acquaintance from Bombay, the wily Mr Bunkusdaas, who had invented the moving picture and whose idea—named Bollywood—would, decades later, become such a rage that the whole Western world would nick it and make their own moving pictures (which, alas, were lacklustre, formulaic and bereaved of the drama that spines all riveting storytelling). Mr Bunkusdaas was excitedly chatting with Tarun Khokla, India's only haute couture designer, who had trained in Paris, apprenticed in London and retailed in Bombay. Spotting Nandini, the thin-framed, bony-wristed Tarun Khokla, clothed in a flamboyant orange suit with a fluffy white chrysanthemum in the upper slit of his vest, looked at her with astonishment.

'Are you a ... star?' he garbled.

'A star?' she said duskily. 'No, my darling, I am an entire constellation.'

Tarun Khokla was speechless. So Mr Bunkusdaas took over and informed her that Tarun Khokla had just returned from Europe, where his fashion had been donned by the Queen of Denmark as well the Princess of Capri, who was, in fact, so stirred by his flair for blending the bravura of the sari into staid European clothing—all those stuffy corsets and bonnets!—that she had pleaded with him to stay back as her personal couturier. He had desisted, and here he was, in the great mountains of India. That was when Tarun Khokla gushed that his achievements were water in front of her luminous beauty and ... and ... in the name of Christ ... would she model for him?

'Model? What an absurd idea! Besides, I'm too ugly to model for anyone or anything.'

'I don't believe that for a moment.'

'Neither do I,' she said with a depraved giggle. 'But Lord knows I tried to fool you.'

'Listen ...' Tarun Khokla was now practically begging. 'Listen ... will you just dance with me? Please?'

'Certainly!'

At the very corner of Barr House, under three ancient mango trees, a certain type of newly discovered music—jazz—was making its debut in Matheran. The musicians, all brought in from southern America, were three beefy, sad-eyed gentlemen, the colour of the night and its absolution. As soaring beauty oozed out of their trumpets, a woman with tied-up hair and a rouge-red scarf around her thin, long, black neck sat on a scruffy old wooden stool and sang in a thick, impish voice which Nandini felt could easily travel from being rascalish to slit-wrist bluesy at the drop of a single chord.

'Be careful!' she warned the designer as they glided to 'Ain't Misbehavin' '. 'Don't you go round crushin' my Churchill!'

'Pray tell me why's he so ... well behaved.'

'You heard of opium, TK?'

But as she was dancing with the legendary couturier, Nandini was overcome by a terrible loneliness: all of a sudden, she hated this place, the people in their chic clothes, their futile chatter, the sizing up and running down of the attendees. Over the music and under the tittle-tattle, she longed for the Irishman. His bright listening, the confluence of veins on his solitary organ, his remarkable patience, the delectable plumpness of his rear, his confidence in his love for her, which somehow made her hopeful about the very idea of love *and* its existence.

She walked off from the dance, drunk and lost and forlorn. Who could she speak to of the heart's pursuits? Who, in this august gathering, could she trust with her secrets as dark as treacle? Just when she decided there was no one here that she cared for, she saw Libya and Khalil, surrounded by a genuflection of admirers and hangers-on.

'And just *what* is so wrong about two men deciding to settle down?' Libya Dass, a cerulean sari wrapping her sizeable buttocks, was fervent in tone. Recently Georg and Erich, two Danish transplants, had settled in a cosy cottage—the Gulistan, near Garbut Point (Nandini had met the tacked-up twosome at the Olympia Race Grounds).

'Why! Georg and Erich are abso*lutely* deviant!' Lady Worthington pursed her lips in revulsion. 'Just how can they even do what they did?' She had often wondered where two men would put it in. Or did they? Maybe it was just a little rubbing and shaking?

'But what'd they do?' Nandini was clueless about what they were discussing.

'Well, my dear,' informed the local pastor, Father Mulligan, 'Georg and Erich got married. It's entirely against the law, of course. And more importantly, against the Word of God. But what would they know of the Word of God.' He gave a theatrical shudder; stout and hairy, he looked like a rare species of evangelical Scottish grizzly.

'I'm assuming God gave you His word personally,' Libya Dass said. 'By the way, is He cute, Father Mulligan? Tall? Burly? Nice buns? Any pecs to speak of?'

'Nevertheless ...' Father Mulligan pretended not to hear Libya Dass's deplorable remarks. 'Never. The. Less ... I shall pray for their souls.'

'Just be happy some of us have still got souls to pray for.'

'Nothing but filthy perverts. A bad example to everyone in civil society!' Lady Worthington was on the attack. 'All these poofters ought to be banished to some faraway place. Put away in an asylum, I say.'

'Oh, aren't they already?' Nandini said in a naive tone. 'I believe it's called Cambridge, Lady Annabel.'

The whitewoman miraculously stopped her cheeks from flushing the shade of new plums.

'I've never understood what the breeders have against us,' Libya Dass continued, quietly riled.

'But Libya, it's so obvious. The unqueer are scared spitless by how queers *live* their desire. And unqueer blokes are the worst ...'

'... because they can't ham it in their own beds they're axe-after the men who can?'

'Now just when did Ms Libya Dass become the resident expert on *men*?' Lady Worthington said contemptuously.

'Ever since I stopped sleeping with them. You see, it made my opinions about them indubitably honest.'

'May I remind us all in this discussion of the simple truth: the Bible forbids it.' Father Mulligan raised his hands up.

'And that is only so men like *you* stay in the business of God. You'd be terrified if everyone decided *not* to breed, wouldn't you?' Everyone looked up when Khalil Muratta spoke—perhaps in defence of Libya Dass? 'I mean, who'd show up at your sermons then? And who would leave their silver coins on *your* platter? From the baptism bath to the funeral prayers, the production of life is what buys the rosewood podium you stand on and the casket which, one day, you too will lie in, Father Mulligan.'

'And,' Nandini added, tilting her head, 'I believe, at the last count, there were six hundred admonitions to the unqueer in the Bible—including death for a leg-over on a Sunday! But only six for queers. Of course, I'm not suggesting that the breeders are bad—maybe they just need more supervision?'

Everyone laughed; even Father Mulligan. Only the hostess remained seethingly unamused. She had had enough lip. 'Now, Ms Hariharan, could I *ever* accuse you of falling low? Seems to me, little one, you were just born that way.'

There were icicles in that moment.

Throats were cleared. Feet shuffled. Very swiftly, the assemblage scattered.

Nandini stood alone, a quietly embittered sentinel, infinitely small but with claws so sharp no one even guessed she had them, or for that matter could use them to effortlessly tear someone's neck in half. If Revenge were even half as sweet as the reason for it was bitter, then in this case the revenge would be sweet, *very* sweet indeed.

32

In her last week in Matheran, the white doves of hope that soared through Anuradha's chest left her giddy with the realisation that because the vigour in her feet had been restored, she would return to Bombay, under the browse of her husband's eyes, and they would, once again, enjoy strolls by the sea and songs at dusk. What it would be, she imagined over and over again, to lie next to Vardhmaan again, to gauge his sighing chest, to watch the changing patterns of sleep on his face. She wore again the silver anklets on her feet and rushed out over the red earth of Matheran and thanked the healing air, the redemptive solace of the forest.

On the day before they were heading back, Nandini asked her whether she would like to take one last walk up to Charlotte Lake. Anuradha jumped at the offer, not only because she loved bringing in the twilight by the lake but also because she could walk up to receive it: a gift of movement she wasn't about to take for granted any longer. Of course, she asked Shloka to come but the lad was so caught up in playing tug-of-war with a red hanky with Tia that he was quite content staying put in the Owl's Retreat until his mother's return. Just as they were past the gates, she turned and saw them playing, laughter and barks, glee and more glee, the inseparable duo, and Anuradha felt uneasy leaving him alone: why such a worry stroked her she did not know. Was it the panthers that everyone talked about? Was it rabies? The monkeys that sometimes harassed children? Only a few minutes into their walk, barely past Upper Louisa Road, Nandini said solemnly: 'Perhaps life is essentially unfair.' She was still smarting from Lady Worthington's insult at the party last week.

'Life essentially seeks out balance. I have found that it is in the habit of trading one sorrow for one joy until one cancels out the other.' Anuradha looked refined in a plain white sari, the tinkle of green glass bangles.

'And then?'

'Equipoise,' she said. 'That precise moment in the ocean when a wave neither falls nor rises.'

'Do you think my parents were ever in love? I mean …' Nandini had always wanted to know whether she was conceived in an act of love. If *that* particular emotion was the impetus behind her existence on this planet. 'But I guess all that love-bove is too strange.'

'It's bigger than us,' Anuradha accepted. 'So we confuse ourselves over it. And of course, its vastness overwhelms. But then that is the only lesson in life. How to love. How to love well, with a detached eye but a concerned hand. How to understand and surrender to its countless contradictions. Most importantly, though, how to *never* stop loving.'

When they got to Charlotte Lake, it was, thankfully enough, bare of visitors, and they found a large black rock at one corner on which they sat to hail the immutable saffron splendours of Matheran's sunset—so entirely unlike any other sunset in its intensity of colour and range.

'Nandini ... If I'm not intruding, tell me what you feel for Sherman ...' Now that Percival Worthington was safely engaged, she hoped that Nandini might receive Sherman with the regard that he deserved.

Nandini removed her rattan hat and aired her short black hair. 'There are times I want to squeeze him only to check if he's real. He holds my every shaggy-dog story, rides out my wilfulness, and who else will bring me my Yeats?'

'I don't know.'

'But he can't be what I need right now. Yes, I know, Anuradha, that he's starch, and I could swim in the blue of his eyes.'

Ages back, when she had told Sherman how her mother had buried her brother, she valued most that he had said nothing, no flimsy sorry, no bogus consolation: a moment of flawless understanding that there was no commiseration in such things.

'And I can talk to him about anything. For hours.'

'It'll take you years to piece *that* one together,' Anuradha said, bearing in mind her unspoken regret. 'How lucky you are for it.'

Nandini put her hand on Anuradha's shoulder. Over the last few years, she had witnessed the gradual rift between Anuradha and Vardhmaan: the quietness sitting between them like an enormous continent or a rough, unforgiving sea.

'Two days ago, I got a letter from Pallavi. She's been in the hospital. Her heart's been acting up. Vardhmaan never even told me.'

'Maybe he just didn't want to worry you.'

'She's dying, Nandini. Pallavi is ... no matter how you look at it ... oh, there, see how hawks are wheeling ...' She tried to distract herself from the mineral ache gathering in her throat.

'We're all dying, Anuradha. The really tough bit is living. And the kites nest on the bluff near One Tree Hill. Three chicks I saw one time.'

'I am learning to count on mercy these days.'

But the lady spoke too soon.

Like the very best of calamities, it happened without warning: on their way home, under a crown of rain trees, Anuradha fell. No, *crumpled.* Like a dream dismembered by wakefulness.

'Anuradha!' A stunned Nandini tried to lift her back up. 'What's the ...'

'My feet!' She winced. 'I can't *bear* it!' Her white sari instantly took on the red of Matheran's earth.

'What d'you mean?'

'The pain ... it's come back, Nandini ... it's *insufferable.*' Sweat rainbowed over Anuradha's wide, lovely brow. What was happening? And why *now*? Just when she thought she was doing OK.

'You stay right here!' Nandini said, herself terrified by Anuradha's sudden, dramatic transformation. 'I'm going farther down the road and I'll try to get a rickshaw ... for you ... Then we can get you home—and to a doctor.'

To articulate Anuradha's anguish would be to capture it for ever: it was as though someone had hauled back a cricket bat and smashed it against her kneecaps with breathless viciousness. Or as if her feet had landed in some poacher's secret trap and the rusty metal teeth had clapped shut to suffocate the flesh and blood out of her.

'I'll be back before you know it,' Nandini promised before she dashed off.

But only moments later, mist from the valley rose up in thick, gloomy tufts, erasing away even the road Nandini had taken. Panic woke inside Anuradha when she heard the rhesus monkeys in the trees bark. Just as she started to push herself forward, grunting softly, feet brushing against the forest floor, she heard, from the ringal bushes behind her, an odd rustling.

She stopped dead.

Mourning doves fluttered through the mist. Bonnet macaques rattled the branches, liberating a shower of leaves over her.

That was when she saw him.

Panther.

Crouched in the verdure, coat as if made of black velvet, ponderous breathing, pink tongue languidly hanging out, green eyes casting an unmoving gaze.

'Why?' she whispered. *'Why,* God, has this happened?'

She heard the leopard rise. With his every step, dry leaves crackled. Shrieks from the monkeys. Then, a silence so deep she felt she might vanish inside it. *Hadn't she already? Hadn't other silences mauled her before?* He was by her toes now, and his bloody odour made her nauseous. She wished he'd do it quick. The Death bit.

Breathing over her nape. Noisy breath. Needly whiskers piercing skin.

He stood there a moment. Glance up. Glance down. He would do it now. *Now* she would feel his teeth in her neck. *Now* she would hear her own bones crack. Hah! But before she knew what was happening, he had slipped back into the bushes.

Gone!

In the snap of a finger.

When Anuradha looked up, there were a scatter of paw marks all around her, like a wild rangoli.

Now she was certain: she had a fate worse than death.

33

Disturbed by that darker-than-need-be glimmer in Nandini's eye, curious about Radha-mashi's reticence, and with her own nape reeling from the beast's touch, Anuradha returned to Bombay hoping for the dependable silence of Vardhmaan (for now, and just for now, she looked forward to it in the same way that she once looked forward to the iridescent flashes of his stories).

That, however, was not to be.

Because his moving out had been so seamless it made her feel that he had never even lived here. The exodus was impeccable, without a trail to point a finger at or a spoor to follow. This evanescent deception, nevertheless, was hardly any consolation for an anguish that would tremble inside her, form patterns over her soul like old seashells that become patterned by spending far too much time in rough water.

'Is everything all right?' She had managed to walk up to his room. *Upstairs.*

He nodded. Handel was shimmering out of the gramophone: an unusually, even illogically, joyous tune for such an encounter.

'We had such a wonderful time in Matheran. We must go there one time, you and I. There's this gorgeous house, Balthazer Court, deep inside Matheran. All one can see from there is the valley, the blue above, and great, tall mountains the colour of pottery. It's so far away from everything ...' *What are you doing here?* she wanted to yell. *Why are your clothes and shoes and your water carafe up here, in this room? What will Shloka think?*

But now it was her time to remain silent.

'I tried to grow flowers. While you were away.' He didn't have the heart to tell her that Dariya Mahal, normally quite responsive to any sort of verdure, had passionately rejected the civilization of Vardhmaan's horticulture: one fine morning he woke to discover his painstakingly planted saplings lying flung out of the wet, smelling-sweet earth.

'But it is all good,' he said, looking down.

She stole a moment to observe how precise and shipshape his room was, utterly devoid of her feminine chaos of scarves thrown carelessly on the settee or silver earrings on the console. This, here, was a plain landscape. Of no songs. No violins. She sighed. His fetching, hard good looks still started a drum in her chest, and now her longing for him was as broad as it was raw. *Will you come down, please,* were the words roaring inside her like an inferno. *Just for tonight. I don't care about anything after. I don't want too much. Where, in this life of ours, Vardhmaan, are the small mercies?*

However, it seemed to her that no matter what she said now, it was unnecessary: he already knew. And knowing that he knew, she turned around and walked down with a sad, sad ache in her ankles and came into her room where, in the next few weeks, she would discover that it wasn't only her waking self which missed him but that her sleeping body desired him even more keenly. Between lovers and their bodies is a secret pact, one that allows elbows to touch and fingers to collide. The coincidence of anatomy. After having reached out for him at dawn, after relying on the sound of him stretching for a glass of water, the vardhmaanlessness of her life was not a state she wanted to wake in, or to.

The small mercies, nonetheless, were not entirely absent: finding relief in her rapport with Pallavi allowed her to disremember temporarily what she could not really place out of her mind for ever. When, one afternoon, over a cooking lesson—Anuradha's sumptuous paani-puri this time—she brought up this peculiar turn of Fate with Pallavi, her kind, exhausted friend steepled her hands before she spoke. 'Did I ever thank you, Anuradha? For your friendship. I don't know how I kept my silence so long ... why I never vanished into its depth. Odd thing is, I didn't even know I wanted to tell someone I was *this* sick. Perhaps that's only because I didn't know who to tell it to. When you think about it, it's crazy, all the things we carry inside us—and these are precisely the things we're just bursting to tell. How do we go through life like this, huh?'

She paused and looked Anuradha in the eye. 'I'm sorry. I'm sure it was just as dreadful for Vardhmaan. After a point of time, we learn to remember things without that horrid sting in the throat.'

Parrots shrieked from the ashoka trees; the clouds cleared; sunlight came weeping in.

'In the old Dwarika house we used to waltz after everyone was asleep. He said he would teach me how to waltz. There were times when he would hold me and I could just let go. Because I was convinced *he* would always hold on.' In the troubled straits of her mind, two unforgettable images, like the hands of a drowning man, shot up: Vardhmaan's brilliant, barmy elation when she had told him, for the first time, that she was pregnant; and then, the sight of a bier on his shoulders. *The west wind blurring it all.*

Anuradha stood up from her stool. 'My ankles, Pallavi, I just don't know what to do ... and you know ...' She stopped to gather the thought that'd come to her. 'The memory of happiness is as heartbreaking as its absence.'

'That's why I never want you to remember me. OK? Have you heard that they have now put sound in the moving pictures?' Pallavi's voice sounded bereft. 'Krishnan said so. We might even go to such a flick. Someone in Calcutta put in the sound. It's quite marvellous, really.'

'Ah-huh. Nandini knows Mr Bunkusdaas, the man responsible for this craze, oh-ho, what's it called now ...

'Bollywood!'

'Yes! We met him in Matheran. I swear, Pallavi, he smelled like an old sock. And so much oil in his hair, why, you could start a refinery on his scalp!'

Pallavi giggled.

'You know what's the *really* dangerous bit? Having your prayers answered.'

'What d'you mean?' Outside, the grey of the sky had graduated; Pallavi thought she ought to leave because Krishnan would be home any moment now (these days they cooked in Anuradha's kitchen to save her the bother of walking).

'In the early days of my marriage, Vardhmaan and I would come to Juhu beach for our evening walks—basically, to get away from Divi-bai. And on our way back home, I'd tell him that I wanted nothing more than a house by the sea. Aw, just look at what I've got myself into. At least Shloka must leave it. I don't want him to see this. Separate rooms.'

A few weeks later, Pallavi's words ricocheted through Anuradha. She was stirring a daal. The ladle fell out of her hand. *I don't want you to remember me.* That's impossible, she told herself, and then reasoned what exactly her friend was trying to save her from. *Where are the small mercies?* Hell, right now, she would even lift a shovel and dig out the mercies or trade all her night's dreams for them. And so, without any snicker from Fate's side, mercies arrived in a growl of smoke and with the dazzle of a million fireflies: almost instantly, Anuradha fled into the succour of the drama that followed.

You see, what happened in the next twelve months was the astonishing rise and jazz up of Ms Nandini Hariharan, aspiring artist, cat lover (so to speak) and everyday enchantress. Before she turned twenty-two, she was a national celebrity sharing front-page press along with freedom leaders, martyrs, royalty and film actors. Not a day passed when Vardhmaan didn't see her boldly plastered in the *Times of India,* a month without gracing the pages of *Tatter's* Native Glamour, and that same year she received her first mention in the *International Who's Who.* She'd been on the radio, where her dusky cadence brought back to life three dying men in the Arogya Nidhi Hospital, and her suggestive beedi-laughter made women woozy with envy. When she went to St Joseph's School to pick up Shloka each afternoon, the bounty of her breasts, the Delphic roundness of her hips, so agitated the pimply teenage boys that they ran home crying and dropped their trousers to their mothers. 'Mama, Mama! I'm going to die! There's a bone between my legs!' Their mothers, suburban and self-conscious, told them this was only God's way of punishing them for failing algebra. A famous sculptor, who went without his shoes, crafted a bust out of her from twenty-four-carat gold, and it was installed at Flora Fountain for all the city to admire, much to her mortification (she held on to the belief that Fame haunted only the mediocre).

But to call her a star would be to reduce her meteoric rise to the top, which was entirely unplanned, a necklace of coincidences that took her to such heights that she secretly hoped her entire past—Uncle; a woman burying a baby; and other sundry details—would, one fine day, fall completely out of sight below her. After returning from Matheran, pregnant with vengeance yet surreptitiously overjoyed that Khalil Muratta was busy working on his masterpieces, for which *she* was the inspiration, Nandini settled in one corner of Dariya Mahal to work on her own art. But a few days after the long rains were due to leave, the house bell rang. Anuradha, who used a cane stick to move around, was flabbergasted to see a spindleshank dandy with damp hair standing at the portal with nine hundred red roses which he claimed were for 'Miss Nandini Hariharan'.

'I am Tarun Khokla,' he announced. 'And if Miss Hariharan does not model for me, I shall shut up shop and become a monk.'

'It's only an excuse,' Nandini chided as she came down the stairwell, a paintbrush in her right hand, 'for you to fool around with the other monks, Tarun. We all know what happens in the name of God.'

'If you don't believe me, I will starve myself right outside your house,' he threatened, and promptly sat outside Dariya Mahal (who was, incidentally, unspeakably uncomfortable that a grown man was fasting unto death simply because a woman wouldn't model for his Monsoon Collection). The next morning, photographers from the *Bombay Chronicle* and the *India Herald* and scores of other papers were snapping up the dejected designer's picture with their clumsy box cameras which made short blasts and released a plume of smoke with each click.

Couturier Will Perish If Muse Will Not Model
Dying Designer Has Only One Wish

'I am *not* a muse-for-hire,' Nandini fumed to Anuradha as she read, the very next morning, the reports that labelled her 'moody' and 'cruel' and 'captivating'. Affronted that everyone might be reading such tush-tush, she stormed out, pulled Tarun right up in the air by his lapel and yelled, 'All right, now what d'you *want,* you li'l' cotton queen?'

'Please ...' yelped the emaciated but enthusiastic designer, 'just wear one dress for my Monsoon Collection. Only one!'

She dropped him to the floor. 'And just what the hell will I have to do?'

'Nothing at all,' he said. 'Just be yourself.'

'But that's asking for way *too* much!'

In any case, she agreed only so she might not be plagued by the press piranhas, and so that she might be able to return to the solitude essential for her own artistic pursuits. That August, a few days after the eternally quiet Shloka turned seven, everyone worth their cigar smoke was out on the grounds of the Billingdon Clubhouse for the launch of Tarun Khokla's Monsoon Collection. Togged-up reporters from newly started magazines like *Vogue* and *Vanity Fair* clustered together for what was described by many as *the* defining collection in World Fashion. Behind the stage, Nandini Hariharan sat on an ottoman as Libya Dass lined rouge over the seething model's lips. In the last few weeks, Tarun Khokla had come to Dariya Mahal frequently, always with his trusty measuring tape, his scissors, his young, thin, androgynous apprentice and realms and realms of ornate fabric: tussore, Burmese silk, hand-woven khadi, Bengali jute. He said his designs were so precious that they had to be stored in vaults after a rival couture house had tried to nick them.

'How can I not be told what you want me to model!' she had complained to him in the grounds of Dariya Mahal. 'And why the hell are you so secretive about what I have to wear?'

'Everything shall be revealed to you,' he said enigmatically, flapping his hands as though they were little butterflies.

And in a matter of days, it was.

A singular design that altered the sartorial history of India for ever.

It was, of course, the mini sari.

At its most generous length it ended above the knees, and at its raffish least it stretched an inch or two over the crotch. Other than that it had all the trappings of a conventional sari—the elegant pallo, the arm-length blouse, the creased length and folds. That evening, as the other models went out, applause rippled through the grounds, but an hour later, as the event was drawing to a close, Tarun Khokla sent Nandini out. A spiral of smoke preambled her entrance; the guests all sat up in their seats; photographers readied for the much anticipated moment: just *what* would she be wearing?

And out she stepped!

In a gold brocade mini sari, with a sandy-maned Yorkshire terrier in her right arm and a sassy beedi blowing rounds and rounds of smoke over the shocked face of Society. Unremitting applause competed with catcalls and sighs of pleasure and gasps of shock and nods of amazement. The next morning, that photograph of hers—gold brocade mini sari, her left hand pegged on her hip—made it on to the front page of almost all the national dailies.

India, being India, was incensed.

This was nothing short of cultural blasphemy. The venerable sari, originally designed to cover every spare inch of an Indian woman's holy body, was reduced to the condition of a garment that celebrated the female form. Nandini's picture on the *Times of India's* front page ran with the provocative blurb: *'The Future of the Indian Garb—Ms Nandini Hariharan models the Mini Sari from the Monsoon Collection of Tarun Khokla'.* Although Anuradha just laughed it off and Pallavi raised an eyebrow to it, neither woman anticipated the social pandemonium that would rise up as quickly as soufflés deflate. Anuradha was stunned to see that demonstrating right outside her house, the next morning, was the conservative Pro-India Nationalist Group—the Rakshash Junta Party, an extremist right-wing group of thugs who, years later, would take over all of India and make it unrecognizable with their vicious brand of politics. Clad in their repulsive saffron garbs (feral, fascist oranges), they hollered slogans such as: 'Nandini Hariharan—Hai! Return to London—Bye-Bye!' and waved banners saying:

The LAND that WORSHIPS the COWS
Will NOT Have WOMEN Showing Their CALVES!

The demonstrators unfurled metres and metres of shoddy two-rupee saris and flung them over the high walls of Dariya Mahal in an effort to educate the chalu Ms Hariharan about its designated length.

'Go all the nine yards!' they screamed like hooligans. 'Down with the mini sari!'

'Down with the mini sari?' Nandini gritted her teeth. 'Oh, Anuradha, how much more farther down can I take my sodding sari?'

Anuradha burst out laughing. (In those moments of altered reality she forgot the sweat-breaking sorrow of not only having misplaced the mobility of her feet but also the fact that her husband now had a separate bedroom.) It was Vardhmaan who pointed out that the leader of a prominent women's rights group was on a hunger strike (*à la* Gandhi) right outside Dariya

Mahal. The humongous, sweaty and unforgivably unsightly—beak-nosed; three chins—activist type nearly died.

'It's like I've got a beached whale right outside my gates,' Nandini told Sherman, who was her greatest champion during the Mini Sari Madness.

'And a beached whale without a bra at that,' he noted wryly.

Very soon, though, the leaderess of the women's rights group gave up her hunger strike, claiming: 'It is all right for that Gandhi to fast; he has nothing better to do anyway.' Not wanting to be left behind in the spree of Nandini-bashing, the wily-oily Culture Minister published an article about how a 'certain twenty-two-year-old Indian individual, heavily influenced by Vestern Values, has corrupted our moral society indelibly and for ever'. He concluded that she should be prosecuted, put behind bars and, as punishment for her sins, be made to grind wheat with a stone mortar and pestle for the rest of her life. Of course, none of this surprised Nandini, for she had long witnessed the country's deplorable history of intolerance as well as its vehement drive to add to its future heritage of censorship. It was expected, she told Sherman, from the Rakshash Junta Party and their puritanical, outdated values which systematically persecuted art and artists. Around the same time, an Indian author was condemned for writing a book against religion. When the freethinking minority press called Nandini for comment, she said: 'He deserves to die; he's too ugly to be allowed to live anyway.' The *Manchester Guardian* and the *Daily Telegraph* ran her photograph, saying she was the new face of Indian Liberalism—erstwhile an unheard-of phenomenon—and carried alongside it the grotesque image of the condemned writer in his copper spectacles covering his bloodhound eyes, his steepled hands, his smug smirk. They also ran a nationwide poll asking readers to decide whether he ought to be shot dead for being ugly, and when 97.3 per cent of the respondents replied he should be, the novelist rushed off into hiding.

'They did him in,' Nandini whispered worriedly to Sherman one night. He could not believe how out of her element she was—but she had good reason. She said that the man responsible for this furore, the ambitious and creative Tarun Khokla, had been hacked apart into teeny-meeny sausage-size pieces with a coconut knife by a seedy member of the Rakshash Junta Party. Demonstrations and protest marches marked the mutilated man's funeral cortège and the few models who showed up to pay their last respects all wore saris that covered even their faces (just to be on the safe side). The commotion calmed a bit, following his murder, but it seemed that the only way to curb this national outcry would be for Nandini to intervene and somehow rein in the crazy state of affairs.

'But what do you expect *me* to do?' She leaned her head on Sherman's shoulder; he had never seen her this way: a parable of elegant vulnerabilities.

'I'm sure there's a way to handle this situation. Now that Tarun Khokla's been done to ground, they might receive you more indulgently.'

'You mean the press feels for me because comrades of the Rakshash Junta Party are also hounding me? That they might come after me next? Oh, I'd *hate* to die under a coconut knife, Sherman!'

'Use their new-found sympathy for you. You're only down—not out,' he urged.

She gave his advice more thought. In any case, what other choice did she have? Leave town? Go into exile in Matheran? But those sewer-sorts would come after her there as well. The one thing blazingly clear in all her confusions was that she was deluged with gratitude for Sherman, his thoughtful ear and his discerning advice: those were the days when she swam in the cool blue of his eyes, captive to the authenticity of his soul. Around two or three days after Sherman gave her that fiendishly sly tip about getting the press on her side, an idea of such brilliance struck her that she couldn't sleep a wink the entire night, and first thing the next morning she sent Sherman to all the newspaper and radio offices to inform them that at noon she would be holding a press conference. Three hundred and seventy-seven reporters clustered outside Dariya Mahal; the roads were cordoned off; police officers stood on guard (lest a member of the Rakshash Junta Party hatch a bomb plot or some such). Anuradha was sweaty from wondering just *what* Nandini now had up her sleeve—and why on earth was she sporting, so brazenly, that cursed mini sari of hers?

God! The girl *really* was tempting Fate.

Nandini did her namastes and her hand-waves before she opened her simple but breathtakingly convincing argument that her infamous garment—her marvellous mini sari—was nothing more than the embodiment of Gandhi's values of simplicity and austerity.

'Tell me, esteemed members of the press, what could be simpler than a shortened sari? And what could be more austere? If anything, I'm merely living the all-important Swadeshi values: I am wearing home-grown cotton, a garment spun in the soils of Gujarat; and because its length is considerably reduced, I am saving valuable fabric. During this time of war and freedom struggle we should all be cutting expenses. To pitch into the fight for freedom. To let Mother India know that her sons and daughters care. At least, I do. And that's precisely why I'm wearing Indian cotton. Indian style. So if there is anyone constitutionally Indian then it is me—Ms Nandini Hariharan, Nationalist Number One!'

Ludicrously enough, it made perfect sense.

In the next few weeks she became the new emblem of austerity and Indianism: all that Swadeshi chic. Promptly enough, the press fell in love with her: spiffed up and mustard, she was deliciously young, liberal and sharper than Leicester cheddar. Who would have imagined that from the minor controversy arising over the abridged length of the national garment, Nandini Hariharan would be elevated to the status of a national hero. If she walked into posh South Bombay book discussions, there was a hush of respect from the loquacious, irascible literati. Percival Worthington and his astrolabe-arsed fianceé Lucinda Cummings were at the Billingdon Clubhouse when they saw, much to their amazement, that a trumpet was sounded to mark the arrival of the Number One Nationalist: she sat at a table overlooking the golf course with her two equally biscuit friends, the enigmatic Afghani artist and the Patron of the Arts. When she went with Sherman for a walk on the beach, hordes of women swarmed around her, congratulated her, blew kisses in the air to her.

'My legs are breathing because of you!' was the refrain she heard wherever she went. 'My legs are breathing!'

College-going women all across India donned the mini sari. Middle-class housewives cut the lengths of their existing saris, wanting to keep with the craze of the moment. Old widows looped it up and displayed their shrivelled fat legs at sombre funeral meets. Legs were *everywhere.* When the women freedom fighters marched down outside the new Telegraph Office, protesting against the colonials, they did so in their white khadi mini saris, their voluptuous thighs shaking sinisterly under the Indian sun: so dazed were the policemen that not a single one of them tried to stop the women; in fact, decades later, historians proved that the mini sari had hastened India's freedom movement no end.

Sherman was pleased to read in the *Bombay Chronicle* that Tarun Khokla, the couturier in question, the dear departed, was given an honourable memorial at Bandra Bandstand, where the Culture Minister himself unveiled a frail bust of the designer, and made a moving speech in favour of the mini sari that was not only saving quintals and quintals of cotton, but also prompting a spree of nationalism that would even give the Rakshash Junta Party a run for their rupee. The final straw was when Gandhi requested a meeting with young Nandini; he wanted to congratulate her on getting everyone to wear home-grown cotton—which, of course, had been the fundamental premise in his fight against the Visiting Whitepeople.

'It has been brought to my notice,' he said solemnly, 'that you too believe in my motto of simple living and high thinking.'

Nandini cleared her throat. 'Well, babycakes, I wouldn't make a habit out of it.'

She confessed to Gandhi that they had met once before, oh, around ten years back, at Radha-mashi's salon, when he was but a wannabe in the brat pack of freedom fighters and she a fourteen-year-old fatakadi who danced with a stunningly naked back to the crowds.

'I *still* think your loin cloth is the last word in cool!' she told him playfully.

'My dear, what I think of your mini sari I will not say.'

'Why?' she asked, rolling her eyes. 'Because it might rally against all that celibacy bollocks you go on about?'

And at that, Gandhi threw back his beautiful bald head and laughed and laughed.

34

Early the following year, in February, when Sherman Miller opened his rickety red postbox, he found a stiff brown manila envelope with smart fonts, sealed with formal black wax. In his kitchen, to a depressing aria that Alvina the turtle dove was crooning for the amusement of his stew-bum, bereft mother, he slit open the envelope and found, much to his thrilled dismay, that he had been accepted at Trinity.

I'm in, he thought. *But that means I'm out of here.*

He glanced over at his mother. Sitting on a bat-wing rocking chair, walled in her grief: how would she receive the news of their incipient relocation to Dublin? He decided to tell her the news another time—when she might have a firmer grip on her senses. Unable to tolerate Alvina's morose singing of 'Ombra

Leggiera', from Meyerbeer's *Dinorah,* he trundled out of the kitchen and over to Dariya Mahal where he sought Nandini's audience because he needed to inform her of his leaving and settle, once and for all, whether she might *ever* be a part of his life in Ireland. Would that billi-ki-bachhi abandon Bombay and all the notoriety she had gathered in it? And would she tag along with someone whose greatest aim in life was finding the cure for an obscure Irish disease?

His dedication to *triste incurabilis* was, without a doubt, commendable, and in the last few months not only had he apprenticed himself to a famous scientist—also researching *triste incurabilis*—he had also scrimped up enough to buy, from the finest jeweller in Zaveri Bazaar, a solitaire that he polished with felt each night—not that the glimmering stone had any need of it.

Some nights, he imagined how it might look on her finger.

'Before you say a word, I have news that'll hit you like a ton of steel!' Her voice was charged with the coruscating flames of gossip; she led him by the arm to the back of the house. 'Lucinda Cummings kicked it! The hag's history, honey.'

'What?' He had met Percival Worthington's fiancée only once, at a party Nandini had taken him to. 'How ... terrible ... I suppose ... how on earth did she ... pass on?'

After sitting him down on the grass behind the bamboo grove, Nandini told him that around a month back Lucinda Cummings had received an adorable puppy sent to her all the way from Matheran. Although she was keen to return the six-week-old golden retriever, she had no one to send the puppy back to: it arrived incognito, in a cane hamper, with a red ribbon around its neck. She decided to keep him. Only a few days later, the puppy was biting everyone in the house, little nips and pecks which they graciously—and mistakenly—discounted as his teething troubles. The following week, he was refusing water. Before long, he went off food. Then he started snarling and striking out at Lucinda when she tried to comfort him.

Alas, on the sixth night, the poor puppy perished.

The next morning, Lucinda Cummings realized that she could not bring herself to bathe, not because she was intrinsically unhygienic, but because she had developed a morbid, overnight fear of water. She found herself sweating and hallucinating; in the evening, she tried to throw Percival Worthington off a balcony in a fit of madness in the course of which she tried to tear apart three housemaids *and* shatter the hallway mirror into a thousand and one pieces. Two days later, her dead, distended body was found washed up on the shores of Chowpatty. It was deduced that she had been trying to confront her rabid fear of water.

'But whoever sent her the puppy?' Sherman was curious.

'For Christ's sake—how am *I* supposed to know! You want me to look in my crystal ball and get back to you on this one?'

He was thrown by her snappish response.

'In any case,' she said in a somewhat calmer tone, 'what did *you* come to tell me?' She would never forget his gallant assistance during the mini sari tehelka.

'Nothing ... when will Khalil Muratta have your paintings ready?'

'Oooo!' She rubbed her hands together. 'That's the *other* bit of good news. In a few weeks, they're unveiling his work at the National Gallery. Museum directors and collectors and art aficionados from across the world are coming for the showing. I'm having kittens over it!' She grabbed his cheeks and tousled his hair. 'Golly! He even wants me to do the honours that day. Batty, huh.'

'Maybe ...' His tone seemed disembodied '... the chap loves you?'

'I never asked him to,' she responded defiantly. 'The first time I met him I told him that if he taught me how to paint, I'd teach him how to fall out of love ... if anything, I've helped him return to his creative impulse ... aw, Sherman, forget all that ... beguile me with what you came to tell me.' She noticed that ever since he had hit his twenty-fifth year he had become downright delectable: shoulders broad enough to use as a clothes line and legs that seemed to be carved out of butter; gloriously tanned white skin which gripped you with the unbiddable lust to lick him, and a jawline so sharp you could file your dagger on it.

'Trinity,' he whispered as pulled out his envelope. 'The eejits took me in.'

Momentarily he saw her face fall several inches but she recovered herself nippily. 'Oh, Sherman! I'm over the moon! *This* is your life's dream ... now you can go look into *triste incurabilis*... oh, I'm so damn tickled for you ...' She kissed his forehead. Then she added with a despondent sigh, 'And now, as expected, you'll only forsake me in this wild land of tigers and elephants and malaria ...'

He grimaced. In the years that he had known her, learned all of Yeats for her, stolen books for her, waited pebble-still for her to sketch him, plotted escape routes in her time of crisis, what significantly minor part had he played in the drama of *her* life?

'Will you come?' he asked. 'With me. 'Cause I'm asking.'

'Need to cut thought on it,' she dodged. 'Dublin's not on my itinerary—but I wouldn't rule it out either, Mr Soda Bread. The cider's smashing, grapevine goes.'

'They'll adore you. Be the queen of the city, you will. And I'll be the medicine man they'll flock to. Me and you, we'll make a pretty ditty, Nandini.'

She looked at him non-committally. He closed his eyes. Was this all there was to Love? That it would pack its bags, put on its running shoes and dash off the very instant you thought it might last.

'OK, fine fella, I got to do my vanishing act,' she said, brushing him off. 'Urgent appointment. Question of life and death and all that bakwaas ... but let's trade notes soon.'

Sherman looked at her with maddeningly inquisitive eyes: just where was she dashing off to in this flurry?

35

Nandini Hariharan had places to go.

At eight thirty that night, she arrived at the Billingdon Clubhouse, where, at a table reserved specially for her, overlooking the expanse of the egret-speckled golf course, waiting for her was a certain gent she had once dismissed as someone who wouldn't know a blow-job from a hand-job even if they were the only two jobs in this world.

'Ah, my Kendal candy! Did I make you wait long?'

Percival Worthington sat with folded hands in a thoroughly meaningless silence. Was his reticence owing to his bereavement after his fiancée's unexpected death? Oh no! He wasn't down, she worked out, but sloshed.

'I'm ... I'm rather pleased ... you decided to see me at such short notice,' he mumbled. 'You see, I wanted to ask you a favour ...'

'And just what is it, Mr Midlands?' A turbaned waiter delivered her usual: a Scotch neat. The slit of her cool crêpe dress came all the way to her hip, which she believed was not sartorial depravity but merely a means to air her legs lest they suffocated and fell out of her waist from this hideous desi heat.

'We're from ... from ... West Sussex,' he clarified, somewhat affronted. 'But that's neither here nor there ... I hear Khalil Muratta is having a showing.'

'At the National Gallery. A bang-up and a ball, sweets. Anyone who's someone in the art world is going to be there.' She couldn't believe how she was playing with him. As if he were a weaver bird.

'Is there any way ... that *someone* could get an invite?' Gin had toned down his genteel demureness.

'Like who?' She was going to make him beg, she decided.

He exhaled audibly. 'Will you go out for dinner with me? *Please.* Tomorrow. There's a spanking new place called Dyer's. The Bombay duck is to die for, I hear.'

'We'll see ... but will you drop me home tonight? I'm just a li'l' hammer from Harrow.'

'Most certainly.'

After an elaborately scrumptious dinner of mutton curry and naan and cool, cool raita, they boarded his black Ford. In two deft strokes she pulled down its smart leather top so that the wind might romance her hair. Just as they were nearing Dariya Mahal, she asked him to take another route—one that led down to Juhu beach.

Velvet night and owls on the prowl, the sea sighing and foam crests curling up, curling in.

'You swim, sonny-boy? Know the backstroke? I can teach you otherwise.'

When she started to unbutton his shirt he resisted.

She encouraged, 'Come, now: it's time we got acquainted, boy.'

But after she stripped him and found him hopelessly inert, she tilted her head and stared at him with fiery, prying eyes.

He coughed. 'Er ... it has no vocation.' As if he were speaking of a wastrel son.

Not one to give up without a fight, she took the small slug hanging between his legs and groped it delicately first and rigorously next. But when neither the shrewd alacrity of her fingers nor her mouth's brilliance for suck could breathe any life into it, she sighed from the conviction that this pretty pink-headed maggot would sooner burrow back into his own flesh than someone else's. Counting on her previously propitious carnal karma, she flipped him: maybe he had a beautiful behind? But when she saw that he was flatter than a butcher's board, she gave his buttocks a resoundingly tight slap in the recognition that he didn't possess a single redeeming body part.

'You mean it's never worked with *any* kitty?'

'Nothing,' he said, shrugging his shoulders.

'Not even for those brown boys that whole armies of you folks came down for?'

He shook his head remorsefully.

'But that was the whole bloody point of the Raj!'

'What?'

To ram someone in the rear. Hard. *Against* their will. For as long as they lasted. Even *after.* But she didn't say it.

'You're thick,' she declared. 'But in all the wrong places ...' Before he could respond she asked him how he got over Lucinda Cummings so quickly.

'We English have a remarkable propensity for recovering from death,' he accepted. 'But only if it's not our own; in that case, we never recover.'

She giggled her freewoman's giggle. 'Dinner tomorrow? Pick me up at nine. I'd love to lift a fork or two at Dyer's.'

'Nandini ...' he said earnestly, like a novice actor auditioning for his first role. 'You fascinate me.'

'It's a common complaint,' she said, and vanished into the night.

Her head was dizzy with the revenge she'd been hatching, ever since the time Lady Worthington had slighted her on the lawns of Barr House. Savages, huh. Pray tell me just what was locking fifteen hundred folks into a walled compound and shelling them till streams of blood dazzled the vultures above? What was imposing a tax on *salt?* And throwing hundreds of thousands into jail when they protested that, now, er, *maaf-kijiyeh,* please, they wanted their land back. Ah, why, maybe all that was just one big tea party. Jolly good! Cucumber sandwiches and scones. Right. *I get it.* She shuddered with laughter and a lily in her right hand swung from side to side as she rocked open the gates of Dariya Mahal and strode in: seawind had ruffled her hair, moonlight smoothed her skin to a shine.

'NANDINI!' Anuradha's voice stood up like a ramrod before her entrance.

'Hah ... drat! You took my breath!'

'While you were out, trouble came calling.' Anuradha's voice trembled like a diya. 'Came calling for Tia. She's taken sick. Vardhmaan is out delivering Mrs Shah's baby. Shloka's too young to go alone ... and because of my ...' Nandini knew of Anuradha's indignity: a woman who once ran down the stairwell of this old house with silver anklets prefacing her movements was now shuffling around with a cane stick in her right hand.

'I've called for a rickshaw—could you please take Tia to the animal hospital? It's all the way up in Parel.'

'Of course,' Nandini replied. 'But where *is* Tia?'

Anuradha took her arm and guided her under the whorled stairwell where she held up a cylindrical beeswax candle over the murky picture: little Shloka curled up next to that picture-pretty boxer. But, oh Deva!, what a change! Tia's little belly was bloated up to twice its size; her mouth was ajar and her tongue was hanging out, a horrifying shade of purple.

'Gosh! Anuradha ... when ...'

'Two hours back. It's had me in a stew. I can't even imagine what it might be. The animal doctor won't come out this late—please ... just take her. Might be her only chance.'

Shloka came out from under the stairwell. Thoroughly shaken.

Shloka and Nandini lifted Tia into the tanga that was drawn up to the porch.

'She'll be OK,' Nandini told Anuradha as the horseman whipped his stallions.

'May there be mercy,' Anuradha whispered under her breath.

In the shaking tanga, driving through a night in which the abiding midnight hush was dappled only with the clip-clopping of the stallions' hoofs, Nandini looked at Shloka and decided that here, now, he was insanely fragile. A lullaby of a thing. She loved that he tried, but couldn't knot up his tie properly: a charming inadequacy.

'Hey, *you*!' she assured. 'No worries! I bet it's only gas.'

But Nandini was doubtful of her own words because the nearer they got to the hospital, the worse Tia seemed. Retching desperately. Yet unable to throw up. Moaning as if a banshee were fighting to get out of her.

Would she make it? What would this do to Shloka?

Itty-bitty li'l' thing. Pond-watcher. Butterfly-catcher. With a genius for melancholy.

The Bai Sakarbai Petit Animal Hospital dealt mainly with the rabid cats and dogs of the city, who, in its small enclosures, were eagerly awaiting death. As soon as the chowkidar rocked open the hospital's tall iron gates, the midnight silence was enflamed by the wailing of dying animals: cold, hollow howls spiralled up and sank into the crevices of their own limitless anguish. Nandini felt somewhat uneasy at the thought of how Lucinda Cummings had bowed out of the business of life.

'Never seen her like this before. Tia gets sick now and then—but no more than a few stomach upsets. An occasional upchuck ... Oh and a waning appetite in summer.' On the metal examination table in the doctor's clinic, Tia lay gasping. An odd spasm raced through her like a sirocco.

Dr Mody hurried around with a stethoscope while Nandini filled him in on the details.

'What'd she eat for her dinner?' The short, wan doctor with grizzly hair had a nervous look on his face.

'Her usual. Chapattis shredded in yogurt and milk. A smack of sugar to go.'

'What time?'

'Oh, around eight or so, I'm guessing.'

After he ran the stethoscope over her chest, he gauged her temperature. Tia's stomach was rising even more. To the point of bursting, it seemed. Nandini wanted to yell at the doctor: *DO SOMETHING!*

So far, Shloka had been standing, hands behind his back, at the edge of the room, but when the doctor spoke he came closer to Nandini.

'I suspect it's bloat. Common to boxers. They have a snubbed face and eat far too quick—too much air goes into the stomach in the bargain. Causing a gastric dilation. Sometimes an intestine twists over the other—and then, *this* happens.'

'But she's going to be fine.'

'We'll try.' He drew out a sinister black pipe which he started to drive down her throat. Tia reacted violently, shaking her head forcefully.

'Hold her down!' he yelled. Nandini was sweaty as she forced Tia back on the examination table. Cold metal. Moths at the window. Was Shloka shivering? As the tube went in a little more, Tia thrashed her legs wildly. Dr Mody pushed harder. She contracted her body again, as if to shove *out* the pipe that was being shoved *into* her. Dr Mody explained that the pipe was one way of possibly sorting out her jumbled intestines. 'OK ... it's there ... I think we have some traction,' he said encouragingly.

She has to make it, Nandini thought. *Has to, has to, has to.*

Shloka was crossing and uncrossing his fingers. Would she be well? His only friend. In a world so wordless.

Right then, Tia gave one unbelievably vigorous thrust and dislodged the tube they'd pushed down her throat.

A ribbon of blood shot out, like a bat disturbed from its cave. Shloka jumped.

'Oh, God!' Dr Mody stepped back. He took a deep breath.

'She's not going ...' His voice faded away.

'I understand, Dr Mody.' She stepped back from Tia, who was no longer bucking or groaning in that mood of unfathomable torment.

'Shloka ...' Nandini motioned him towards Tia.

Unfazed by the blood reeling out of her jowls, the little boy touched the white flash on her heart. He touched her delicate deer-red ears. He stroked the black sheath of her paws. It seemed like only yesterday that Radha-mashi had got her for him, the wicker basket she had come in, the big blue bow on the handle outside. How they had played tug-of-war with old rags. How she followed him around Dariya Mahal, how they had divided each other's infinite solitude and deepened the meaning of companionship. When he put his ear flat against her chest, Nandini felt something slam against her heart: Tia's ribcage was no longer rising.

They got home an hour later, the leather leash and collar wrapped around Shloka's bony brown arm. Anuradha opened the door. Dariya Mahal pretended that nothing had happened. *But the boy has to leave. Or there's more coming.*

'I don't know what to say,' Nandini whispered.

Anuradha feels her chest heave. How much longer before this house may lay it all down? What else will they have to witness here? Will their eyes burn right into their sockets? In a moment of terrifying unexpectedness, Shloka lifts a gaze over his mother's lustrous, lovely face and, for the first time ever, speaks with a tenderness that defeats her valiant resolve. 'She is gone for ever, Maa.'

PART FOUR
Silver Anklets

36

'Pappa ... why don't you speak?'

Vardhmaan could not believe that his son, who, until the last few weeks, hadn't uttered a word from the day of his birth, had just asked him that. Not even Anuradha or Nandini had ever questioned him so plainly ... and now Shloka ...

'I do.' No conviction tinged that reply.

'What's the colour of the sky called?'

'Blue.'

They were in the garden, by the pond, under the cool shadows of the kadam trees: Shloka was holding a tattered copy of the *Oxford English Dictionary*—which, these days, he couldn't be seen without.

Around a month had passed since Tia's death.

'Do you know how to fly a kite, Pappa?'

'Yes.'

'I don't know how to tie a tie, y'know,' Shloka continued. 'It's worrying, when you think about it.' His voice was unusually soft, a tone one might imagine a summer breeze to possess. 'Why d'you and Maa have ... have ... different rooms?'

Vardhmaan started to walk away. *Because love is not enough.* Shloka followed him. Had he said something silly? Or hurtful? He tried to bait back his father. 'I mean, could you teach me how to tie a tie? I have quite a few. Radha-mashi gave me three for my birthday. Nandini said it's crucial that I learn how to if I want to be a part of Civil Society.'

Vardhmaan swung open the gate. He was about to walk out when Shloka, desperate to hold him back, twisted his arms around Vardhmaan's legs. 'Teach me, please.'

He shook his right leg and untugged his son from his body. 'One of these days.'

Wounded beauty enveloped Shloka's almondine eyes. 'Pappa ... *where* are you going?'

'Sea ... To the seashore.'

'Please don't ...' But he didn't say the word. *Go.* 'Pappa!'

Vardhmaan pretended that he hadn't heard his son. He kept walking towards the sea—the same sea that'd been his solace on the day Anuradha had told him she was expecting a child for the second time.

'Please, Pappa ... *please* ... just come back ...'

Convinced that he had irked his father, Shloka kept calling after him—a heartbreakingly tender cry, barely rising—long after Vardhmaan was out of sight and out of earshot.

The day after Shloka started speaking, as sudden as a sneeze, as unexpected as good fortune, two things occurred: never again did the doves perch on his shoulder; and never again did he see the blurry shards of a whiteman gazing out of the pond. Even Dariya Mahal noticed. Aware that the boy was now in the landscape of language—that he could now *tell* its story—it pulled back its sighing trees and drew away the lianas that'd grown so close to him. Shloka, however, was too caught up with his fledgling love affair with language to notice any of this: right now, just tumbling into his dictionary, bathing in the alphabet, perfuming himself with a phrase, why, that was all there was to life. Even if there was a long time to go before he would grasp that words could only allude to what was essentially ineffable—the real story was and would always be the *experience*—for now, he hungrily flipped through his hard-bound dictionary and tried to assign a word to a sight or a thought or a phenomenon. That was why, when he came across, on Page 197, under I, the word *indisposed,* he realized that, yes, it was perfectly applicable to his mother—but could it also really describe the times Anuradha wept in her sleep not only because she was too brave to do it during her conscious state but also because pain had weaselled smack into the sooty depths of her rest? Is that what words really were: the illusion of the reality? Or the other way round? Undeterred in his quest to identify, to classify and to nail things down with words, he came to see that a *staircase* was never just a staircase: it was that sweeping length from which, he had been told, Nandini had fainted for the first time in Dariya Mahal. And a *balcony* was where his mother sang him her songs and saved him at birth ... just as a *veranda* was full of the songs of Schumann and Mendelssohn making apparent the silence to which his father was hostage ...

Only Anuradha understood that his pleasure was rooted in his relief: now he felt that he was *one of them.* Now he could speak. During those exploratory days, when he would tear up to her with a new-found word, she would embrace him in the grim knowledge that each passing hour brought them closer to his going away. Far away. From the wretched, infectious sadness of this house. Of course, she had no clue as to when he would leave or where or how—such mutilating details would require time and breathtaking bravery to arrange. What she did see in those times of spectacular clarity was that the only way to love was by standing outside it: to look in, to watch, but never indulge totally. To hear Shloka gasp from a perfectly spoken word—but to never stand with him *in* his joy. To hold him with immeasurable care but with the consciousness that he was hers only for safe-keeping, a breeze of the Heavens brushing her as it went along its way.

'Maa!' he cried to her one afternoon. 'Have you seen how hard the cocoon tries to become a butterfly?'

He held out a bakul branch with cocoons feeding on the leaves.

'Heed this much, Shloka: the cocoon can only become a butterfly when it no longer is a cocoon.'

It was, of course, easy to deal with queries as wee as that.

And with ... well, why was the moon silver? What exactly did *redemption* mean (a newly beloved word)? Who put flowers into buds? What did *solace* convey? Tell me about the peacocks that sang on the day you left Udaipur. Tell me about the pergola again. And she did. Gave him the stories that his silent world had resisted—lest he break. One time, however, shudders put their icy legs on her chest when he came up to her with a large wooden case wrapped in a faded olive sari.

'I found this under Pappa's bed.' His eyes had an echo of green in the iris. 'What, Maa, is a *violin* for?'

She was resting her legs in a metal bucket of steaming, salted water with an ointment that eased her swelling a little. She touched her breast bone. 'There's a tale I will tell you ... it is about songs and the evenings we sing them in. It's about me before I came here. And it's about your father. Your brother too.'

'My *brother?'* Disbelief dropped his jaws.

'Yes,' she said. 'Come here, little one. And listen ... on the day I left Udaipur, to marry a man I had never even met, my mother said to me, *In this life, my darling, there is no mercy ...*'

That same night he tried to verify the ghastliness of Mohan's death with Nandini. Who was Divi-bai really? Could someone have no eyelashes? And Mohan, did he really sing so that everyone dropped what they were doing and listened? Had his mother's hand actually touched Mohan as he was hanging on for his life in the shingh tree? Nandini, that night, alas, was too distracted and nervous and moody to entertain *his* qualms. In her room, surrounded by clothes and newspaper clippings about herself (most of which Sherman had dutifully cut out for her), she was working hard on staving off her own trepidations. Just when he decided it was best to leave her alone she said, 'And I want you to come too.'

'Where to?'

'Oh, my khari biscuit! Don't y'know? This Saturday Khalil Muratta is showing his paintings. Of me. It's what I've been waiting for since seven lifetimes.'

'I'll come. But I'll need a suit.' His voice was serious. He wasn't going anyplace without a suit—not that he'd worn one before.

'Of course! I don't want my favouritest itty-bitty li'l' thing coming in threads that don't do him service. We'll get you in something quite suave, Shloka.'

'I'll have to polish my shoes, of course. And I'll need my tie. Is it *really* fancy?'

'Like you wouldn't believe. The works, tootsie.' She snapped her fingers. 'But one look at the marvellous Master Shloka Gandharva and all my friends will be clawing for you—and tell me, who wouldn't for a gent as genial as yourself?' Her eyes were playful. He slicked down his hair nervously. *What if ... what if ... what she said was ... truly true.* And *Master Shloka Gandharva*—now didn't that have a tidy ring to it, huh?

Now it was absolutely certain that he would have to know how to wear a tie.

'Oh, and about your brother? Hmm ... it's all true. Mohan, violin and all. That's how I met your old lady. When she came to Udaipur and I was living with her folks. That just makes us even.'

'Huh?'

'I also had a little brother. He croaked it too.'

'How so, Nandini?' Did everyone have a dead sibling? And parents who lived in separate rooms?

'Natural causes,' she replied nonchalantly. 'He fell into a ditch.'

'But why didn't his mother pull him out?'

'Because she put him there in the first place ...' She shook her head and pegged her hands on her hips. 'Now I don't mean to be lippy, nobby thing, but I'm planning my outfit for Saturday ... and as you know, I do me best solo ...'

'Of course,' he said, and left, his head bowed, his hands behind his back.

Nandini's curtness was grounded in her couturial quandary: she just didn't know what to wear for Saturday's showing. So she flung open her mother's wooden dowry chest which she'd brought along from Udaipur and pulled out its tidings—necklaces, brooches, corsets, saris, serapes—until she found, at the very bottom, a thin black dress with string straps and a wickedly low décolletage. Dusting it and holding it up to herself in front of the oval mirror in her room, Nandini remembered that her mother had told her she had got this number from a couturier just off the Left Bank for her date with Picasso (a rendezvous that left her repulsed because Picasso had a penchant for smelling armpits, and the only way she could put him off was by warning, 'Now, now, they're dusted with sulphur to keep out the fleas'). This was also the same black number Mrs Hariharan, failed artist, walk-on-water child producer, had worn that sweltering afternoon in Udaipur when Nandini was five and she had dragged her by the elbow to the Pichola. There she chucked Nandini's childhood photographs into the serenity of the water, which drank up the images without so much as a ripple of regret.

'Because of *you* I had to give up Paris. Because of *you* I had to marry your father. Because of *you* I never got to be who I was. Oh, you little witch, you'd better make up for all this!'

For years after, every opportunity Nandini got, she paced over the lake trying to find the monochrome photographs and daguerreotypes, scanning right down to the bottom. But she never once found anything. Not a fucking trace of her childhood. They'd all just vanished. And joining them had been that chillingly sad painting she had made of Anuradha bidding farewell to a child—the painting she had drowned.

'Perfect,' Nandini decided, tickled over the choice of her outfit. '*Just* what I needed.'

37

On the day of the Muratta showing, Anuradha struggled out to the veranda and sat up on a pine armchair, a beige embroidered Kashmiri shawl draping her legs: infinite elegance over finite ruin.

'You look stunning. A cupful of moonlight and nothing short of it.'

'Only for the act ... by the way, will you please tell Vardhmaan I won't be coming with him and Shloka? I'm going to some other place first. I'll nip by later.' Nandini seemed somewhat unsure of herself.

'Where? Aren't they expecting you there to unveil the paintings ...' Anuradha was completely thrown. Why wasn't Nandini heading to Khalil Muratta's showing right away? Was it because she was the guest of honour that she wished to arrive fashionably late? Who would be accompanying her there? Resisting any further probing, she said, 'I wish I could see Mr Murutta's paintings. You must be in some dither, Nandini. What an amazing privilege!'

'Yup ... so I hear as well.'

'Although I know little about art, my instincts suggest that perhaps all art is love in some avatar. Its longing and rejection. Its first flower and its finale.'

'I never told you how sorry I was, Anuradha ...' She put her hands on her cousin's feet, over the Kashmiri shawl. These days Anuradha didn't even step out of her room; to be sitting on the veranda was a treat.

'Ah, well. *That.* Some things in this life, we pay with dances,' she said, her gaze pointing at Shloka, who was coming down the stairwell. In his Abdul Rehman suit, the smartest shade of tan, his spiffy leather belt and shoes bought from Princess Street, he looked mighty pip. Anuradha's chest twisted. She couldn't bear the thought that he would, one day soon, be sent away.

'Oh, Nandini!' he cried, eyes wide and hands spread out. 'You look *so* unusual!' What lovely long painted nails she had, and that cloche cap, and her flapper's bravura! But even before he might inspect her ostrich-feather fan or verify whether or not she really did have such long, curling-up, cat-like eyelashes, she bent and kissed his cheeks. 'Sorry, can't stay ... have to rush, honeydove! But we'll meet later.' Sure enough, someone was behind the gates of the house. 'My escort for the evening is here.'

'Who?' He strained his neck to see who had come for her. 'Is it Sherman?'

'Gosh, Shloka, y'know ... I'm plain *awful* with names.'

She blew a kiss at Anuradha before racing out, her shoes clapping up an echo on Dariya Mahal's chest.

Who was in that carriage?

Lord, what was the girl up to *now*?

When Sherman arrived at the National Gallery, that majestic structure with royal ashlars and intricate masonry, it took him over twenty minutes to negotiate the formidable crowd of automobiles and horses and buggies before he made it to the magnificent doorway at a little after eight. Because he was all tacked up in a grey sacque suit and a peach silk shirt, the doorman winked at him when he showed him his invitation card. Even before he had the time to feel entirely out of place in the artistic echelons, a dandy with a high-pitched voice pinched his immensely humpable derrière. 'With buns like that, it's rude to clothe them!'

Sherman turned beet red.

Before long, though, he was lost in the modish menagerie of Basque dresses and bobbed hair and feathered headbands and oiled moustaches: all that garçonne glamour. *But where is she?* He searched. In his left pocket, he could feel the contours of a small blue box wrapped tight with ribbons.

A diamond gleamed inside it like a secret.

As he stood lone as a lighthouse, Sherman's eyes glisked through the toff junta he'd seen before only in the society pages of the *Bombay Chronicle*: the Mandalays; Eric Claude Fromm, the inventor of the world's first erotic vibrator made of used car body parts; Lord and Lady Worthington; Tara Shroff, star of the first moving picture *with* sound, a glorious invention of Mr Bunkusdaas, the Father of Bollywood. On spotting Vardhmaan and Shloka, he dodged through the throng and put his hand on Dr Gandharva's shoulder. 'She make it here with you?'

'No,' Vardhmaan replied. 'Anuradha said she's coming with someone else.'

'And *I* thought it was you she was coming with!' The innocence in Shloka's voice was like dewdrops.

Sherman shrugged. 'I guess not. But with whom, then? Everyone she knows is already here. Maybe I should ask Libya?' he said when he saw her a little way away.

Clothed in a lilac crêpe-de-Chine blouse that barely restrained the exuberance of her breasts, Libya Dass had organized the catering to keep with the mood of the event. Gliding through the three-hundred-odd guests who'd come from all over the world for this remarkable occasion, the waiters served authentic Afghani fare: grapes brought in from Pul-e-Khumri; a distinctive cheese, with the consistency of fresh mozzarella, from the Shamali Valley; and a wine that caused a breezy, potent intoxication three minutes and twenty-seven seconds after consumption had been requisitioned from the cellars of Ahmed Matahideen, Kabul's most celebrated wine-maker.

'Well, I haven't seen her either,' she told Sherman. 'Maybe she got held up someplace?'

But at eight thirty she looked at her watch in infuriation: where on earth was Nandini? The guests were antsy for her arrival; after all, Khalil Muratta wanted her to unveil the paintings (Nandini had desisted, of course, calling it a bit over the top; but he had remained adamant).

'She'll be here,' the Afghani assured her. 'I had never believed I would meet this much happiness again.'

'I can't wait to see the paintings,' Libya Dass burbled. 'The finished work. They'll be spectacular. Oooo ... look at Mrs Bilachand's daughter. Luscious enough to peel out of her clothes and eat!'

An hour later, when she saw some of the guests begin to hat up and blow because they'd run out of patience waiting for that barefoot, beedi-smoking firecracker, Libya fumed: 'I can't believe her nerve! We ought to start without her. She's probably forgotten.'

'That's *im*possible!' Khalil Muratta countered, although he too was somewhat anxious. 'Please let's give her another, say, ten minutes?'

Libya told him that even the curators from the Rijksmuseum and the Spanish Prado were ready to do their bye-byes if the artist was not inclined to show his work. Was all this a farce? some folks were tattling. Just a means for an artist who hadn't painted in years to garner some publicity? An elaborate prank? Khalil Muratta, however, was unconcerned, because for him the only satisfaction in all this had been meeting Nandini—and then, painting her. *How wonderfully strange love is,* he thought. *And how strangely wonderful!*

The plague and the panacea.

The ruin and its repair.

The question and the answer.

But what the poor Afghani never fathomed was that Love could be *all* those things in one single night—and often enough, at the same bloody time. Fifteen minutes later, right in the middle of a mêlée between Babe Ruth and the stage actress Avantika Sheth, Nandini Hariharan arrived to a clap of light bulbs and a swarm of exasperated whispers. Soaring through the constellation of gazes and remarks, she reached out for Khalil Muratta.

Embracing him, kissing his earlobe, she said, 'Remember, I promised to teach you how to fall out of love, Khalil?'

'What do you mean?' He was elated to see her, but now also quite baffled.

'Come now!' Libya Dass urged. 'Say a few words.'

'Me?' she hissed, her hand on her décolletage. 'Never! I'm an artist. And this evening, merely the muse. Khalil should say what he needs to.'

'You know how Khalil is in public situations. He'll freeze. Spit a few words, draw the string over the first painting, and get the evening rolling! You're late as it is!'

'I am but your humble little slave-girl,' she said, waving her ostrich-feather fan.

Sherman saw her through crowds six rows deep: black stringstrap dress and ostrich-feather fan. But she seemed to be in the hands of a troublingly vigorous confusion. What was the matter? Where had she been all this while? What startled him most, however, was the sudden realization that his old friend, neighbourhood outrager, sari militant could not really be with any *one*: there was no room for a lover simply because she was too much her own self. Right then, the anxiety on Nandini's face flew away: light from the seven-hundred-and-seventy-seven-crystal-teardrop chandelier above draped her with a faded radiance and the ground beneath her feet was a chessboard of stylish marble.

'Ladies, gentlemen, and everyone else ... how utterly charming of you to make it for the showing of one of my dearest friends ... I'll keep this short because I'm allergic to speeches as well ... earlier this evening, I was talking to my cousin Anuradha.' She rolled her eyes, as she recalled the exchange. 'And she said something about all art being love in one of its avatars. Love's rejection. Love's desire. Love's sullenness.

'But I look at it another way.

'Perhaps all art is nothing but a road *from* lovelessness. A means to manage the void. Because love, in its ripeness, annihilates the impulse to create simply because it *is* creation.

The lived experience seeks no outward expression; private and secure in its own self, it just is.' She paused and altered her voice, making it more slapdash: 'But hey, what do I know, kids? Maybe art is nothing more than paint and easel—and what the eye perceives. Maybe art is nothing but pretzels and cream and quietness ... 'nough said ... it's such a fantastic honour for me to ...' And she hurried over to the first painting. She pulled back the cloth: *The Hand.*

Almost instantly, the audience broke free from their spell and came alive to the reality of art.

Resounding, deafening applause.

Flashbulbs and gasps; shaking heads and stunned ones.

Shloka was propped on his father's shoulders so he might see this marvellous painting. Everyone peered in, like spikes of metal careening towards some enormous magnet. Ten minutes later, as Khalil Muratta and she were posing for pictures for the *New York Times,* Nandini saw Sherman and waved to him.

He fought through to get to her. 'Can I see you after all this is over?'

'Of course ... did you like the paintings, Sherman?'

'They are as you are.' He was dying to give her the diamond.

'Oh, how terrible!' She sighed, and returned under the spotlight upon the request of Libya Dass. The two women posed for a photograph for *Tatler.* But barely had the flashbulb gone off when Nandini smacked her hand to her head. 'Oh, and before it slips out of my mind ... I forgot to apologize for coming in so late. But you see, earlier in the evening, I got engaged.' The breeziness of her voice threw them all off; it was as if she might have mentioned that her dahlias had dry rot or that she'd tasted the perfect pomfret at Dyer's. All the reporters stopped dead in their tracks: some looked up from their wire-back notebooks; others put their cameras to their side. Contagious murmurs spread through the throng: *She was what?*

Engaged?

To whom ... well, what, even ...

But isn't Khalil hoping ... oh well ...

At first Khalil Muratta thought maybe he was only imagining this. One of those Artistic Moments when everything undergoes a drastic shift in perception. But when she repeated herself, he grew short of breath: it was as if someone had booted him in the gut. Sherman dug his fingers into the flutes of the column behind which he was standing. Maybe it was true what they said. About how playing with fire leaves you scorched.

Shloka looked at his father with widened eyes: what would Anuradha make of this?

'And just who's the lucky chap?' someone yelled.

'Oh, *him* ... I bet you all know him already ... Percy ... Percy ... come say hello ...'

Dressed in a black bowler hat and a suit cut by tailors on Bond Street, Percival Worthington walked timidly forward, like a child being awarded a debate prize at a school function.

'We're getting married in two months!' She slipped her arm around him.

Percival wondered why she had chosen such a momentous public occasion to announce their engagement. Was it so that his mother could do nothing to wreck it—certainly not after all the world knew about it? Witnessing all this, Lady Worthington felt as if she'd suffered a spontaneous expulsion of her normally unyielding bowels, and off she scuttled like a railway rat for the toilets—and with a bit of luck, even a pistol to shoot her son in the head. In all of this hungama no one saw Radha-mashi dash after an unspeakably distressed Khalil Muratta, frantically trying her best to stop him from leaving so abruptly. *I'm responsible,* Radha-mashi blamed herself, *for this debacle.* Why had she even invited that wench to her Thursday salon? Why hadn't she warned Khalil when she had seen something like this coming from quite a long ways back? By the time Radha-mashi returned to the National Gallery, the attention had shifted from the Muratta paintings to the news that the son of the Governor of Bombay was affianced to the muse of the artist Khalil Muratta. *No one saw an Irishman fling a tiny blue box into the night he was running from.*

'And how do *you* feel?' someone pestered Lady Worthington. She was in a daze: just *how* could her son decide to settle with a card-carrying member of the curry classes? Taking a moment to gather her wits, she said in English as crisp as the crackers she was raised on, 'I'm absolutely speechless ... you *blooming* twit!'

38

Did *anyone* ever know what finally happened to Khalil Muratta?

Or Libya Dass?

Truth be told, no one *ever* pieced together where Khalil Muratta had vanished to, although the widely held rumour was that he'd returned to Kabul, where, as the honoured guest of the King of Afghanistan, he lodged in the west wing of the palace: three nightingales were commissioned to sing outside his window at seven in the morning. Others said he was in Peru, shacking up with a native woman of ravishing loveliness, a tame rattlesnake curled around her neck. But one harridan, a noted clairvoyant to the swell set, insisted that she had seen Khalil Muratta's ghost—robed in his customary pairon-tunbon—

weeping a stream of ochre-coloured tears that collected in a perfect semicircle around him: a half-moon of mourning.

In the two months after the day Nandini broadcast her engagement, Anuradha read—to her disbelief—that Radha-mashi had also left Bombay. 'Canapé Maharani Flees City' was the heading of the article in the *Bombay Gazetteer,* which also informed Anuradha that her aunt had moved to a small town near Sydney where a new colony was coming up: in that culture of new faces, Radha-mashi hoped to lessen the weight of her troubled heart. Dilute the density of her guilt.

Libya Dass, on the other hand, everyone soon uncovered, had moved—alabaster bathtub in tow—up to Ooty, into a two-storey gabled house in a tea plantation (where, years later, she would find a love as true as she was lovely and the two ladies went on to raise three children, one of whom was later sent to Eton, where he excelled in Medieval History and English, and much later made a name for himself as a publisher in London).

And so that left Sherman Miller.

With the house sold and his bags packed, all there was room for was nothing: his house, like his mother's heart, was bare, and it was for this empowering bareness that he learned to develop a lifelong fondness. Perhaps that was the true nature of life: things boiled down to their essence.

Love defined by the depth it may never occupy.

Since Nandini's wedding and his departure were roughly a week apart, he dropped by to see her on the day before he was leaving from Bombay harbour on a ship called *Patience,* which would briefly berth at Singapore on its way to Dublin. They sat at the back of the house, in the bamboo grove, where, after the tailor-birds hushed their song, he promised to send her a wedding present from Dublin. She nodded; somehow she didn't seem all that keyed up about her own nuptials. She touched the earth on which they were sitting. *This,* she remembered, is where she had painted him. *This* was where they had discovered a wry, invincible affinity for each other. Could she have ever become the artist she was today if he hadn't sat for her with heart-melting patience? As he was telling her about how Alvina, after she had been freed, began performing arias in the Hanging Gardens, Nandini interrupted him with a sigh of ineffable regret: 'Some days I'd give my arm to start over. Clean slate and all. I only want to be safe, Sherman. How did we go so askance? And wham into the path of other people's violations. Only to get blown into pieces that'll need several lifetimes to collect.'

'That's why you're knotting down with Percival? Safety?'

She looked away.

'Here,' he said, taking her hand and putting it upon his chest.

'This is my heart, Nandini. Just so you know.'

She listened with her skin. Memorized that beat. Its abiding sincerity.

'Remember the first time you came to Dariya Mahal? Did y'know someone died inside of it? Waiting for love.'

'There was a book in your hands. Red gown with a long train. Anuradha hollered out for you. Aw, you were *so* nasty to me. Wasn't the chap called Edward? The fella who died in here.'

'I was *not*! And it was a play of Ibsen, if I recall right. Edward it was. I almost banished you from the house, didn't I?'

He laughed. Maybe she was right. His mind raced to what she'd told him ages back: *Miss God put me down here to bring joy and sunshine into the lives of millions!*

'I didn't know better,' she owned up a minute later. 'We do what we see, Sherman. But I'm standing on my two lovely legs, and most mornings I don't ask for more.'

'Not even for your legs to be lovelier?' A tortured twinkle in his blue, blue eyes.

'Darling child,' she said waving her hand airily. 'Is it *even* possible to improve on perfection?'

He said that his ship was leaving the dock at seven the following evening and that his mother, for one, was eager about returning to Dublin. Nandini said that she was quite 'looking forward' to married life—and all that it entailed. But their lame, haphazard talk was a hedgerow of syllables. Formal. Divisive. Because neither knew how to bid farewell to such sweeping innocence. Like shutting your eyes to the broad blue sky for its beauty is too much. How could you part from someone who loved you not for your secrets but in spite of them?

Before their exchange acquired any burden, he got up to leave.

She followed.

At the water fountain, he takes the tips of her fingers and presses them into his palm.

'Will you watch for me, Irishman?'

What is the thing next to love? Or above it? She feels *that* for him.

'*Always.* And with the Yeats.'

'Promise me you'll do something about your hair?' The despair in her voice is liquid, the bravery of her gaze formidable. 'Try hair wax. Or a salon. Something, Sherman. Look at it this way. We'll probably never save our souls—but hell, at least we'll get our hair sorted.'

39

Although the Taj Mahal Hotel, the Billingdon Clubhouse and scores of other venues eagerly offered their grounds for Nandini's wedding—they figured that the uppity guest list alone would chalk up incalculable goodwill—the bride resolutely decided that she would get hitched no place else but on the lawns of Dariya Mahal. House painters were called in to erase away the shamble of the walls. Gardeners mowed down the four-foot-high grass and its mishmash of ravenous weeds. Two days before the wedding, Anuradha sat out on the veranda and watched Vardhmaan organize the workers. Merely the sight of her tall, muscular husband in his dashing white kafni-lehnga made her blood race. It seemed as though the gaiety of Nandini's wedding had brought him provisional eloquence, and Anuradha thought:

maybe *this* is the sliver of good news that he has been waiting for. Maybe, after all these years, he will tell again the stories he used to. *My beloved anecdoter.*

Shloka had started speaking, hadn't he?

Things change.

Through the tumult of the preparations, when Vardhmaan stole glances at his wife, bound to her chair, lending her insights to the workers, suggesting precise alterations, he wanted nothing more than to run down the path on which he'd left her behind. With a frangipani braid in his hand. With an unremembering heart. He saw, however, that he hadn't merely left her; rather, she too had wandered away into a geography of such physical agony that it would take an entirely different map to reach her. He was aware of this agony because her room was directly below his, and he would often hear her moan in the nights from a pain that bewildered her by its relentlessness. In such moments a dizzying need to embrace her would grip him—but he would desist when he considered the solitude she had cultivated to manage her suffering.

To alleviate her condition he had asked scores of his doctor friends to intervene. They had suggested pills and X-rays and various kinds of modern ointments: but all their efforts had been in vain. For her part, Anuradha had taken on each remedy with optimism but later, when their futility was established, abandoned them with a magnanimous smile. Even Nandini had tried to help. Around six months ago, the roving fascinator had brought home a 107-year-old Chinese healer who thrust long pins and needles into her ankles and drew out a pus-like liquid, saying it was impure and needed to be removed; the swelling in her joints had settled for a few days, but then one evening it returned as though it hadn't ever been away—it had simply sunk back somewhere, retracted its claws for a while, only to reappear with the vehemence of the rested. The memory of one attempted cure, however, was particularly bitter to Vardhmaan—and to Shloka. During the summer of the previous year, a hermaphrodite shaman had placed Anuradha's swollen feet in a tub of brackish water and applied tiny black fleshy knobs to her knees and ankles. A while later, when a striking pain suffused her—as if she had walked into a vicious, implacable eddy of ache—the shaman said, in a calm voice, that those black things on her legs were marsh leeches from the Bengal backwaters, and that they were hungrily sucking out any poisonous blood that might be causing the inflammation. When the shaman pulled the sucking leeches off her flesh, a thick reddish-brown liquid whooshed out of her veins. Her fingers tightened their grip on Shloka's wrist: and the two individuals, mother and son, were briefly and perfectly bound in one flare of excruciation.

'Vardhmaan ... Thank you ...' she said, trespassing into his recollection.

'Huh?' He hadn't realized that he was so close to her; she touched his kurta.

'For managing all this so splendidly. Nandini has no father, but if she did, I think even he would not have done this the way you have.'

When he leaned down and kissed her forehead she was overwhelmed; this closeness was more than she had expected, and charged her enough to keep her pain at bay for many, many hours.

On the night before her wedding, Nandini caught a timid knocking on her door.

'May I … er … talk to you?' Shloka saw clothes and flowers and chocolates littering her room. 'Nandini, Maa said … you'll be leaving us … for ever?'

'Oh no, my kachori!' she cooed. 'I'll be very much around, and I'll visit when I can. Besides, you can come to Worthington House *any* time you like. You'll adore it. It's got thirty-six bedrooms, and I could *easily* find a place for you.' Beneath her poise, she seemed edgy.

'But just why'd you want to live in a house with … with … thirty-six bedrooms? Do you really like Percival?'

'Percival? What does he have to do with my marriage?' She chuckled. 'He's merely my accidental occidental. As for you … Aw, baby … you're greener than asparagus. When I was your age, probably even younger, Shloka, I was parcelled around from house to house,' she said, removing a pearl necklace and storing it carefully in a pink silk batwa. 'My folks were chutney by then. No one knew what to do with me. One morning, I landed up at a house with custard-apple trees in the back yard. Oh, I don't know how to explain to you … imagine if I pulled your arm out of you—how'd you feel?'

'Bad?' he said uncertainly.

'People tear. Did I ever tell you that? We break and tear. Like cloth and furniture and everything in between.' Her voice was a curious blend of reverie and disdain. 'Awful truth is, we're in this alone. And there's no help coming. Of course I don't have any answers. But getting someplace with thirty-six bedrooms to hide in is *definitely* the way to bet. Now tell me what you think: lilies for my hair or white hibiscus?'

'White hibiscus!' he cried enthusiastically.

Waking to the rambling sweet refrain of koels on the morning of Nandini's wedding, Anuradha bathed with a sandalwood soap, used a pumice stone against her skin and wrapped herself in a ravishing bottle-green kanjivaram sari that had an ornamental brocade border. When she caught her reflection in the mirror in the drawing room she giggled: after years of austerity, this was a bit much!

Even Dariya Mahal shared the sentiment.

Vardhmaan had arranged for the wooden pelmets to be strung with loops of yellow and crimson marigold flowers, the valance was tasselled with lilies, and the vases abounded with roses of many colours. Anuradha felt as though the house had risen from its relentless dust and grime to shine for the occasion. Just as Vardhmaan spotted his wife and walked towards her, he heard it. Cold cawing. White crows. *Somewhere.*

The sound *rippled* through his blood.

'Vardhmaan ... is everything under control?'

He seemed distracted. 'Did you hear any crows?'

'There are crows all around ... probably hunting out scraps of food, nè?'

She was disappointed that he hadn't noticed she was wearing the same jewellery she had worn for their wedding, in Madhav Bagh, nearly two decades ago.

'You look miraculously lovely!' gushed Pallavi as she walked into the house half an hour later, elegant in an orange tussore sari, a small batwa under her right arm.

'Because it'd take a miracle to make me look lovely, huh?'

'Hush now! How's the bride? And where's Shloka?' When Pallavi embraced her, Anuradha found her thinner but with the same brave, soft eyes. *My closest friend,* she thought, *my sister.*

An hour before the wedding, everything started happening at once. The pandit arrived and laid out his paraphernalia: the banyan leaves, the holy strings of naada-chadi, the wooden platform, the pellets of camphor and his fading, tattered booklets of shlokas: ancient Sanskrit verses to summon divine blessing. Then the nine adipose cooks who were busy cooking in the back yard, over large black bhattis, said they needed more oil to fry the jalebis: so Krishnan sped down to Church Maarkit for seven litres of oil. By the time he got back, the first set of guests were already trickling in, and he had to make his way through the phlegm of reporters and awestruck bystanders. The Mini Sari Madam was getting married! To the son of the Governor of Bombay no less! Anuradha and Pallavi were welcoming the guests—most of them English gentry invited by the Worthingtons—directing them to their tables and urging waiters to bring out the numerous aperitifs. Ten minutes later, a grand trumpet announced the Worthingtons: Lord and Lady Worthington and Percival stepped out of a smacking-new black Rolls—all decked up and pretty-poo.

'They're here!' Pallavi's hands were cold.

'She looks like she hasn't been to the potty in seven months!' Anuradha whispered, gesturing towards the tight-faced Lady Worthington. Shloka couldn't stomach that his mother could be this humorous; he had only known her ailing.

Firecrackers were going off on the road outside as Vardhmaan and Anuradha welcomed the Worthingtons into Dariya Mahal. After they were seated at their assigned place upon the velvet gallecha, the Brahmin, with three tyres of navel fat, started to recite the sacred shlokas over the exultant tunes of the flute-caller. The guests were now waiting for Nandini to step out of her bedroom door and walk down the stairs and to her place: alongside Percival Worthington.

'If these hibiscuses don't stay on,' Nandini hissed up in her room, 'I'll glue the frigging things!' She hastily put out her beedi.

'OK, world—here I come!' She threw open her bedroom door, picked up the ends of her sari, went out on to the landing and down the stairwell. Instantly, a conspicuous hush swept over the proceedings: Nandini looked illuminating, an embodiment of pure Shakti. The pallo of her rouge-red sari was brought over her head, and its delicate gold tasselled hem fringed her forehead: you could only half see her face. As she walked down and eyed the crowds, some three hundred-plus mostly white faces gazing at her, a small, unnamed part of herself begged for Sherman. Not for either consolation or attention but for an acre of their simple understanding in which she might throw back her head and laugh like a witch at the gall of her own affectations. Perhaps he was the only one who had understood her act enough to accept it. A shared code. His blue eyes, to swim in, to never rise out of.

She sat next to Vardhmaan.

White crows were on Dr Gandharva's mind.

The pandit leans forward and smiles at her; she nods back politely, although she is suddenly secretly revolted by his bulbous eyes, his sweaty navel and its wheels of fat. She is queasy. Aware of the watching guests and reporters, she muffles a retch. Now just why this pandit seems so disturbingly familiar, she knows not. Thankfully, Percival smiles at her and dilutes her anxiety. She turns around and winks at Shloka. But then there is a touch on her arm that she does not like. It is the pandit. He is asking for her hand. So he might tie the sacred naada-chadi around her wrist. She extends her wrist very slowly, very reluctantly. His fat, coarse fingers grip her skin. Tight. Almost unyielding. That is when it lashes her like a whip. *Uncle! He's here.* She frantically yanks back her hand with a gasp everyone hears. Vardhmaan stares at her. But she cares not, and inspects the pandit closer. *Is that Uncle? Has he rushed down from Udaipur? With custard apples in his metal suitcase. And can his hands still tear me apart?* Like cloth and furniture, and everything in between. Or *am I only imagining all this? The repulsive smell of him. Ghastly touch.*

Even before she can fully process her thoughts, Anuradha looks up: just what is this furious flapping?

White crows swoop in, cawing wildly, coldly.

They startle the guests and agitate the groom. *Uncle is here.* She has not even noticed the birds. *With his nursery rhymes. Baa ... baa black sheep ... Have you any wool?* Some guests are flailing their cane walking sticks at the birds. *Yes, sir! Yes, sir! Three bags full!* Shloka is dazed too. Something curdles in Vardhmaan's gut when he hears some of the children shriek manically. The corpulent pandit pauses in his rites. The flute-caller abandons his soothing melody. And seconds later, a frothy-faced, angry-lipped, famished Fit sits up inside Nandini and rattles her from her soles all the way up to her skull, causing her to foam at the mouth and howl like a rabid beast. She shudders violently, and understands that *this* is the inexorable moment when Fate has chosen to fold in its wings and roost in her, to never leave, and to assure her that no matter what you do, how high you fly, how low you drop, what magic you pull off, the truth of the matter is this: you are never safe.

40

For the next few days, all the newspapers were abuzz with the story of how Nandini Hariharan had 'wildly attacked the guests at her wedding' or how 'she was caught in a most devilish fit like someone of occult bearings' or 'that she seemed unhuman, entirely unbecoming of a muse to famous painters—is that why Khalil Muratta had vanished?' She was crazed, they concluded, and it was a good thing that the Governor of Bombay had found this out about her *before* she married his son rather than after.

The real story, of course, was considerably different.

Minutes after Nandini fainted, Lady Annabel, the embodiment of decorum, grabbed her husband by his elbow. 'If you don't come with me *right* now, Benedict, I'll ram a rod up your rear and rattle it till you see the Queen Mother!

You HEAR me?' Percival ran after his mother meekly, like a whipped mongrel, and promptly enough the guests followed suit, muttering and stuttering on their way out.

Dariya Mahal was left as bare as it preferred to be.

The Gandharvas' only concern, that dastardly afternoon, was Nandini—whose fit had caused her to fall face forward into the ceremonial fire. Because she had been ablaze many moments before they finally managed to put it out, her sari melded into her neck with a vicious zest she would remember all her life: that eerie sound of cloth crinkling as it singed her nape ... white crows were nowhere in sight but the house smelled of smoke.

Pallavi and Vardhmaan remedied the situation somewhat as they doused Nandini's face with cold milk and basted it with honey which comforted her scalded skin. Vardhmaan assured his wife that Nandini's burns were only superficial and they would heal very soon—it was the shock of the incident that she would need time to recover from. Anuradha nodded, thinking that, if anything, he had bolted back into the cave of his Quietness—not that she blamed him any longer. It reminded her of the day of Mohan's funeral: one calamity competing with another until she was so busy sorting out where one started and the other ended that she forgot to shudder under the potency of their collective anguish. There was one thing, in all this frenzy, that Anuradha did with admirable efficacy: just as Lady Annabel's Rolls was storming out of Dariya Mahal she reached for a pewter vase on the telephone table and hurled it with such dazzling precision that it shattered her car window and launched splinters into her malevolent snakish eyes.

The next morning, the *Times of India* carried a report about the wedding debacle.

'I'd heard all sorts of things about her,' Lady Worthington was quoted as saying in the article. 'I disbelieved them because my son loved that girl. But what has happened is just unforgivable. I'm surprised we were *never* told about her ghastly faculty for the grand mal. Everyone said it was a form of madness.'

Pallavi read in the *India Dispatch and Courier* that Lady Worthington was only too grateful that Nandini's inclusion in their clan had been duly shelved because her blood would have defiled future generations of the Worthingtons in ways no one could *ever* rectify. What stunned Vardhmaan was that no one had even once asked them for their version of the incident. He was also infuriated that almost all the guests of the Worthingtons chose to remain silent over this carefully planned, brilliantly executed charade. Was it because Nandini had so far enjoyed such a disproportionate run with fame that now everyone was keen to rub her face in mud? Or was the rumour true—that Lady Worthington, the Governor's bitter half, had paid the hacks she could and bullied the ones she couldn't, only so that Nandini's side of the story never made it to the sheets?

'I'm the last person to think discriminatorily of the human race in its various forms,' Lady Annabel explained on the radio later that week. 'But I have to admit there's a certain element of the savage in all of *them.*'

Over the next few weeks, witch hazel and turmeric healed Nandini's burns. Anuradha's scrumptious fotrawalli khichdi with yogurt satisfied her stomach. And she woke to the exquisitely red amaryllis blossoms Shloka had so thoughtfully left for her in her room. Plucky but tired, defeated but still prepared to struggle on, Nandini was sure of one thing: she wanted out of Bombay. So the very day that her strength was somewhat restored, she packed her bags and said she was heading for the mountains of Matheran. Anuradha insisted she should stay a while longer but Nandini brushed away her concerns: 'This house is *wicked.*'

In Matheran she shacked up with Supari Iyer, a friend who had a large country house at Maldunga Point: an outhouse had been offered to her, and Nandini lived there for over a year, deliriously and gratefully alone.

Painting.

Thinking.

Reading.

What stayed with Anuradha most was the day Nandini left for Matheran. The orphan was on her way out when the tanga halted. She jumped down. Barefoot and beautiful, dressed in a torn blue gown, she ran up the drive and to the threshold, where she embraced Anuradha almost madly. 'I know you think it's odd. What I did to the weaver birds. And you're probably right. But what you don't know is that I loved Sherman in a way you cannot ever imagine. Take care of my itty-bitty li'l' thing, OK?'

She sprinted back to her tanga, which trotted away, leaving behind a sparse cloud of dust inside which Anuradha found herself shaking with a fiery, compelling emotion she had no particular name for.

41

In the next few months it became common for the telephone to reverberate in the lush midnight silence of Dariya Mahal and rattle sleep out of the eyelids like ghosts being exorcised out of old peepuls. By the third or fourth time, Shloka was no longer in a frazzle: Pallavi-aunty, his mother would explain, was under par. And because she could not go herself owing to her legs, Vardhmaan would assist Krishnan to get her to the hospital. *It is nothing,* she would console Shloka, *Pallavi-aunty will be just fine.* She, on the other hand, was inconsolable. The nosedive that Pallavi's health had taken recently had left her woozy with despair, and she came darn close to going into Nandini's room and hunting out the bottle of Scotch hidden in Mrs Hariharan's dowry chest. During those times Anuradha did, however, come to understand the respite of the cigarette—although she would never own up to her habit out of a sense of voluminous shame and guilt which she always experienced after a few puffs (not only was she a Hindu woman who ate chicken club sandwiches, Lord, she was now down to tobacco and such).

Pallavi kept the calls at a minimum because she considered it rude to disturb Vardhmaan in the middle of the night, and because she knew well enough what effect they had on Anuradha. Therefore when she spent an extended time in the hospital she didn't allow Krishnan to inform the Gandharvas (but they came to know inadvertently, when Anuradha sent Shloka to their house, and he got no answer for his patient, timid rat-a-tat-tats). Restless from her curiosity over Pallavi's condition, Anuradha picked up all the force left in her legs and went to Nanavati Hospital, to seek out her friend.

Lying in the arms of a ghastly solitude, Pallavi was in the postscript of her siesta when two knocks at the door roused her awake.

Was it Krishnan? Or that nurse with a habit of digging into her nose?

'Arrè! How on earth did *you* manage to come here?' She couldn't even imagine what it must have taken for Anuradha to walk all the way up to the second floor of Nanavati Hospital.

'They couldn't find a storm mad enough to stave me off, or animals wild enough to hold me back, and here I am, Pallavi, giving my eyes the calm they need and my ears the sound they seek—how are you, huh?'

'Well. I suppose, as well as I can be ... and Shloka is here too! How lovely! Come ... come by me ...' He dawdled over to Pallavi, somewhat uneasy at the cold pallor of her face, the defined veins on her neck, the sterile white bed sheet drawn to her chest as if she were a corpse.

'Pallavi-aunty ... does it hurt?' He offered her a single wild yellow flower.

'What? Ah, thank you ... how thoughtful you are ...'

'All this ...' He pointed to the tube and needle at her wrist. The white pills in a small bottle.

'You little angel ... y'know, I had to almost swim through rainwater to see your debut on this earth? On the last day of the Storm of Nine Days. In August.'

Shloka looked at his mother, as if to verify what Pallavi had said was true. Anuradha shook her head: she would never forget the relief she felt at Pallavi's words—*I'm here, Anuradha*—on that fierce, rainsome night.

'It does not hurt,' Pallavi replied. 'After a point of time, nothing hurts any longer. You heard from that scamp at all?'

'She's still in Matheran. Pallavi-aunty, I miss her. Do you think ... she'll come back maybe? I want to kick Percival.'

'Now, now,' Anuradha pulled him up, although there was no sternness in her pitch.

'That Nandini of yours has had a bumpy few months. She's just recovering. Some of us do it best alone.'

Anuradha sat on a rexin-bound chair by Pallavi while her son continued his artillery of questions. 'But I thought she was better. That's why she went to Matheran, nè?'

'Oh, beta ... she has plenty to recover from. There are some things that you and I don't know or ever will. So let your thoughts of her be unbound for now. Because your house will not move a step and she will be back before you can forget her.'

'I will never forget her!' He was aghast that she'd thought his loyalty this flimsy. 'But when will she be *there* ... that place where it will no longer be acheful for her?'

'Shloka!' Anuradha slapped her hands on her thighs. 'Why don't you please play in the corridor? The nurse has given us only half an hour as it is.'

'Hush now, for I pinched you some food,' Anuradha whispered after Shloka left the room. She pulled out two crisp chakris carefully wrapped in a blue hanky and tucked into her blouse.

Pallavi's eyes cheered. 'I swear hospital food will make *anyone* sick!'

'Your life get any more exciting than mine?' Anuradha folded her hands but leaned closer to Pallavi, who was wolfing down her surprise treat.

'Some ... did you read about that building which crashed in Apollo Bunder? One of the few who made it through was an uncle of Krishnan.'

Two or three days ago Anuradha had read in the *Mumbai Samachar* that after a hoary rain tree crashed into a building, it had come crumbling down, like a ribbon freed from some goddess's locks. Only thirty-seven of the two-hundred-odd trapped inside survived. A few were welded alive into the rafters. Some jumped off the balcony: they never made it.

Three men had been found buried in the rubble two days later—and they, miraculously enough, were breathing when they were dug out.

'That uncle of Krishnan worked there?'

'Oh yes,' Pallavi said. 'He was the man responsible for bringing the sitting toilet to Bombay. He survived.'

'Must be all the blessings from folks who had a clean go on the pot!'

'But seriously, Anuradha, it made me question why some men were returned to their families. And others died without a prayer to their name. What sort of balance is there in life?'

'I've struggled with it ever since the day I sent a child out on his father's shoulders, and never got him back. I *still* cannot forget the white lilies on Mohan's bier.' Anuradha paused, not out of distress at what she was remembering but because what she was about to say revealed the fruit, the essence, the gist of how she had come to some sort of acceptance of her first son's death. 'It must be karma, I think. Mohan's karma was what he was to work out in his brief spell with us. And ours was what we were supposed to receive out of him. That continuous exchange between people—what we also call a relationship. But I always wonder what it was that he left behind in me and Vardhmaan. Violins? Memories? A terrible fear for love? I still wrestle with such things. Because there are no clear-cut answers, are there?'

'You know, last night, as Krishnan was reading aloud the paper, telling me about that building and his uncle's escape, it amazed me. The heart of the man, how I had fallen into it. Drowned. Then I thought, what has *he* done to deserve this? A wife who is only inches away from the time when she will be the ash that old rivers crave. Who never brought him the children that he always wanted.'

She told Anuradha that she liked the *idea* of karma, and that even though it made sense on some levels, it seemed absurd on many others. Her point was: if life was about doing the right things, then she could claim boldly but humbly that she had hurt no one intentionally, done no wrong knowingly—and yet she had elicited such a cruel verdict on her life. What justice lay in this? Had her karma not been decent enough? Why were some of the men in the building still alive—even two days after the crash? Unearthed from the dust of things. Returned to the life they feared they had lost. How could some women lose the vigour of their ankles and some, like Lady Annabel, go sniggering through their time down here?

Anuradha took a deep breath. The evening sun was fading. It was her favourite time of day—dusk, when the light never dazzled nor did the darkness alarm.

'A long, *long* time ago, Pallavi, you and I started out as a thought in the head of the Universe. When we were sent on our way, it was with the understanding that if we did good, it'd be returned to us. And if we did what was not appropriate ... well ...' She shrugged. 'The point is, if we perform the right actions, do our dharma *now,* we may receive its dues in this life. Or ... or it may be carried forward, bestowed on us in another life.

Death isn't the end. Each life, well, think of it as bead after bead on some divine, unfathomable necklace.'

'But don't you believe in Heaven?' What a comforting, reliable notion it had been to Pallavi.

'There be no Heaven, Pallavi, and no Hell that I haven't lived through already ... and so I see now that it is all here, the compassion we hope to give and the cruelty we beg to escape. Right *here.* In my palms and on your soles. Over this room and 'neath your bed. But you know what my mother told me ages back? In some fundamental way, we all are in total control of destiny. Because destiny is what we build each day with our correct actions. With our work, our dharma, with the actions that are in complete abeyance to the Law of our Being. Now that's precisely what makes it so crucial that you should never again see your life in terms of one singular existence, but rather try and imagine as if it were like water. See the rain that roused you from sleep during August? See *that* rain? Well, our life is like the water that tumbles from the sky and into the stream.' Anuradha's hand pointed floorward. 'And then, some day, the stream arches into the river. Running with a mad fever, this river heads for the ocean. Where it rests and it plays. See? But before you know it, that same bead of water will rise up from the ocean's chest and soar into the great old sky to become the cloud it came from ... and so, Life starts over and over again. Thunder unfrees the drop, lightning announces its return and the earth sighs at its inception ... oh, the old sky we all are, and always the ocean we will be ...'

Her words trailed off. Pallavi shut her eyes: a peaceful, wise anguish gathered in her chest. When Anuradha saw the anguish spread over her face, slink into the brow, she sensed it was caused by the one unwavering worry Pallavi had battled with all along: what would happen to Krishnan?

Who would look out for him when she was gone?

Anuradha, on the other hand, knew what it was like to lose a lover: one not snatched away by death but by life itself.

'Even love comes with its own season … and relationships with their own kismets. They start through us, Pallavi, and then love loves *through* us. And when the give-and-take between two individuals is over, the relationship fades. Like a fruit that must fall from the bough if it is to carry its life into its next avatar. There is nothing more critical than to exercise the generosity to let something end with the grace that it started with. By your dying … your love doesn't vanish. Oh no, *no*! Never! It survives. Quietly. Under the skin of things. Trust that the love you brewed for Krishnan will see him through. It *has* to, Pallavi, and it will—if it has been right and strong. And I believe,' she said, looking right into her friend's soft, oval eyes, 'it has.'

Pallavi touched Anuradha's chin, as if recording its shape, its delicate, perfect cut.

'There was a time …' Pallavi strained as she spoke. '… when I thought life was about joy and regret and fury and radiance and all of those things both of us have known in our own way. Nowadays, though, life's only about getting tired. But there's one thing I am sure of, Anuradha, and it is broad as the sky with as much depth. A few months back, during the long rains of July, thunder stirred me awake after midnight. I sat up with a gasp. But Krishnan was undisturbed. In his sleep he seemed so fragile, so handsome, only the breaks of lightning were illuminating him for me. There is only one truly important work for all of us. I drew the bed sheet up to his chest and I shut the window. And that work is to love cleanly, with considerable heart, with love's inexplicable instincts taking full control of us. I lay down next to him knowing that if I did not wake, my job, at least in this life, was done.'

Anuradha looked out of the window. The sky was pearl grey with fringes of orange. 'I should go ... Shloka is probably bored out of his head by now ...'

Pallavi thought, *What if this is the last time I see her?* 'Thank you, Anuradha ... My life has been so much larger because of you within it.'

When they got home, Shloka ran up the drive, went over the lawns and came up to the pond, its decrepit fountain burbling ever so faintly. Anuradha followed.

Behind them, the sandstone ruin stood still in an aloof dignity.

'Shloka, what a beautiful day it is. And despite what you think, I could not be happier. My heart is full and I ask no more ... did you forget any of your toys back in the hospital?'

'No.'

'We have to do things for the sake of love that we cannot even imagine doing in the midst of our abhorrence.'

'No matter what happens, my heart will always want you.' He had no clue where this had come from, this trespasser sentence. When she touched his elbow, almost against her control, she felt the tight, perfectly concealed knot of rage she'd carried inside against Divi-bai for all these years loosen and melt away. *This is why you asked me to leave your house, Divi-bai,* she wanted to inform the vicious old hag, *so that one day I might come here. Into this moment. Yes, this house has a heinous heart and perhaps I will never dance a waltz in it again. But never mind all that! I came here for this: my son, by the pond. This holy whisper.*

'Please forgive me, beta.'

'But ... for ... what?' His face tilted as he looked at her.

'For what I will, one day, have to do.' And her voice was draped with a black mysteriousness that left him terribly, terribly nervous.

42

In the cupola-topped gardener's cottage with crenellated veranda columns that overlooked a bottomless gorge, Nandini painted with blood on her hands. Firmly bound in a solitude that came from being rejected by the same society that had once feted her, her paintings captured the rubble of her deliriously flamboyant past. Her host and friend, Supari Iyer, tall and imposing, ever clad with gold necklaces, amethyst garnets in the ears, the only hermaphrodite to have shared correspondence with Rilke, found Nandini's work reminiscent of the Varazdinian painters trained in places as varied as Zagreb, Budapest and Prague. The same everyday city sights: spires and squares and boulevards infused with an impassioned sternness that reinforced the idea that life, only inches beneath its campy wit, its casual loves, its fleeting joys, was formidably solemn.

'It is no longer even art,' Supari Iyer said of one painting. 'It *is*.'

Nandini Hariharan could ask for no greater compliment and she went walking into the forest filled with gratitude for the observation but also the nagging belief that she had, in the last few months of living a reduced existence, forgotten who she really was. It took her a long, long time to understand that in the tenure of her isolation she had evolved on many levels: her irreverent flash, though not entirely domesticated, was calmer; her wit had sharpened, and because it was laced with her changed circumstances it sparkled with irony. With her eloquence sculpted, the rough, exuberant edges of her genius chiselled, what remained was the gist of a woman who had tried but, alas, couldn't escape the authenticity of her kismet. When, in those mad days, she was seized with a compulsive urge to tear out her wild short hair or fly into the valley, she distracted her feelings with her thoughts: the mail had come and a parcel post marked from Ireland had been redirected from Bombay by the Gandharvas to her present address. Keeping it aside, she painted for the next few days to gather the guts she needed to open that brown package, because already she could smell in the contents inside his blue, *blue* eyes. Finally, a fortnight later, she tore open the package in the belief that this particular incident of destiny might remind her who she was, and how that version of herself had so gracelessly abandoned the entirely honourable love of a young man, and his hesitant poetry recitations.

Dear Nandini,

Apologies for the delay of my response to you, but the last few months have been absolutely chaotic and have altered my life in a way I had never foreseen. The same, I imagine, must hold true for you: married and settled, you must have moved into your new life with great enthusiasm. Hearty congratulations on your wedding! I am writing to you from a wee little apartment in a house whose first level is a noisy pub called the Flying Pig. The amazing bit of news is that I thoroughly detested Trinity—so campy and crooker — and we are leaving Dublin for England in a week. It took a while, to come to terms with how I could want something for all of my life—and then when I finally had it, I realized that its reality was far too bitter to be swallowed.

It makes me want to start all over again, and I am doing just that.

Last week, Mother, who is doing plenty better here, got a canary who performs Celtic ballads that range from the festive to the morbid; thankfully, this one croons mid-afternoon. I don't know where I will go. You were right, we walked into the path of other people's violations. Some nights I watch the patterns the rain leaves on the cobblestone path, under my bedroom window. Leaves and stones and dragons surface. Part of me believes that one day, walking on your road, wherever you are, you too might see the same motif of water on stone, and briefly we will stand in a togetherness of our own construction. Unfettered by time and distance and fact. How odd are the ways the heart finds its intimacy. Nandini, I wish you infinite happiness with Percival and wish that your art finds its discerning audience, its reasonable critics.

This will be my last letter to you.

Did you ever wonder why I was so bent on finding a cure for triste incurabilis? *I'd never imagined it could be so difficult. Farewell and all that. The moon here has, as Yeats rightly pointed out, 'dark leopards' which no one can reach. Far away and fierce, its beauty brightens the closer you get to them: but come too close and you leave blinded. Underneath the ounce of regret, the guilt and the grief, there is a clearing I know for you. A place to come to after everything, when you need nothing at all and everything too. I leave you now, hoping that you find faith in the morning, and compassion at dusk.*

Yours,
Sherman

Along with the letter came the finest pair of black felt gloves with the message: *For Paris;* and a copy of *The Complete Works of Verse: W. B. Yeats* with an inscription, *For Life.*

She opened it at the page where the deckle edge had been folded over.

How many loved your moments of glad grace,
And loved your beauty with love false or true,
But one man loved the pilgrim soul in you,
And loved the sorrows of your changing face ...

For the next few days, at sundown, on some nameless bluff, she fathomed the full anatomy of longing: how the lips could howl like wolves for the sake of someone's spittle; how one's crotch might feel desolate enough to want to burst open like a volcano that can no longer sustain the magma of its own isolation. Looking at trees, she wanted to split open their trunks and haul the boy and his kite out of them. Looking at the moon, she was fevered with a need to bay at it, to unfurl such anguish at it that its haughty silver would alter some inches. *Come here, you sons of bitches. And all you marketplace harlots too. Do you know just how wide of the mark you are? Because even if the scars vanish under witch hazel, the wounds run deeper than ever. Oh, you don't know nothing about a cut if you think you can patch it up pretty. Make it all OK. Maybe you've all just got a memory worse than mine, and I am baying at the moon for it.*

Heard me? I am baying at the moon for it!

She would jump into the valley or she would know the mountain top.

Where would she go from here? Back to that old house still waiting for them all with a butcher's knife in its fist? Back to Udaipur and its weaver birds? So when Supari Iyer suggested a certain escape route, she gave it much thought, and one sleepless night she came to the conclusion that there was no better way out. Of course it was crazy—but at least it was a chance. And these days she was counting on chances because her faith in safety had petered somewhat. Before she could weigh up the risks, the sound of thumping paws outside her panelled door alerted her.

The hour past midnight.

His low whispering snarl she will recognize from all others in the forest, and when he walks in, his tail knocks down the hurricane lamp. They unite in a darkness as black as his coat, snarling some, biting a little. But for the first time, she is suddenly nervous. Tonight his passion is like hers: it knows not where love ends and fury commences. So she wants out. He will not let her go. In the lightless gardener's cottage she starts to scream till window panes shiver; he is unrelenting. His growls contest with her screams. That's when she shoves open the door and rushes out into the forest. Poor thing, she leaves a spoor. The juices of *his* loins dripping out of hers. He sniffs her out and chases after her. She slides through the forest. Monkeys barking. His cantering paws crushing twigs. She tries to climb trees. Fails. Thicket smacks her face. Blood on her neck. Gasping. Takes a right. Almost goes down a damned gorge. Turns and scrambles up some rocks. Out pours the moonlight she has bayed at and branches that whack her flat. She rises again. Keeps going. She runs because she can hear him running after her: two legs competing with four. Where she will go, no one knows. And how far before he might catch up with her?

Or will she escape? For the first time, the girl understands that there is only so much you can give of yourself to Desire before it takes you all in. Opens its seductive mouth and gulps you without a trace. It rubs you into its own canvas—and Nandini is not ready for this yet.

So for now, she is running, and she is free, and she is as wild as wild can be.

43

In late October of the following year, at dawn, when the sudden, thrilling shriek of the marsh kingfisher rode over her brittle sleep, Anuradha Gandharva ascertained that she was alive, but her feet were dead. She tried to lift them out of bed but it was as if they had got up and walked away, abandoning her to a sweaty, startling immobility. Out of an uncured habit, she reached out for Vardhmaan: the space nearly sank her (as it had him, when she was in Matheran). She would wait, she decided, until someone was up and ask what'd happened, although it was obvious what had occurred: but she needed someone else's validation that what she had thought when the leopard had prowled around her was true: she had a fate worse than death.

Oh, easily.

From that moment on, Anuradha didn't disclose her inertia as much as she established it: like a new flower whose fragrance covers an old garden, her condition swam over the house. That same morning, she convinced Shloka that she would now walk only when it was most vital. When he asked when that would be she just gave him an inscrutable smile that seemed to suggest that although that day would be here soon, he should certainly not be looking forward to it. In the evening, when Vardhmaan came to her side because he had missed her familiar, sweet humming in the morning and, later, her presence at the dinner table, she sat him on her bed, touched his arm. 'It is time you put away the Spikav. There's absolutely *no* place for waltzes in my house.'

Vardhmaan gathered together his records—songs to which they had surreptitiously danced, years ago, in the Dwarika house—and packed them in a wooden chest in the attic.

A few days before Diwali that same year, Anuradha sat up in her bed with a writing board on her lap. But before she started to write she wondered if theirs was the only house on the street on whose door sill no bright lantern swayed. No terracotta lamps lined the balustrade. No marigold toran hung above the door. Was this the only house where the woman indoors was not breathlessly busy whipping up copra paak and sakar para during the festival season? Did it plague Vardhmaan: that maybe he ought to have come for the walks on Juhu beach when she had asked him years ago? She reassigned her mind to the letter growing inside her: her words were poured out over a lined page, in a script that was clean and right inclined.

Dearest Radha-mashi,

Did I ever tell you how thankful I am for the birdsong outside my window, in the madhumati arbour. Tailor-birds and bulbuls and mynahs broaden my mornings with delight and bring consolation to the afternoons. How is your heart? Sparrows roost after twilight, noisy little tattletales. One day I hope you see this, the extent of my everyday joy, its unwavering brilliance. Nandini, who never did marry Percival, moved to Matheran several months back and writes of the hawks in the valley outside the gardener's cottage she now occupies. Why did she faint on her wedding day, Radha-mashi, she who tried so hard to reverse everything? She who walked on water but fell on land. I have stopped walking. But I will again, one time, one day.

Over the last few years I've come to the awareness that all that my heart affiliates itself with will be taken from me: and perhaps this has only been arrogance at its stealthiest because I began to feel that I was ready for such losses. Many years ago, I accepted Mohan's leap into his own destiny, so much braver, with so much more velocity. When I returned from Udaipur, with Nandini and songs and conviction, I saw Vardhmaan move away into his own world and I told myself: 'Yes, in this too there is the hand of something Larger than me. Something which will not allow me to lose myself in my love for him.' So I stepped back, and then I saw him for the first time: vulnerable and broken and true. I suppose life is a process of looking clearly at things. But this will find its greatest trial when I send my little Shloka away. Even if we all leave this old house, its sadness has tainted us in inconceivably various ways, and it will find my boy and extract its dues. He must leave. As promised.

A promise I made long, long ago.

Do you believe arrangements can be made for him in Australia? I want him to go to one of the better boarding schools there; all expenses will be taken care of. My only wish is that you look deep into his growing years. I am infinitely tired. I want to go back to where the peacocks will not be silent around me. I want to go home. To the lake outside my window. I have gone this long without asking about your new life, Radha-mashi, and all its new faces. Do your Yorkshire terriers still drink gin and tonic each evening? I think of your cook Picasso and how he taught me to make soufflés so light we had to chain down the ramekins, and I miss your naughty laughter.

Anuradha

Barely had she signed the letter when she heard Shloka ringing the doorbell; first politely, then furiously. He was back from school—and there was no one to open the door. His childish impatience made way for disquiet: who now would let him in? Where would he go? Sweat murmured down his nape and he loosened his faithful brown tie—clumsily looped around—as he sat by the pond and waited and waited for his father. *No whiteman in the pond now.* Goldfish. Black ferns. Pebbles. When Vardhmaan let him in at the end of the day, Anuradha gave him his own little key which she asked him to tie to a string and wear around his neck so he would never lose it. No sooner had he put his shiny copper house key around his tiny neck than he rushed to show it to her. But she only asked him to sit beside her on the bed.

'Remember I keep talking to you about Australia?'

'Hmm ... yes ... maybe.'

'Do you remember?' Her voice lacked the gentleness he associated with her.

'Yes.' He didn't like where this was going.

'Well, I believe the time will come soon when I will have to send you away. There.'

'Why?' He folded his hands defensively.

'Because ...' But even before she could say another word he shouted: 'NO! I'm not going anywhere! You can't send me ANY place—do you understand?' It was ludicrously incongruous: the big voice of a small boy. He knew what happened to people when they had to go and live with strangers. Nandini had told him all about it. The tearability and breakability of people.

Anuradha sighed.

What could she tell him in the circumstances? Was there any rational explanation for this? Maybe *he* was the last song of dusk. He would carry the Story everyone else had lived. No matter where he would go now, the Story would be the same, even if the characters differed in colour or height or cadence of speech. What would distinguish it from all other stories would be the bravura of its sadness, the humility of its joy, the subtlety of its fury.

'Maa?' He was waiting for her to speak.

'This house ... when I was carrying you, around eleven years ago, I tripped in the chowk behind. It rained as though spears were cutting me into bits. My water bag burst and I was stranded for two hours in a storm, bleeding, unable to move. That was when I saw the mad heart of this house for the first time. I promised Dariya Mahal that if no misfortune struck you, then I'd send you away. When the time was right. Before it sat up and licked you with its sorrow. Like it has me. And your father. And Nandini. You cannot understand a love that does not bind. But you will. Hear me? You *will*.'

Trembling hands and a torn face didn't loosen his mother's gaze on him: her unalloyed, unmoving, drinking-in eyes.

'And Shloka, one more thing.'

'Yes, Maa?'

'Say my name.'

'Hmm?'

'My name, say it to my face. I want you to call me by my name from today.'

He looked away.

'SAY it!' Her voice reached a note so high, it tore. *'Aloud.* To *me.'*

'Anuradha,' he muttered.

Pond-watcher. Butterfly-catcher. Itty-bitty li'l' thing.

'I didn't catch that.' Who would have imagined that Anuradha Gandharva, who at one point in time had inspired the swain poets of the Udaipur Sonnets Society, would grow up to become a mother so heartless she would send her only son away?

'Anuradha,' he repeated, this time a few notches more audible. 'Anuradha ...'

She raised her hands up. 'Louder!'

'Anuradha! Anuradha! *Anuradha!'* Yelling his mother's name to her face, he ran out of her room, shaken by her brutality, wounded by her capacity to walk right out of his life and wipe her feet on the shreds of his childhood.

Is *this* what he has to forgive her for?

Years later, as she will be dying, she will call him at the other end of the world.

'Shloka ... beta ... will you please call me what you used to call me before you started using my name?'

And his masculine baritone will ask in return, 'You mean before *you insisted* I use your name?'

44

Before the monsoon swept out the leaden clouds of August, Pallavi died. Dawn crept over the sky outside her cottage and tailor-birds started work on their nests and ants went on their way. She had died inside poems and gazes and a little regret and a bewildering expanse of love.

Krishnan walked over to Dariya Mahal and told the Gandharvas.

Anuradha noticed how his eyelids never blinked as he spoke.

Now, more than before, it was true: life was a process of expanding the imagination till it could contain reality. Never in her wildest dreams had Anuradha Gandharva foreseen that she would not even be able to walk to her closest, perhaps *only,* friend's funeral meet. But then, as Vardhmaan was carrying her in his arms, down to Pallavi's place, she buried her face into his nape, its coltish elegance, and she was heartened by the awareness that this was the nearest she'd been to him in years, and that underneath the grief of Pallavi's passing, this moment, this palanquin of arms, was lovely: a solace she had never expected in a sadness that she had.

Looking at Pallavi's supine form, on the bier, strewn with lilies, covered with a white cloth stretching up to her neck, Anuradha was struck by how deeply centred inside the seed of death she was. Unlike the restless mien of Mohan's face, of he who had never wanted to die, Pallavi's face was serene, without argument. She shut her eyes. And her mind raced back to the afternoon when she had met Pallavi for the first time, outside Church Maarkit, how she had offered to drop her home. For a moment she arranged and rearranged the memories of their friendship with unambiguous detachment, recalling the anxieties confided, the jokes bartered, the wisdom pondered, and the uncertainties they grew to accept out of a reverence for fortitude, and, oddly enough, the fortitude that came out of such an acceptance.

When she opened her eyes, it was time to take Pallavi away.

They lifted her, the bier-ends resting on the shoulders of Krishnan and Vardhmaan and two other men. As they passed Anuradha, she leaned forward and they stopped.

'Go well, my friend ... there is so much beauty in you ...'

Around a week after Pallavi's funeral, Shloka brought Anuradha a few letters that the postman had left under the gateway.

'Shloka?' He seemed so distant these days.

'Yes, *Anuradha?*' He would hurt her in the same way that she had savaged him.

'Well ... never mind,' and she started to open one of the letters, the first of which was from Radha-mashi, who wrote saying that she would be more than willing to have Shloka over in Australia, that a splendid boarding school stood very near where she lived and hence she could visit him often and watch over him. *I will be visiting Bombay in two months,* Radha-mashi wrote, *and I'll take him back with me. I will be there. Always. Tell him to be brave; life makes us that in any case.* Anuradha held Radha-mashi's letter to her chest, unsure whether to be comforted that someone would take her son away or flail her hands at a house with a butcher's knife that raged to strike out at them every now and then. Anuradha started rereading Radha-mashi's letter, and learned that her aunt was happy in her new home, that she had made many new friends and rediscovered old ones.

Towards the end, she asked—circuitously—how Nandini was, and whether she was recovering. Truth be told, Anuradha, over the last few months, had lost track of Nandini, who had pretty much moved to Matheran. Was she still living with Supari Iyer? And painting with blood on her hands? Was she OK? I'll write to her, Anuradha thought hopefully.

But, as it turned out, the following week, she got a note from the walk-on-water wanderer.

Hoo-hah and tiddly-winks but I got to Paris. Flat tyre and all. Who'd have thought I'd get here in one scrumptious piece of cherry, but I did. The place is tiny, where I'm putting up at, just off Montparnasse, He's a friend of Supari Iyer, an art collector who threads up so sharp you could slice cheese with his winter jackets. He takes me around the scene, and last week Atget, the bloke who snapped me for Muratta's catalogue, introduced me to Ozenfant, who's offered me studio space. Been busy I have, Anuradha, and the thing about the toil in art is not that it's an act of remembrance, but an act of forgetting. Till memory is blank and the artist may entertain other sorrows, with less weight. Should have telegraphed you or something. But I didn't want to leave with more heft than I had. It's impossible, how brave and beautiful you are. Did I ever tell you that? And look at me. Damn! No one but street dogs will make any claims on me; I'd claw their eyes out if they made an offer, tho. But whatever that 'home' bollocks is about, I'm letting go. I'm footloose, I'm free. Paris. It's home. Till something gets ghastly and I got to fly again. And Shloka, my itty-bitty Li's' thing! All packed? Know what I told you that one time? Well, I was off base. Some of us do mend. It's all about time and stamina.

Because when we get broken up bad, it takes time. And no, no, no—don't you believe somebody when they tell you time heals. It heals boiled eggs, time does. Time only allows us to become as large as our boo-hoo until we are, one day, larger than it, and it tumbles right out of us. I'll watch for you. You do the same. I'm the pretty one with the dimpled thumb. I'm the one the cats follow. I'm the one who got away.

Well, almost.
N

Even before she put the letter down Anuradha's mind raced back to a geometry lesson from her childhood in which the teacher had said that two parallel lines never intersect. They mirror each other and they keep going—but they never intersect ... then she remembered the addendum to the theory which stated that two parallel lines *do* intersect, at some unnamed point, in some unnamed place in space. Her heart brightened up. Would Nandini ever know the listening shade of Sherman again? Would they once again laugh at their lives and the lives of others, not from bitterness but surrender? Oh, would that barefoot, beedi-smoking, mini-sari madam's heart ever be in safe hands? At that moment Shloka happened to pass her on his way out; when she told him that Nandini had been holed up in Paris for the last couple of months he just shrugged his shoulders. Everyone was somewhere but here. Nandini. Tia. Sherman. Everyone had to leave. Later that evening, sitting by the pond, he touched on many queries. When did Nandini leave Matheran? Why didn't she say goodbye? Would she ever come to Australia?

He remembered one of their last conversations, when Nandini had returned to Bombay for a brief spell to pack up her remaining belongings. Anuradha had not yet spelled out the terms of his departure, but he was becoming uneasy at the hints she kept dropping.

'Do you think that maybe ... perchance Anuradha's angry with me?' It was a little after midnight; an owl flew through the house.

'Now why would you think a thing like that?' Nandini was cleaning her paintbrushes in turpentine. Two suitcases had already been packed.

'Was it something ... that I did?'

'No, Shloka, don't be silly.' She noticed that his eyes were barren and innocent. 'Remember this much. If someone pulls out your arms, don't let them come back for your shoulders. Because that's what they'll do. Look after your arms. All right?'

'I'll ... try ... but where's Australia, Nandini?'

'Oh ... the middle of nowhere. Keep your head low in boomerang country, baby. A lot of kangaroos they have out there.'

Shloka nodded. He had read about kangaroos in a dusty encyclopedia. They were brown and big, cheeky, furry creatures with long tails and shiny eyes that ate loads and hid their babies in vein-lined pouches on their bellies.

'Say I were to stand on a hill in Australia,' he said in a speculative voice, joining and unjoining his hands. 'Would 1 be able to see you from there?'

'Your eyes see strong?'

'Oh, I can see for miles,' he replied confidently. 'Miles and miles.'

'Then it may be possible. Besides, how could you ever miss my beauty?'

'And would I be able to see ... my mother?'

'Shloka,' she said, her voice urgent. 'Listen up, bean ... you'll come see me. And my paintings. My time in India is coming to a close. It's time to cut and run. But no worries. Some day I'll have a grand showing of my paintings ... at ... oh, at some place spectacular ... in Europe, perhaps ... and then I'll get you over on the back of a for-hire angel if need be.'

'I'll wear my brown suit. And my camel tie. Think I'll have learned to knot it by then.'

'What about your black leather shoes?'

'I'll start polishing them.' Shloka never understood it. Why he felt as if he might burst from being inside that moment.

45

Nearly twenty years ago, Anuradha Gandharva came to Bombay to marry a man she had never even met. She had married, of course, and she had loved. In the early days, she would sit on the balcony of the Dwarika house, listening to some glorious song by Schumann, and imagine that she would meet age in the friendship of this man, Vardhmaan. That she would anticipate his return in the evening, and her waiting gaze would mitigate the fatigue of his day. Her dream was neither romantic nor too optimistic: this had been the life of her mother and her grandmother, and she had assumed that this would be the path that she too would follow. But somewhere in between a song by Schumann and a melody freed by Elgar a few months earlier, she had been evicted from the reverie she had hoped to live in: and how!

But if anything, she no longer missed Vardhmaan as she used to because they had now learned to extract each other's companionship in ways that suited them best. Each morning, for instance, she woke when he, in the room above her, shuffled his feet to put on his shoes; and if he overslept she would hum a ditty that would banish his sluggish tardiness. When the confinement of her own bad health maddened her, he would, without her asking, come into her room, lift her in his arms and walk her through the house, and she would look at the fig trees taking root in some of the vacant rooms, the chaise upstairs, the wooden landing, and she would feel refreshed that she was where she was. *It is all good,* he had said to her once, and today she saw what he meant by it.

A few days before Shloka was due to leave for Australia, she realized that perhaps none of this would ever have happened if her ordering chicken club sandwiches at the Billingdon Clubhouse had perturbed Vardhmaan enough to stay away. She laughed and laughed. Perhaps because she finally understood that the street slang of life was one word alone: irony. Sometimes she would talk about a new movie she had read about or comment on the freedom struggle, and he would pleat the newspaper in his fingers and look at her from behind his steel-rimmed glasses and listen attentively. But even after her words were folded and put to one side, they would continue staring at each other in the knowledge that the endurers of a common fate have an association that outlives calamity and joy, strengthens over time, and deepens into a clarity that allows them to accept that love was nothing but the fragile excuse that enjoined them in the first place, and that after its cessation, after the haunting emptiness of its passing, this silence they were now sharing was, in fact, nothing short of divine eloquence.

Over the last few months, Anuradha had discovered amusement in the vice of the cigarette, and like a conspiratorial teenager, she had also introduced her husband of twenty years to it: their delight only deepened because they kept it a secret from Shloka, who, she swore theatrically, ought never to know that his mother was a 'smoker of the first order'. Vardhmaan promised to keep her confidence if she would return the favour. She was, however, never sure why he would only ever bring her one cigarette—was it because he didn't want her amusement to become a habit?—but they shared it, and his lips touched what hers had, and the cigarette was exchanged many times before its red, burning tip was extinguished: it died into itself, the greatest death of all. Waving her hands to dispel the smoke, she would briefly admonish herself and then him, as though it were he who had suggested this most vile of cravings in the first place. Those were the evenings when she started to read to him, from her Sharat Chandra novels, and in this way night would come and pluck them apart and remind them that the only purpose of two people being together was that they might encounter the solitude curled tightly inside them. Now one such evening, perhaps it was the week Shloka was scheduled to leave, Vardhmaan was sitting beside her, reading her the review of the newest Gujarat play, *Jeevan nu Raas.* Quite abruptly, she interrupted him, 'Say what you will, Vardhmaan, I'll miss him. Things rake deep enough to alter the flesh of the soul.'

He put down the newspaper. 'Shloka will be fine.'

'That much I know. Perhaps it's even easy to forgive. The forgetting bit is what takes us to our grave.'

She laid her hand on his knee: how blissful that felt, her touch. She giggled. He looked at her: what was that twinkling laughter all about? She would not tell him that her mind had oscillated back, to those breathless, lush nights in the Dwarika house, when her loins would squeeze him with brilliant ardour, and in order for him not to spill into her too soon she would distract him by reciting the prices of the vegetables in Dwarika market. Nearly twenty years on, she was giggling as she wondered whether Taru or Sumitra-bhabhi had ever overheard a grown woman moaning out the rates of tomatoes by the kilo in the middle of the night, in the throes of ecstasy.

'Do you remember Mohan?' he asked after a moment.

'I remember most how he would sit in the bird bath and sing. But mostly I've forgotten, Vardhmaan, because it's been a long while. And a lot of things have happened since.'

'Did you remember what he told you? I mean the last time you saw him.'

'Of course. *I want my violin.* His last words. He'd wanted it ever since Taru had told him it had been brought into the house.'

'And do you know what his last words to me were?'

'He didn't say anything to you, Vardhmaan. He was unconscious by the time you arrived. Unless you mean in the morning or the evening before.'

'Neither. He spoke to me. Just before he died he spoke to me.'

'Vardhmaan ...'

'Remember I carried him to the hospital? And then I found a doctor friend and he let me in as well?'

'Yes ... yes ... I do.' *My beloved storyteller,* she thought. *Tell me not this story.*

'A few minutes later I'd come out with the X-ray and told you about what had happened.'

'Mmm.' She remembered how he had gone back into the operating room, his form fading behind the glass bracket in the door.

'When I went back in and they were about to sedate him, he came around. Just for a moment. He opened his beautiful black eyes, looked at my face, touched my face with his tiny hands. And he said, *Save me, PaPa ... please don't let me die.*'

Evening sun slid into the room: a gentle, nourishing spray of golden light.

She took his hand in hers. 'I was wrong, you know.'

'About what?' He wanted, after the longest time, to embrace her. To fill himself with her.

'Remember many years back I—well, Shloka and I and Nandini—were leaving for Matheran? At the Victoria Terminus, by the peanut-seller.'

'Yes.'

'I was wrong to the bone of me. Because love is enough, Vardhmaan.'

46

Not knowing what it would take for Anuradha to change her mind, he tried everything. Shloka lit up the terracotta Diwali lamps one evening (practically blinded Dariya Mahal, that did) and he painted a wall mad pink. When he hung Anuradha's old saris from the landing they came fluttering to the ground floor, majestic, stunning curtains of silk, in colours ranging from emerald to heart red. She was puzzled; he was indefatigable. He brought in a few of the deathless goldfish and took out the furniture. He deweeded the garden and then smashed to bits the teardrop chandelier over the dinner table. She was puzzled. When she asked him why he did it, he would not say, and it was much later, long after he was gone, that she realized what he had been trying to do. Provoke something that would translate into his staying.

Press some trigger. Push one particular button. *Anything.* Lit lamps and hanging saris. Because he simply couldn't fathom how she could have promised this house, in the estuary of a storm, to send him away? How bizarre! And why could you *not* go against that absurd promise? Did her choice arise from mad whim—or from great and inexplicable love?

When his child's bewilderment calmed, remarkable insight poured in, like the tiniest chink in the cathedral windows that invites in the light dancing outside it. With that chink of light he paused to wonder whether perhaps what his mother had said was right. That there was enough sadness in this house to break your back. Was that *really* so? Or was this house plain wicked? All cobra venom and stormlight. With that chink of light, he was the only one who eventually saw what everyone else had missed: even Vardhmaan and Nandini and, most of all, Anuradha. That it wasn't sadness. Oh, no, no, no! Aw, Lord, it was only love. Thick as molasses; hungry as a leech. This was the love someone had died for, and it was still here: tripping up pregnant women and causing grown girls to faint.

Shloka was the only one who got it.

That Edward had not died waiting for love but merely from waiting to *give* it.

Because this awareness reeled through his head and made him dizzy, he decided to counter it by immersing himself in his packing—and since there was only a day left before his ship was due to leave, he decided it was time to start now. Carefully and diligently he hauled out his clothes, and before long a vaguely neat pile had gathered on the bed: imprecisely folded half-pants, his checked half-sleeve shirts, his white underwear, his socks and all the bits and bobs he knew he just *had* to take. A perfectly preserved swallowtail. A black rose. Tia's leash. There was one more thing that he absolutely would *not* go without: his collection of ties. And there were well over a hundred! There were gold ones and blue ones. Striped ones and ones with motifs of vines and roses. But when he held up a particular cream silk tie, it harked back to an incident steeped in regret, the colour of ash. Around a few weeks after he had started speaking, he mustered the courage to ask Vardhmaan to teach him how to knot a tie. Vardhmaan was in his bedroom that evening when Shloka walked in.

'I've tried, Pappa.' He extended the tie towards his father. 'But I just can't get it on. Could you please show me how to ... ?'

Over a violin aubade reeling in the background, Vardhmaan took the tie and started to tie it on himself: it was, of course, ridiculously small for him.

Shloka chuckled, and Vardhmaan unravelled it with a sheepish grin.

'Show *me* how, Pappa,' he clarified. What was the point of Vardhmaan putting it on, after all? Vardhmaan started looping it around Shloka's neck. But Vardhmaan seemed to have his sense of proportion mixed up because the tie came trailing all the way to the floor.

'Er ... I think it's a bit long, nè?' The tact in Shloka's voice was well beyond his years.

When Vardhmaan tried again, in earnest, it turned out too short—and Shloka ended up looking like one very adorable circus aspirant. Vardhmaan pressed on, and Shloka surrendered to the gorgeous, grieving succour of his father's touch: it reminded him of his secret list of Things To Do with Father. Like flying kites. Or strolls on Juhu beach. And trips up to Matheran. His heart lit up. Right then, though, the skin on Shloka's neck trembled. Warm teardrops had landed on his nape. A weight so gentle, it was unbearable.

Like the weight of a child's bier.

I'm sorry, Vardhmaan whispered. *I'm so terribly sorry ...*

What could Shloka say? What was left that had already been painfully unsaid? The violin played on behind both of them. (Many years later, Shloka would recall that moment as the one in which he had ascertained he would never be the son that he was expected to be: and oddly enough, this bound him to Vardhmaan with a feeling wider than love but as wretched as hope.)

Shloka folded the cream silk tie and placed it in his suitcase.

He would take it with him.

To Australia. To boomerang country.

Later that evening, after his bags were packed and he was sitting in his room watching the egrets fly over the marshes, a voice rose through the house, reined him by the wrist and pulled him out: 'Shloka! Come with me, beta, I must talk to you.'

'Anuradha!' He ran out. He was greeted by the sight of Anuradha walking towards the stairwell: he caught his breath.

'How are you ...' It was difficult to believe that she was walking again. Was he imagining this?

'Be not afraid. I've been saving for this day. Come, let us go to the balcony. Help me climb the stairway.'

Shloka ran down and held her hand.

As he used to when she could still walk.

'How beautiful it all is!' she said when he threw open the long doors of the balcony. 'There is nothing more I love in this house than this balcony. On the first day we came into Dariya Mahal, we sat out here to enjoy our evening meal. How limitless the sky was then!' As she moved slowly, he watched her with the insurmountable fear that any moment now her feet would give way. That she would fall like dust falling to the floor.

'Come, sit by my side.' For a shutter-snap of a second she experienced what Edward had the evening he waited for his brown-skinned lover.

She patted the chaise. Shloka sat beside her.

'Very soon, you will be gone. And this house will be empty. Did I ever tell you, on the day you were born, you just couldn't sleep. Left your father in knots. But when I awoke, I think a day had gone by, I carried you and brought you here. You seemed so without ease. So I sang you a lullaby. After a while, you drifted to sleep as the rain left and dawn came.'

'But where did you learn them? Your songs.' He was in his going-away clothes. His brown half-pants and his cream shirt. A camel-coloured tie. Tied badly.

'In Rajasthan. When your brother died, I returned to my mother's house. Those were the days when I could not understand how *such* a grief had reached me. I thought to myself: how could I have stepped so out of the course of normal existence, for surely, this must be the grief of another, greater life, entirely unworthy of me. And I wondered what it was that lay in it that I was supposed to see. The defining *point* of this experience. Of course, many people told me the usual wisdom of grief. That it makes you stronger. It builds you. And yes, all of that holds true. But there must have been some greater intention that I was meant to fathom, to know *why* it had happened ...'

She smiled. 'Then one evening, my mother dragged me by my arm to the water's edge, under the wooden pergola. An old aunt of hers was also there, and together, the two of them unleashed a song of ineffable power, of countless nuances, and you know, Shloka, it was more than a song. It was a surge of history. A tale of endurance, of what she had seen, and what others had seen before her: all of it came through.'

Anuradha stood up, and when she walked to the end of the terrace, he followed. With her hands on the balcony railing, she shared an extract of the song she had heard that evening. A slow, fine tune, unfurled lightly, without burden. When it was done, she collected her breath. 'And the thing I accepted that day was this: for some things there are no reasons. Beyond the reach of all logic they lie. And the only way past them is through them: we have to live them *out* of us. So all I asked was that if I had to shoulder this, then there ought to be a way I could do it better, something that would rise from inside me, and hold me up. That evening I learned that this grace was my songs.'

A twilight of startling beauty: scarlet dying in black unfolded over them.

'I want you to have these.' She handed him a silk drawstring pouch. 'Open it if you like.'

When he pulled back the strings and inverted the pouch, a pair of silver anklets poured out. He lifted them against the cheek of the evening sky, and he shook them to unspool their rhythmic *zhan-zhan-zhan.*

'Take them with you,' was all she said.

Years later he realized what she had *really* given him. The sound of her feet. The preface to her movements.

'I wonder, Shloka, if you will remember me with an angry heart. You who will be so far. But my being here and your being there is no divide for a mother's love—which knows no restraint. *None* whatsoever. See the green in that tree? That too is some mother's love. And the blue in the sky above? Why, that *too,* Shloka, is what a mother's love is all about. It'll hold you when you miss a step; will lead you out of a path where there is only darkness. Ah, Shloka, you just reach your hand out, and I will hold it. But promise me one thing, Shloka. No matter what, you will live your life, endure your destiny—in fact, go forth and beckon it, and hold its full tenure unfailingly. Deny nothing; live *everything.* And when you have allied yourself with your kismet perfectly, almost as if it were some noble dance, a day will come when it will repay you. Suddenly, you will find yourself in the custody of something that will let you bear any weight you have to. For me, that mercy has been my songs. On the day I left Udaipur, my mother told me there is no mercy in this life. She was wrong, so very wrong. For Nandini it will be, I believe, her painting. In your father's case ...' She drifted away; but Shloka knew perfectly well what she meant. 'One day, it will be your turn. To hunt it out, to ask Fate for the motive under its actions, and when you find it, it will save you. It may be anything. A new land. A lover. Simple as a story it may be, or a kind breeze. Always stay alert enough to receive this. Take it with you. Because you, Shloka, will have paid for it with all of your life.'

Before dusk folded its wings and night slunk in, it was time for him to leave. He was going to spend the night with Radha-mashi because his ship was leaving at the unearthly hour of four in the morning. His two brown leather suitcases were placed in the boot of the car; his travel documents were in order; and kitted up with a gold watch on a chain that opened at the slightest touch (his going-away present), he was all ready to depart.

Anuradha reached down and tightened his tie. 'How handsome you look!' she said at the doorway.

It overwhelmed Anuradha, the small mercies of her life: that Vardhmaan and not she was sending off this child. *My poor, poor Vardhmaan,* she thought under the eyelid of the moment, *how many children will you have to give away in one lifetime?*

'Keep your tie knotted tight. Hold your head up. Always say thank you. Open doors for ladies, and read loads.'

'Should I ... write to you?' He seemed to be taking permission, this feather of a creature.

'I would be ...' What was the word she was looking for? ' ... devastated if you didn't.'

She stood at the foot of the tall black gate.

He was, now, already in the car.

Vardhmaan pressed the pedal. The car rolled down the steep black drive, and she followed. In comparison to what she felt in her chest, the ache in her feet was nothing. From his window, Shloka extended his small hopeful hand, and for the briefest moment, their fingers touched.

The car went down the road.

Shloka looked ahead. The Arabian Sea was in the distance. Rain trees peered down.

'Pappa,' he said looking out. 'About the ties. Forget it.'

He touched the boy's earlobes. Would his son ever forgive him? If not his love, could at least he hope for his atonement? When the car came to the other side of the road, Vardhmaan slowed as they passed Dariya Mahal: Anuradha, he noticed, was still standing at the gateway, under the kadam tree, her fingers webbing her face.

Waiting.

'Could you please stop ... just for a moment ...'

Jumping out of the car, Shloka faces her on the other side of the road. She looks up. And she sees what Nandini had painted over a decade ago: a little boy in brown half-pants, cream shirt and a camel tie.

The tiny leaves of the albizia tree tumble in the breeze. The scent of coming rain.

Should he run across? Or should he stay? *I want to see the goldfish ... one last time. Please don't be angry with me, Anuradha ... my heart will always want you ... May I come back ... some day?* Pond-watcher. Butterfly-catcher. Itty-bitty li'l' thing. With a genius for melancholy. They gaze at each other for an exquisite, enduring minute: past sentiment, fearless, iron-eyed. She nods once. When a light rain drapes over everything, he returns to the car and they drive away into the kind, kind mist.

No matter the distance now, her mind will always trace him out: lying on her bed, with birdsong for solace and not a prayer she can count on, Anuradha Gandharva will see her son clearly, quietly. All she has to do is close her eyes and he will appear before her. She will wince at his first shaving cut; and it is her hand which, despite his never knowing it, will caress his back when nightmares unsettle him. She knows that this boy will wander, always wander. She closes her eyes, and sees him. Now a grown man, he is walking through sun-burnished bushland, an ascetic, solemn animal.

Simple, hard good looks. *Beautifully brown.*

When he looks up at the evening sky, in its burning orange he hears her, the under-her-breath hum, the lullaby that saved him. Years have gone by. Decades. In this much time, they have spoken only once. *Will you please call me what you used to call me before you started using my name.* She hungers for the word. *Maa.* He does not oblige her.

He follows her life with the grasp of his ear.

Today he is neither old nor young, at that point in life where things are not analysed or probed but accepted. He thinks about her songs, and he lets them go. To himself he says the word. *Anuradha.* A private spell, an incantation. He wishes to tell her that he now knows what she had known all along: that one day, this world will burn down from the love it cannot bear. Fire will reduce flesh to bone and bone to ash, ash to smoke, smoke to air: this is how we shall all go. Here is when she sings—and at the other end of this evening, he catches her song. The song is whole and wondrous and it alludes to the truth that there are mercies in this life so small and humble that they will break you more easily than the cruelties ever could. Now a crimson-winged butterfly quivers past him. Lying inside that heartbroken old villa, Anuradha sees a butterfly—crimson wings; shivering panache—rest upon a tiny black rock in a barren landscape. *He has his father's hands,* she thinks, *long and noble.*

Much later, when Shloka does not sleep alone, he wakes one morning to a *zhan-zhan-zhan. A* woman touches his neck, and he acknowledges her gesture in the flattering amber colours around them. The recherché idiom of lovers. He steps out of her caress and into the garden, where the wind moves through tall pines, a haunting, old-coloured sound. Where is this place? Where the sunsets are dazzling, but the dawns even better. He has made it *here.* Shloka hears it again. The swish of the anklets. *She is here.* A bird calls out from the trees. The horizon empties its dark secrets and the sun, slow but sure, sends up its coruscating flares.

Staring into the new morning, Shloka accepts that Anuradha has been right. He was to tell the Story. The sudden lightness in his chest he cannot name, and he cannot deny. All he knows to be true is this: there is a song, an evening song, which, when you take to the great and old mountains, will return no echo. A melody released with a volcanic contralto, it rises up and reaches far and it touches the bluebells hiding and the weasels and the smallest harvester ant that ever breathed. *But it returns no echo.* Of course, the ear, small and without the necessary wisdom, presses against the crepuscular radiance and hunts out some kind of ricochet. But this song, this last song of dusk, now it demands no reply nor permits imitation simply because it is full in itself: a breath that will never be breathed again. All things under its bough will be healed and returned to the place they came from: silence. There is a song, an evening song, which, when you take to the great and old mountains, will return no echo.

There is a song.

Acknowledgements

It's hard for me to believe that I wrote this novel: it's easier for me to accept that perhaps I only stumbled into an inheritance: a story that was handed down to me to be passed on. But even this safekeeping, this fleeting possession, has been made possible only because of a fierce and fantastic love that has graced my life. And this love has come from many, many rivers: because even if one hand pens a story, the blood, the memory and the gaze of all of these people is right behind it: Y. Anjani, Roopa Banker, Elnora Cameron, Diana Divecha, Parul Doshi, Niki Gomez, Barbara Greenway, Sylvia Lim, Vasavi Mody, Nehal Parikh, Kamlesh Pawar, Felicity Rubinstein, Ali Shah, Urvashi Thacker, Dr Arvind Vasavada and Helen Garnons-Williams.

And most of all, to Sai Baba and Meher Baba: from whom come this work, and this worker.

A Debt to Music

The lives of the characters, in my imagination and in my deep heart, have turned radiant and full-bodied by the music of these exceptional artists: Kishori Amonkar, Johann Sebastian Bach, John Barry, Claude Challe, Pt. Hari Prasad Chaurasia, Chicane, Dido, Edward Elgar, George Frideric Handel, Lata Mangeshkar, Paul Oakenfold, Orbital, Cheb Sabah, Franz Schubert, Robert Schumann, Begum Parveen Sultana, George Winston, Gabriel Yared.

About the Author

Siddharth Dhanvant Shanghvi's first novel, *The Last Song of Dusk*, won the Betty Trask Award in the UK and the Premio Grinzane Cavour in Italy, and was nominated for the IMPAC Prize in Ireland. His second book, *The Lost Flamingoes of Bombay*, was shortlisted for the Man Asian Prize. *The Rabbit & the Squirrel*, with illustrations by Stina Wirsen, and *Loss*, essays on death and grief, are published by HarperCollins India as well. Shanghvi works and lives in a village in north Goa.